SUZANNE FERRELL

CLOSE TO THE EDGE

WESTEN SERIES, BOOK 2

Copyright © 2013 by Suzanne Ferrell

All Rights Reserved

Cover Art by Lyndsey Lewellen

Release date: Mar 2013

Please return / renew this item by the last date shown above
Dychwelwch / Adnewyddwch erbyn y dyddiad olaf y nodir yma

P.S. Thank you for all my fantastic covers!

Chapter One

Her ass was by far the finest he'd ever seen in this town.

Westen Township Sheriff, Gage Justice, pulled his cruiser in behind the brown sedan parked in the alley between the town's only bank and Gold's Foodmart. His deputy Cleetus was right. Someone was definitely digging around in the trash dumpster.

A satisfied smile of pure male appreciation split Gage's lips and a warmth spread over his body as he sat back and admired the view. This didn't look to be your typical dumpster diver. The woman stood tiptoe on the hood of her car, the top half of her body bent over and into the container's edge. The way the perp's jeans clung and stretched around her thighs and nice round bottom warmed more than his smile.

Oh, yeah. A man could spend all day holding those

round cheeks in his hands. Wonder if the top half of her was as nice as the bottom?

He gave himself a mental shake. The more important question was why was she rifling through the trash?

Without making a sound, he eased himself out of the cruiser, leaving the door open. Careful not to step on anything to alert her of his presence, he moved past her car to stand just below her and off to the side. He looked at her feet.

Awful small, even for a woman.

The jeans clung to her legs, which weren't supermodel thin, but nicely shaped. He resisted the urge to reach up and squeeze her calves.

"Exactly what do you think you're doing?" he asked in his best bad-cop voice.

Startled, she jumped and lifted her top half out of the bin. For a brief second he caught sight of her face. It wasn't the kind that stopped men dead in their tracks, but the curious brown eyes, the arched dark eyebrows, and the soft lips rounded in an *O* of surprise caught his attention.

At that moment her foot slipped.

In almost slow motion her balance shifted. Dark hair flying about her, she waved her arms around in big helicopter circles, papers drifting down like confetti. She twisted to one side as if she meant to catch herself on the edge of the dumpster, only to slip again. This time that lovely butt came directly at him. Despite something wet dribbling down on his shirt, Gage shifted sideways and did the only gentlemanly thing he could do. He held out both arms to catch her.

2

Just as her bottom and thighs filled his arms, she threw her arm around his neck, emptying the contents of a brown paper bag on top of him. "Oh, crap! Thank you…" her voice trailed off as she looked at him.

He couldn't help but smile. Her voice reminded him of a soft summer night, warm and whispery. "Gage Justice, Westen's Sheriff. You're welcome, Miss?"

"Sheriff Justice? That name's just too perfect." She laughed softly as she lifted the half-eaten chicken salad sandwich off his shoulder and tossed it back to the trash bin. Then she smiled—a genuine hundred-watt stunner from the heart. "I'm Roberta Roberts, but my friends call me Bobby."

Gage turned to set the shapely woman on the ground then glanced over her shoulder through the driver's window and froze.

The contents of her purse were scattered on the car's passenger seat. Peeking out of the bag was the butt-end of a gun.

"So, Bobby," he quickly set her on the ground and moved so he stood between her and the door handle, "want to tell me why you have a gun in the front seat of your car?"

"I'm a private investigator and I have a permit for my gun, Sheriff." She gave him another smile.

The words private investigator chilled whatever response he'd have for her. "Don't suppose you have some identification and a permit on you, do you?"

"They're in my bag."

She started to reach for the door handle, but he caught her arm to stop her. "I have to get them out to show you."

"How about I get your bag for you?"

"Sure. Help yourself."

"Don't mind if I do."

He released her and she stepped back, giving him a mutinous stare, those deep-brown eyes narrowed like a mad cat. Opening the door, he forced her to move away farther. Careful not to turn his back completely on her he retrieved her things, handing her the bag, but keeping her weapon in his hand.

Still casting him a rebellious look, she snatched her bag and dropped it onto the car hood, fishing around inside.

"I know it's in here. I put the permit in before leaving home."

"And where is home?" he asked, watching her rummage.

"Cincinnati," she said, starting to pull items out—wallet, bottle of water, notebook, granola bar, collapsible umbrella, reading book, sunglasses, lipstick case—laying them on the hood of her car one at a time. Every time he thought she reached the bottom she'd pull something else out. She rifled through each set of folded papers. "I know it's in here."

"How big is that bag?"

She slanted her head toward him a moment, disgust in her eyes, before turning back to her mission. He fought hard to swallow the grin that itched to pop out at her schoolmarm expression, the gun in his hand reminding him of the seriousness of the situation.

Finally, she turned her bag upside down and shook. The only thing that fell out was a gum wrapper.

"I can't find it." Her shoulders slumped a little, she reached for her wallet. "I can show you my PI license."

"How about we take a little trip over to the jail and I'll run a check." He gripped her arm and stopped her, turning her to face the car.

In all her life, Bobby Roberts had never seen a man turn from a knight-in-shining-armor into an-ice-cold-robotic-cop in a matter of seconds.

"Excuse me?" He couldn't be serious.

"You heard me, hands on the hood, lady." His voice, which had been warm and teasing a minute earlier, had turned as cold as a Midwestern snowstorm. She didn't doubt for one second that he meant business.

Not wishing to anger him any further, she placed her hands on the hood of her car and spread her legs. "This really isn't necessary."

"You have the right to remain silent, which I highly suggest you take advantage of."

He was really going to arrest her. Oh crap! She'd never even had so much as a parking ticket in her life. "This trash is in the alley, which makes it public domain. You can't arrest me."

She glanced over her shoulder. His jaw was as hard as granite, his lips pressed into an angry line, and those stupid reflective aviator glasses kept her from seeing his eyes. The metal badge, pinned to the blue denim shirt stretched over his wide shoulders, reflected what little sunlight filtered into the alley.

Oh, yeah. He was the town sheriff and he meant to let her know he was in charge. She recognized the silent intimidation. It was one of her favorite tactics to use on any number of her students over the years.

He ran his hands down her back all the way to her feet. If she didn't know better she'd swear he went a little too slow over her bottom. Next he brought those big hands up her legs and the outside of her torso. Despite the situation, she found herself wishing he'd do it again.

She gave herself a mental shake. Stupid woman, he's arresting you, not starting foreplay. Get your mind out of your pants and his. This is reality at its worst.

He leaned in, his body's heat warming her and she closed her eyes. It took all her willpower not to moan. Suddenly, he grasped one arm from the hood and brought it around her back. When she felt the metal of the cuffs encircle her wrist, her eyes snapped open.

"Officer, won't you just listen to me? I told you, I'm a private investigator. I know my rights. I was simply looking for a letter my client sent to this bank."

"Private investigator?" He looked from her head to her toes again. "Yeah, right."

"But I haven't done anything wrong." She tried to turn and wiggle free of his grasp.

"Keep it up and I'll charge you with resisting an officer. For the moment, I'm taking you into my office. We'll talk about your suspicious activity and this unlicensed handgun."

"Suspicious? You can't arrest me for searching public trash."

"Keep talking and I'll add a noise complaint, too."

"You can't be serious!"

"How about public nuisance?"

"Because I dumped trash on you?"

"You don't know how to remain silent, do you?" He pushed her against the car and cuffed her other arm behind her, then hauled her backward.

Abruptly, the internet warning about women being stopped and raped by fake cops along the interstate popped into her mind. He wasn't dressed in an official uniform—just a blue denim shirt, jeans, cowboy boots and that stupid badge. Panic spread over her like a whirlwind. Her heart jumped into hyper-drive. All she could think of was she shouldn't let him put her in that car. She started to wiggle as he led her toward his cruiser.

"Stop wiggling." He opened the back of the car.

"How do I know you're really a police officer? You haven't shown me any identification."

"Let's see, cruiser, badge, gun." He pointed at each item as he named it. "Don't I look like the sheriff?"

"No. You look like a farmer with an Indians baseball cap and badge."

He growled, opened the front door, leaned in and picked up the radio. "Cleetus?"

"Yes, Sheriff? What's your 20?"

"I'm out back of the bank with the suspect in custody. I'll be there in a few minutes."

"Roger, Sheriff."

The big man looked down at her, still no smile. "Satisfied?"

"Okay, I believe you're who you say you are, but I don't see why you've handcuffed me. I haven't done anything wrong. I can sue you for false arrest."

He closed the door on her threat and went back to

her car, shoved her things back into her purse, closed her door, then returned, climbing into the driver's side. He set the bag and her gun on the passenger's seat then started his car.

"Wait. You can't just leave my car out here. What if it gets stolen?"

He huffed—the same masculine sound she remembered her father giving her mother when she was a child—and took off his sunglasses, rubbing his fingers over the bridge of his nose. "Your car will be fine. And to be sure, I locked all the doors. Happy?"

"I'd be happier if you'd take off these ridiculous cuffs."

"Lady, that's not happening until you're back at the jail." The stony look he gave her in the mirror told her any further discussion was a waste of her breath.

"Fine. But when you find out I really am a private investigator, you're going to feel really stupid."

As he pulled the cruiser out of the alley, the radio sounded.

"Sheriff?"

He palmed the mic. "Yeah, Cleetus?"

"We've got a situation out on the state highway."

The sheriff stopped the cruiser. "What kind of situation?"

"Ralph Fenway's herd is loose and blocking the traffic in both directions."

"I'm bringing in the perp, after that you can go out and handle it."

"Sheriff, Doc Clint called from his car, he's one of the people stuck behind three semi trucks. Says one of the truck drivers just got out of his rig and Ralph's standing in the middle of the road holding a shotgun to protect his cows."

"Oh, hell. I'm heading there right now." He put the car in drive and headed out of town.

"Hey, you can't take me with you. I'm—" Bobby said from the backseat.

"Not another word." He pointed at her in the rearview mirror, the intensity in his narrowed eyes silencing her reply. He opened the glove compartment and removed a handgun.

Bobby closed her mouth, her protest dying on her lips. She glanced at the cruiser's windows. She hoped they were bulletproof—especially if a farmer with a shotgun started shooting.

A few minutes later they pulled up to where several trucks sat blaring their horns at the small herd of cows mulling over the road and the creek running nearby. The sheriff maneuvered the cruiser past the angry drivers and into the grass right near where the cows had obviously knocked the thin wire fencing to the ground.

Bobby watched in fascination as the sheriff climbed out of the cruiser, slipping his gun into the back waistband of his jeans. Hands in front of him, he slowly approached the farmer—who was indeed holding a shotgun, albeit he had it pointed at the ground—like he was out for a Sunday stroll. She leaned forward to hear through the open driver's window.

"Tell the old guy to get out of the way!" a burly trucker yelled from his truck cab. Two other truckers sounded their horns.

"Just hold your breath, sir." He held a palm up as if commanding a dog to sit and stay. Once the man complied, the sheriff turned back toward the farmer, his tone low and respectful. "Ralph, seems we have a problem here."

"Ain't no problem, Sheriff. My girls wanted a drink over in the creek. Seems like these fellers here would just run 'em over if they had a chance."

"How about we give the girls a nudge back to your property so these people can get on down the road?"

"I suppose I could get 'em moving that direction, but who's gonna keep these fellers from hittin' the gas before they're back home?"

The Sheriff held out his hand. "How about you give me the shotgun and I'll make sure no one moves until the girls are back safe and sound."

The old farmer eyed the truckers on both sides of the road. Bobby thought he might refuse. After a tense moment, he nodded and handed the weapon to the sheriff. "Guess you'll do."

As the farmer started shooing his herd back across the highway, Bobby exhaled with relief. Where she came from people didn't carry weapons unless they meant to use them, and unfortunately they did.

What impressed her most was how the same man who'd unreasonably handcuffed her, had just very quietly disarmed a dangerous situation. Maybe she could work with him after all?

"Ralph, you have to get this fence repaired," Gage said as he held the gate while the old farmer shooed the last of several errant cows back into the pasture.

"Well now, Sheriff, I could get some of that new fencing I saw at the county farming fair, but neither your daddy nor I could see the sense of putting up something these ladies are just going to knock down first chance they get."

Ignoring the reference to his dad, Gage closed the gate and signaled the line of cars and trucks to pass. He resisted the urge to arrest a few drivers who kept hitting their horns. If he didn't already have one questionable detainee in the cruiser, he might've done it anyway. "This is the third time since the spring thaw that your cows have blocked the highway."

Ralph pulled off his hat and wiped at his brow. "Ain't my fault the county put the road smack between my pasture and the creek over there."

Gage took a slow breath and counted to ten. "I'd sure hate to lock you up if one of your cows causes an accident or someone gets hurt."

"I'd sure hate for you to do that, too. I'll see if I can't get that lower section mended a might stronger."

Gage doubted that the threat of jail would make much difference to the farmer.

God save him. His life had gone from the dark and seedy world of undercover narcotics investigation to herding cows from the highway.

As he walked to the cruiser his cell phone rang. He stopped and pulled it from his pocket, glancing at the caller ID.

Moira Dudson. The Franklin County Assistant District Attorney, herself.

Just reading the woman's name made his teeth grind. He hadn't exchanged two words with her since before his shooting, and hadn't laid eyes on her since the divorce proceedings. But for some reason, for the past two weeks she'd been calling him almost daily.

He clicked answer immediately followed by *end call*.

Message sent. She could wait until hell froze over.

For a moment he took off his cap and ran his hands through his hair, studying the woman in the back of his cruiser.

Private Investigator.

Next to politicians, private dicks were second on his list of people he wouldn't save from a burning building. Didn't trust them as far as he could spit. In his life he'd come in personal contact with two PI's. One had been hired to take out a hit on his cousin Emma, and the other had helped to nearly get him killed. In his opinion, they were nothing but trouble. Yet the memory of watching Ms. Roberts' bottom wiggle as she'd searched the dumpster sent heat directly back to his groin.

Oh yeah, this one would be trouble for sure.

"Done saving the world from runaway cows?" Bobby asked as soon as he climbed back into the cruiser.

Without commenting on her sarcasm he started the engine and headed back to Westen.

They fell into silence as he drove through the few streets of the small town. Finally, he pulled into an alley and for a moment her fear that he wasn't on the up-and-up crossed her mind again, until he parked behind a door that had an official sign stating Westen

City Jail above it.

Despite the real threat of being arrested, relief poured through her. When she passed her PI test, she'd dreamed of adventure. Being handcuffed and raped wasn't one of them. An hour in jail was definitely a much better scenario. Heck, hadn't every television PI been in jail at least once?

The man opened the door. She'd half expected him to haul her out and shove her in front of him. Instead he held her firmly by the upper arm, and helped her get out of the backseat as gracefully as she could, considering she wore cuffs. Thank God they were in back of the jail. She'd be so embarrassed to be taken into the jail in front of the whole town.

"If you'd just look in my purse—"

"Quiet."

He might not be manhandling her, but he wasn't any less angry. And for what she didn't have a clue. Sure she had a gun, but she also had a permit to carry it. Was there some town law she'd unknowingly broken? Her book said trash in a public container was no longer considered private property. It hadn't said she needed to check with the local authorities before searching the trash for information.

"I got a cell ready, Sheriff..." The giant standing in the hallway, dressed from head-to-toe in an official uniform, stopped mid-sentence as the sheriff walked her inside. "She's the suspect?"

"Yes. I caught her rifling through the trash." The sheriff turned her so her back was toward him then he unfastened the cuffs and gave her a gentle push into the cell.

"I thought we were going to talk. Why are you arresting me?" Bobby asked, just as he closed the cell door. The automatic lock clicked loudly. Her breath caught at the sound. This was not a good thing. Despite the openness of the bars and the window, the confining space wrapped around her like a smothering blanket.

"I'm not. For now you're in protective custody."

What? "Who are you protecting me from?"

"No one." He pointed to his shirt. "I'm protecting the citizens of Westen from you."

"That's ridiculous."

He ignored her comment and stalked through the open door into the other room she assumed was the main office to the jail. She tried to rack her brain. Wasn't she allowed a phone call? But whom would she call? Certainly not Chloe. Her sister might be a lawyer and at the moment her client, but the last thing she wanted was to give her younger sister a chance to say, *I told you so.*

And she couldn't call Dylan. Her youngest sister was getting ready to graduate from med school. She didn't need the distraction of bailing her oldest sister out of jail.

No, she'd save her phone call for later. Right now she needed to figure a way out of this mess. She paced the cell a minute then stopped to listen for any information from the front room.

"What are you going to do with her, Sheriff?" she heard the other officer ask.

"I don't know, Cleetus. She's carrying a gun and claims to be a PI. Hell, she looks more like a schoolteacher than a PI."

14

How was she supposed to look? She *was* a schoolteacher—or at least she had been the past eighteen years. Her handbook hadn't said anything about looking different to be a PI. In fact the thing said the best ones blended in. What did the man expect? A trench coat and hat?

A drawer slammed in the front room. "Until I know for sure, I'm locking her weapon up and her too. Maybe that will keep her out of harm's way."

"Who's she gonna harm? She's just a little bitty thing."

"Herself for one, me for another. Where's my clean shirt?"

Several more drawers opened and closed.

"It's in the back storeroom. Ruby said it wasn't right to have clothes in the filing cabinets."

Bobby hurried to sit on the cot that passed for a bed in her cell, just as the sheriff stomped back through the hall. She sucked in her breath at the sight of the man. Apparently she'd gotten more than just an old banana peel on him when she'd fallen into his arms. He'd stripped out of the shirt and was naked down to his waist.

Lord, she hadn't seen a naked man that looked like this...ever. From the brief side view she could tell he didn't have weight lifter six-pack abs, but he was all muscle, and she was sure that if he stood still she'd be able to count his lower ribs. The man had locked her up, humiliated her by cuffing her, and all she wanted to do was run her hands over every inch of his torso? There had to be something seriously wrong with her.

Maybe she had a fever? She put her hand to her

forehead. Nope. Cool and dry. This was not good. Not once in her life had she let a man get her flustered. Not one male teacher or administrator had ever interested her romantically. Because she wouldn't date any of them some had even assumed she was a lesbian. They'd been wrong, but she hadn't tried to convince them otherwise.

Flirt. Oh, there was an idea. Lord knows she'd watched her younger sisters use the trick on their boyfriends for years.

She shook out her hair, and went to the cell door. "Sheriff?" she called in as sexy a voice as she could muster just as he started back up the hall. He'd put on the new shirt—same faded blue denim as its predecessor—and had it almost completely buttoned.

"What?" He still sounded surly as he removed the baseball cap and ran his hands over his short, military-cut, sandy-blonde hair, then slapped the cap back on.

This close she noticed the pierced holes in his left ear. *How odd.*

"Can't we come to some compromise?" She cocked her head to the side, just like Dylan did when she was a little girl, and peered up at him.

He'd removed his glasses and she saw his eyes were the color of winter spruce. His lips twitched and he seemed to be buying her act.

The phone rang in the front room.

"And just what are you offering, Ms. Roberts?"

Heat from him radiated through the bars. She licked her dry lips. Nerves or excitement, she wasn't sure which, but the man certainly had the effect of a desert storm on her mind and body.

"Well…"

"Sheriff, there's a fire out at Aaron Turnbill's place." The other officer stood in the doorway.

"Shit. Call the county fire department." His attention completely focused on his deputy he stomped away from the cell to the front room.

Crap! She'd lost her chance.

"Aaron already did, both the county and the local volunteers. That would be me, too, Sheriff."

"I'll meet them out there. You'll have to stay here this time." Sheriff Justice grabbed his hat and glasses and hurried out back. He stopped in the doorway. "And Cleetus?"

"Yes, Sheriff?"

"She stays here, got it?"

"Yes, Sir."

With that order, he was out the back door.

Bobby's heart sank. So much for sex appeal. She'd known it was a long shot, since she'd never had any before, so why had she thought she could conjure some up today? This day, her very first day on her very first case, was turning out to be a complete disaster.

What was the sheriff going to do with her when he got back? How was she going to convince him she was a legitimate PI investigating a case? And just how long did he plan to keep her in this jail?

Chapter Two

Gage turned from the asphalt onto the gravel country road, spinning dirt as he hurried to the Turnbill's farm. However, his mind remained on the woman locked up in his jail.

What the hell had come over him? He'd never used his power as a policeman to manhandle someone, especially not a woman. So why had he gone off the deep end this time?

Simple. He'd liked holding Bobby Roberts, even though she'd dumped garbage on him. It'd been a long time since a woman had intrigued him, even if what intrigued him had been mostly her bottom half. But the minute he'd seen that gun, he'd reacted on instinct. Three years ago he'd naïvely let one woman's looks almost get him killed. He wasn't going to let another, even if she did look more like a schoolteacher than a dangerous criminal.

His radio crackled.

"Gage?" John Wilson, chief of the volunteer fire brigade was on the other end of the line. "You on your way out here?"

Gage lifted the mouthpiece. "I'm less than a mile from the farm, John. How's it look?"

"Aaron called it in, but the fire isn't really on his property, over."

"Where *exactly* is it?"

"On that abandoned land next to his back forty."

Shit. If he'd been told that before he left, he could've taken the paved road all the way to the property. He knew exactly the area John described. Driving the gravel road around the Turnbill place took him the long way round.

"I'll be there in about three minutes."

Once he'd come on board as a deputy, Dad had taken him on a tour of their patrol area, telling him which lands the bank had foreclosed on before he'd moved back to Westen. At least with all the recent spring rains the brush around the abandoned place wouldn't be dry. The fire shouldn't spread to the Turnbill farm. Had it been the dead of summer, with the occasional drought and dry grasses the area had, the story would be different.

As he drove by the Turnbill's the smell of smoke filled the air. Farther up the road the gray-white fumes hovered over the charred remains of an old barn. Both volunteer fire engines flanked the road, the men milling close by continuing to pour water onto the site.

He parked his vehicle behind one truck to leave room for the county fire truck, whose approaching sirens filled the air as he climbed out of his cruiser. One of the best things the town—with his dad's prodding—ever did was form and train the volunteer fire teams. The county's response time was under four minutes in the larger city and county seat, but out in the rural areas it took more than ten minutes for them to get to a fire. The volunteers kept the fires contained until the bigger units with full-time fighters arrived.

Before closing the door he pulled a pair of latex gloves out of his glove compartment. A solitary figure separated from the group of men keeping watch on the barn's smoldering wood and headed his way. John Wilson's tall, thin, and slightly bowed frame announced him as a man who worked long hard days in his farm's fields eking out a living for his family.

"Glad to have you here, Gage." They shook hands then approached the burn area.

"Do you have any idea how the fire started?"

"Not really." John pointed to the barn's side. "My best guess is it started on this side and spread. Aaron said he's been seeing vehicles go past his house late at night lately, ever since the weather warmed up. What with all those warnings about the dangers from crystal meth labs the State Fire Marshal's been sending out, I kept my men out of the actual fire area. Figure the professionals have the equipment and experience, so they can go in and figure out the cause."

"Makes sense to me."

Meth lab fires produced toxic fumes, and he'd too just as soon the volunteers, who were mostly farmers, stay clear until an actual cause was determined. He looked around at the volunteer fire team. "Is Aaron around?"

John shook his head. "Said he had to finish planting

his soybeans before dark, but he'd come back over as soon as he finished."

"Good. I'll see if he can give me a description of those suspicious vehicles he's been seeing."

The county fire truck and EMS squad arrived. While John stepped over to fill the captain in on the fire and their actions, Gage circled the perimeter, careful to stay out of any area that might still smolder. Off to the rear of the barn he found a pile of empty beer cans. He squatted down and with a pen he lifted the can and sniffed. Just beer.

Several butts of rolled cigarettes littered the area. He pulled on his gloves, lifted one and sniffed. Grade A pot.

"Find anything, Gunslinger?" A deep gravelly voice spoke from behind him.

"Hey, Deke." Gage shook his head at the high school nickname as he stood and held the butt toward his old friend, Deke Reynolds. "Looks like someone's been smoking pot and drinking beer out here."

"Any sign of a burn pit?"

"Nope." Gage scanned the area once more. A burn pit was an area away from the building where a meth lab was housed, with stained soil or dead vegetation from the meth cooks dumping their chemicals or waste. "I don't see any trash other than beer cans and pot, either. I'd guess just some local kids partying."

"Maybe we'll get lucky and that's all this will turn out to be." Deke bagged the cigarette butt and beer can before walking to the perimeter of the fire area where several of his men had donned hazardous-chemical suits and masks.

As County Fire Chief and a detail-oriented man, Deke donned his own suit and mask and led them through the nearly dilapidated pile of charred lumber.

As he watched his friend give orders to his men Gage's stomach rumbled. Once he finished here, he'd best get some lunch over at the Peaches 'N Cream café. Low blood sugar wouldn't make dealing with his other problem—one small, nicely shaped female with the impaired belief that she was a private detective—any easier.

Just as the café owner's daughter, Rachel, refilled Gage's mug with fresh coffee, Mayor Tobias Rawlins slithered into the booth with him. Two members of the town council and the owner of the local paper, Rawlins' constant entourage, scooted in with them.

Great. Just what he needed today. First his dispatcher breaks a hip, next a PI comes to town, errant cows cause a traffic jam, a fire, and now small-town politics.

Couldn't he eat in peace?

Seven more months to play sheriff in this town then someone else would be elected to watch over the crazies and he could move back to the city. Nothing could induce him to stay one more second than was absolutely necessary. Sometimes what this town needed more than a sheriff was a zookeeper.

To relieve the ache talking to the town's chief politician always caused, Gage rubbed his forehead and looked at each of the other men. "Something I can do for you gentlemen?"

"Sheriff, we want to discuss the situation with regards to Ruby Martin," Rawlins said just loud enough for anyone in a two-booth radius to hear.

And that's exactly what they did. Lorna and the café's staff stopped serving, the banker and his two managers stopped their daily lunch meeting, even the two ladies from the antique store all leaned his way to hear the news on Ruby. In this town, no matter what you tried to keep secret, sooner or later the whole town knew your business. You couldn't fart without someone spreading the news.

"What situation do you mean, Mayor?" he asked, as he cut another bite of Lorna's killer meatloaf and ignored the multitude of curious stares.

"Well, frankly Ruby should've retired years ago. And now, with her falling on her way to work this morning, we're just wondering if she'll try to sue the town for not providing adequate transportation." The mayor sat back and adjusted his suit, waiting for his reply. The three councilmen nodded like bobblehead dolls.

The sheriff's office had employed one secretary-dispatcher for the past fifty years, Ruby Martin. Working for the department was what kept her young, that and the fact she walked to work daily. Unfortunately, today she broke her hip on the way into work which had left him shorthanded. And here Tobias was trying to score political points at her expense.

Gage cut another chunk of the meatloaf with his fork, scooped it through thick brown gravy and ate, chewing slowly and letting the quartet wait on his answer. He hated politicians, he hated attention seekers, he hated people who used other's problems to make themselves look important, but today he really hated anyone getting between him and Lorna's meatloaf special.

"Gentleman," he said as he finished, setting his fork on the rim of the plate. "Rest assured that Ruby has no intention of suing the town."

"Are you promising us there will be no

repercussions?" Richard Davis, the newspaperman asked, taking out his pad and pencil.

"No, Dick, I can't. *But off the record*," Gage said loud enough for everyone to hear him, "I'd say Ruby won't want to bother. Everyone knows she kept working because she liked the stimulation. She walked to work because she liked the exercise. Now if you'll excuse me, I have work to do."

He managed to leave the café with only a dozen people stopping him to inquire after Ruby's health.

***

Bobby looked at her watch again.

Breathe. Exhale. Breathe again. It wasn't that bad.

She'd managed to survive her first hour locked in a jail cell. Albeit a very *small* cell.

Cut it out. The cell was probably a standard size.

From her sister's conversations over the last few years she knew the overbearing sheriff couldn't hold her for more than twenty-four hours without formally charging her with something. So technically she had twenty-three hours left to go. She could do this.

Her stomach growled.

Great. This morning she'd been so excited to get started she'd inhaled a sausage sandwich and coffee on her way out of Cincinnati and nothing since. Weren't they required to feed prisoners?

She leaned into the cell's door. "Officer?"

No response. Up front the deputy's shoes shuffled across the wood floor and his low muttering filled the silence as he talked to himself.

"Deputy?" She called a little louder. "Excuse me, Deputy?"

A moment later he filled the doorway. "Yes,

ma'am?"

"Could I have something to eat and drink? Please?" Her mother always said a man loved a sweet voice more than a sour face.

"Ma'am, Gage didn't give me permission to leave."

"Please call me Bobby, Deputy. You don't have any water or snacks up there in the office? Or maybe you could give me my purse. I have a bottle of water and a granola bar in it."

He looked like he was going to refuse, but her stomach picked the most opportune time to growl very loudly. The deputy grinned at her and turned away. A moment later he returned carrying her bag. She reached for it, but he held it out of her way.

"Now, the rules say you're not supposed to have access to your belongings while in jail, but Miz Ruby told me never to rummage through a lady's purse without her permission. So, I'll just get those things out while you're watching. Okay?"

What was she supposed to do, refuse? Besides, he was being nice enough to give her the water and snack bar. That was more than she could say for the pigheaded sheriff.

"That'll be fine, Cleetus." She smiled when he blushed just like one of her middle school students. "Say, you wouldn't happen to have known Gilbert Byrd?"

"Sure thing, ma'am. Gil lived here in town all his life." Cleetus handed her the water then fished out her oatmeal-and-chocolate-chip bar. "He died about six months ago, found him dead in his house. Doc Ray said his heart finally gave out."

"Doc Ray? Is that the local doctor?" She twisted the plastic cap until the seal broke and took a long drink.

Even warm it felt wonderful. Who ever knew being arrested could make a person so thirsty?

"Used to be. Doc Ray retired not long after Gil died. Said he didn't want to end up the same way without taking Caroline to see the world. His nephew, Clint, is the new town Doc."

Doc Clint. Okay, there was someone she'd need to talk with just to be sure Mr. Byrd died of natural causes.

She took a bite of the bar, hoping to seem innocent in her questions. "Did Mr. Byrd have any family close by?"

Cleetus rubbed his chin, staring up at the ceiling. Again he reminded her of one of her students who always looked just the same way when he was trying to find the right answer to a history question. She hid her smile behind another bite of the unexpectedly delicious granola.

"Can't say as I ever met any of Gil's people."

The phone rang before she could think of any other questions, and blessedly before the deputy could question her interest in a dead man. She settled herself on the corner of the mattress and nibbled on the bar. So the deputy didn't know Mr. Byrd's nephew, Norman—the man who hired her sister to investigate Mr. Byrd's holdings as listed in the will.

Interesting. She doubted Cleetus was lying to her. After eighteen years of teaching, she knew when someone was telling her the truth and when she was being fed a line of horse crap. Did anyone in the town know Mr. Byrd had a nephew? If so, who?

And what had happened to the letters her sister sent the bank? When no one could find them in the files when she called yesterday, she *knew* she had to come to Westen and investigate in person. Dumpster diving had been a long shot, but she'd hoped someone had panicked and simply thrown the letters out.

All that great idea had done was land her in this itty-bitty cell.

Looking around she sucked in a breath as the room seemed to shrink a little more.

Slamming of file drawers and muttering from Cleetus in the front room caught her attention.

"I don't know where Ruby kept that file, Mayor. I looked under T for tickets and S for speeding." Cleetus paused as if listening. "Yes sir. I'll keep looking...yes sir, I'll tell the sheriff when he gets back...No sir, I won't forget."

Who was Ruby? And where was she?

A few more file cabinets opened and closed hard.

"Dang, Gage isn't gonna be happy about this." The poor man sounded really distressed.

She went to the cell door and leaned far to one side to see into the front room. Cleetus paced past the door. "Cleetus? Is there something wrong?"

He stopped mid-stride, turned and came to the door. "Our dispatcher fell and broke her hip today."

That answered the who and what about Ruby.

"The Mayor wants the quarterly traffic violation reports and I have no idea where she filed them. Ruby has her own filing system that no one else can make heads or tails of."

"Aren't they on the computer?" she nodded at the monitor sitting on the desk behind him.

Cleetus shook his head. "Nope. Ruby said she'd been doing the filing for fifty years and didn't need a computer to tell her where things were."

"And the sheriff didn't want to update the system?"

She couldn't imagine the man not ordering his dispatcher to learn and use the computer system. He'd certainly had no qualms about ordering her around. "Seems like a waste of taxpayers' money, not to use it to its full potential."

"Gage's dad, he used to be sheriff, purchased them just before he took sick. Lloyd said he wanted to bring our department into the computer world. When he died, Gage took over his position, but hasn't gotten around to changing things. Says he'll leave it for the next sheriff."

So, the sheriff didn't plan on being re-elected. Given his public demeanor toward her, she'd guess his evaluation of his chances was correct. "You know I'm pretty good with filing. Maybe I could figure out Ruby's system for you."

Cleetus looked at her, then up to the front room and finally back at her. "Gage said you weren't to leave here, but he didn't say you had to stay locked up."

"I'd still be in the building and you'd be keeping a very close eye on me." She tried not to act too enthusiastic, but the idea of being out from the enclosed cell really appealed to her. How did prisoners do this on a daily basis for weeks, months, or even years?

Her argument seemed to convince the deputy. He retrieved the key from the front room, and opened the cell door. The clicking of metal against metal had never sounded so good to her. Stepping out of the cell, she took a deep breath.

Funny, it was the same air inside and outside of the cell, but it felt so good to inhale it out in the hallway. She rubbed her arms with both hands to ward off the chill she'd been feeling.

She smiled at the congenial deputy. "Now, show me

where those files are and we'll see if you and I can't find them before the sheriff returns."

Twenty minutes later, she understood the deputy's frustration. She'd gone through the files as best she could. First, she'd gone alphabetically—the most logical way to find something. She'd tried T for tickets and traffic, S for speeding, and even M for moving violations. Nada. Next she'd tried her second organizational choice—by dates. No months, years, or dates listed anywhere. So where had the lady hidden the files?

"I don't suppose you could call Ruby?" she asked, hating to admit defeat so soon.

Cleetus shook his head. "Doc said she'd be in surgery all afternoon. I don't think she'll be able to talk much before tonight."

Bobby clenched her hands in fists on her hips. "Okay. We just have to try to think about this in another way. Is there any other term you might use to name the tickets when you write them?"

"Fines?"

"Good." She grabbed the file marked F. Flipping through the files, she found nothing marked *Fines*. "Nope. Anything else?"

"Not that I can think of, ma'am."

"Is there any particular way you mark them? You know, to identify them as tickets to be collected?"

"Well each one has the person's name, driver's license number and car tag on them."

Bobby stared at him, a sinking feeling in her stomach. "You don't suppose she'd file each separately by their name do you?"

"No ma'am. There must be at least two thousand

registered drivers in the town and surrounding area, not to mention out of town drivers just passing through." Cleetus rubbed his chin a moment. "But I'd say we give more tickets to the people living in our county."

He slowly grinned. "You don't suppose she'd file them under county, do you?"

"Who knows? It's as good a place as any to look." Bobby grabbed the handle of the C drawer and prayed he was right. There, in a thick file marked COUNTY TICKETS, divided by months and years, were hundreds of tickets. "Voilà! I think you solved the mystery, Cleetus."

She took the file to the desk, and found the monthly listings. White slips of tickets for the month of May were neatly arranged by date.

Cleetus leaned over the desk. "How will we know where to find the out of town plates?"

"I guess that's one bridge we'll have to cross when we get there."

After she listed all the tickets by date, name and license plate number, she sat back and tried to think like Ruby.

If all the locals were in the "county" file, would the others be under "state"? Not likely. They could've been issued to drivers from other states as well. So where would she have put them? What was an out-of-towner? Stranger? No. Foreigner? No, that might be confused with someone from another country.

Out-of-towner. Could it be that simple?

She wiped her hands on her jeans before pulling open the file drawer and flipping to the back.

There it was. Out of Town.

"I found it!"

"I'm glad you did."

The Sheriff's deep voice startled her from behind. She jumped and nearly scattered the contents of the file.

"But what I want to know is why you are digging around in my files and what the hell you're doing out of your cell?"

Chapter Three

Gage couldn't believe the scene before him. "Cleetus, didn't I tell you to keep her locked up?"

"Not exactly, Sheriff." The deputy shifted his weight from one foot to the other. "You told me to keep Miz Bobby here."

"And I'm still here," Bobby said, just a little too chipper for Gage's liking.

He shot her a silencing glare before focusing on his chief deputy. "Not only have you let her out of her cell, but you let her have access to confidential police records." Manila folders lay scattered on his desk, the floor and the tops of the open file cabinets. "Apparently, *complete* access."

Two quick phone calls to the state licensure board on his way back from the fire had confirmed her claim of being a PI and her permit to carry a weapon. His temper cooled, he'd decided after lunch to let Ms. Roberts out of jail and find out why she'd been searching the trash. Now that she'd conned Cleetus into thwarting his orders—and he had no doubt she'd pulled that same cute-but-innocent flirtation act on his deputy she'd tried earlier on him—he had half a mind to lock her back up for the night.

"Uh, Sheriff," Cleetus maneuvered around the stacks of files on the floor, "Miz Bobby is helpin' me get together the monthly traffic violation report that Mayor Rawlins said he'd be by to get before the town council meeting tonight."

Gage inhaled deeply, shoving the air back out in one long rush. With all the bizarre happenings today, he'd completely forgotten about the town council and his monthly crime report. Big crime, like today's fire, he could summarize without a list to the council, but traffic tickets his deputies issued required documentation of statistics. A task usually completed by Ruby.

"So did you solve the mystery of Ruby's filing system?" He paused to study the room's chaos. "Or was it an exercise in futility?"

"Miz Bobby figured it out." His deputy grinned at the dark-haired woman standing at Gage's desk where she'd been sitting to make her list.

Gage shoved himself away from the doorframe, stalked to his chair and sank down into the aged leather. Oh man, the seat was still warm from that nice cushy bottom of hers. His anger dissipated once more and he fought the urge to close his eyes and sigh.

"I didn't do it alone, Cleetus. You were the one who really had the key to where we should look."

The woman was killing him. Every time she spoke the soft sensuality in each word stoked his body like a lover's touch.

Cleetus shook his head. "But I wouldn't have figured it out without you askin' me the right questions, ma'am."

Great, the pair had formed a mutual admiration society while he'd been gone. "So you two are telling me you've completely figured out how Ruby files things?"

Bobby turned toward him and the smile she'd had for his deputy faded. Gage didn't know why that disappointed him, but it did.

"Cleetus said Ruby worked here for nearly fifty years. I doubt we even cracked the surface, but we did find the information needed for your report."

Cleetus lifted a stack of files off his desk. "I'll get that report typed up as soon as I put these back, Sheriff."

Gage glanced at the clock. Nearly six. "Cleetus, I'll put the files away. If you don't leave now, you won't make it to the hospital in Columbus to see Ruby before visiting hours are over like I promised."

The deputy looked around the room. "Are you sure, Sheriff? I mean, you don't know where any of these belong."

"I doubt it's going to make a difference. Neither you or I knew where any of it belonged before you started." Gage gave a rueful laugh as he shoved himself out of his chair and walked over to take the files from his friend, clapping him on the shoulder. "You go see Ruby. Don't tell her we've destroyed her files. I'll clean up this mess."

"Don't you want me to type up that report?"

"I can do it, Cleetus," Bobby offered. "I mean if the sheriff doesn't mind a little help. You really should go see your friend."

Both she and Cleetus looked at him expectantly. Gage knew he should refuse her help. Since the minute he'd met her, she'd caused him nothing but trouble. However, if he did that Cleetus would insist on staying.

"I'd appreciate the help," he said, his voice sounding reluctant even to his own ears. He fished out the cruiser keys from his pocket and some money from his wallet, handing them over to Cleetus. "Take my cruiser. It'll get you there faster than your old truck. If you have time, stop and buy Ruby some flowers from both of us."

"I sure will, Sheri...er...Gage. She likes tulips." Cleetus grinned. "'Course she'll fuss and tell me it's a damn waste of money."

"That she will." Gage set the files back on his desk and led the way down the back hall. "I need to get some evidence out of the trunk before you leave."

His deputy loped to the back of the office in front of him. The man had the body of an NFL offensive lineman, the maturity of a fourteen-year-old and the heart of a kid. He never would've made it in a city police force, but Dad had seen Cleetus' kindness as an asset in Westen. Gage just prayed nothing occurred in town that was really dangerous. He'd never forgive himself if something happened to the man.

Behind him the computer booted up with a lyrical chime. Wonder if Bobby could figure out the security code his dad had installed on the system. Maybe she was more bloodhound than she looked.

Bobby stared at the screen a moment. Why in the world had she agreed to help the overbearing man with his report? It wasn't her responsibility to help him. Since the minute she'd met him, he'd caused her nothing but trouble. More than likely he planned to lock her back in that cell for the night.

35

Icy-cold prickles ran over her skin at the idea. She didn't think she'd make it a whole night in that place. If asked, she'd admit her newfound claustrophobia wasn't the only reason she wanted to type up the list. Working with Cleetus this afternoon, she'd listened to him talk about his friend Ruby over and over. She liked the man and would feel guilty if assuaging her own pride prevented him from visiting her tonight.

On the other hand there was Sheriff Justice. The man might be high-handed and arrogant, but he had agreed to her help, albeit reluctantly. The fact that he'd made a promise to his deputy and went out of his way to keep it told her he was a man of principle and a good friend.

"You could use the old typewriter next to the computer," the sheriff's deep voice said from behind her.

She nearly jumped out of her skin. "Jeez! Do you have to keep doing that?" she asked, once her heart started beating again.

"Do what?"

She turned and found herself face-to-face with his belt buckle. She tilted her head and let her gaze travel up the long length of his torso to his face. He wasn't smiling, but the arch of his one brow suggested he'd sneaked up behind her and scared her for his own amusement. His close-cut sandy hair made her want to run her fingers through it, not too mention all that lean muscle she'd seen earlier.

Lord, the man was both handsome and intimidating. She swallowed, feeling her tongue stick to the roof of her abruptly parched mouth. This was no time to let him know how much his tactics worked. "I wish you'd quit sneaking up behind me and scaring me."

This time his lips spread into a slow, lazy smile and

he leaned closer, stopping mere inches from her face. "If just asking a question scares you, Ms. Roberts, perhaps you should quit playing detective and go back to whatever schoolroom you left."

His breath caressed her cheek, but his words irritated her temper. She narrowed her eyes, turned and typed *JUSTICEFORALL* in the computer's password box, quickly popping up the wallpaper and desktop.

He let out a low whistle. "How'd you figure that out so quickly?" he asked, the arrogance gone from his voice.

She pointed at his father's campaign poster. "I've been staring at that slogan all day."

He chuckled, a deep sound that sent warmth shooting over her slightly frayed nerves. It reminded her of being held in his arms earlier.

"You are good at solving puzzles, I'll give you that." He walked around the desk and retrieved a pile of manila folders from the top of one cabinet. "I appreciate you helping with the report. Cleetus has an overdeveloped sense of duty, and I didn't think I'd ever get him out of here."

Apparently that was as close as he'd come to issuing her an apology.

After a quick scan of the computer's programs, she opened one for making reports, set up the file and began typing the information he needed. Funny, she'd started helping because Cleetus sounded so distraught, not because she wanted to help the sheriff.

Well, okay, to be honest she'd seen a way out of her cell and she'd taken it.

Guilt nibbled at her conscience. Despite his treatment of her, Sheriff Justice seemed to like his deputy. Would that friendship keep him from reprimanding Cleetus for letting her out of the cell? Or would he fire the big-hearted deputy for showing her such a kindness? She hated thinking someone would suffer because of her. Her fingers paused on the keyboard. She stole a glance at the sheriff, who'd just about finished clearing the loose files from the tops of the cabinets.

Don't be a coward.

Yeah, right. Look at the man. Nothing but solid muscle and steel for a backbone. *If I mention the cell, he's more than likely to toss me back in for the night.*

All ready feeling the walls crowding in around her, she struggled to drag in a deep breath. *Don't think about being locked in such a tiny closet of a place, just ask him. You owe Cleetus that much.*

She shoved the whole little-closet image to the back of her mind. "Um, Cleetus is a very nice man."

"That he is," the sheriff said as he grabbed another pile of manila folders from the floor and shoved them haphazardly into a drawer. Apparently, he was no more concerned with proper filing than his dispatcher, who at least had some sort of system.

Bobby typed another few lines and swallowed again. "I hope you won't hold it against him that he let me help find this missing information *you* needed."

Good girl, make him feel you were helping, and it was all for his benefit. Nothing like a little indebtedness to prevent him from locking her back in the slammer.

He shoved some more files into a drawer before turning to fix his cool green gaze on her. She tried to ignore the butterflies jumping around in her stomach.

"Technically, Cleetus followed my orders exactly. I told him you weren't to leave." The left corner of his mouth turned upwards. "You're still here, aren't you?"

Air caught in her throat. She exhaled and took another breath before answering. "Yes, I am."

"Guess I don't see a reason for me to punish Cleetus, do you?"

God, she hated to ask this. "Does this mean I'm free to go?"

"Perhaps."

Leaning one arm on top of the file cabinet, he continued to watch her like a giant cat waiting for his prey to make the wrong move. Her mouth grew dry once more and she nervously pulled her lower lip between her teeth. The only noise in the office was the low hum of the computer's tower and the gentle whirring of the ceiling fan.

Suddenly the office's front door opened. "Gage, I need that monthly traffic—" the man stopped mid-sentence. He appeared to be in his forties with salt-and-pepper hair, deep-blue eyes and movie-star good looks. He fixed his attention on Bobby, flashed her a toothpaste-commercial smile and approached with his hand extended. "Well, hello. I'm Mayor Tobias Rawlins."

"I'm Bobby Roberts." She shook his hand, expecting it to feel soft and sweaty, like a sleazy politician, but instead it was firm and very masculine.

"I didn't know Gage had hired a secretary." He moved closer, still holding her hand.

Blushing, she gently pried it loose. "Oh, he didn't hire me."

"Bobby is just helping out." Gage stalked over and stepped between them.

Bobby studied the two men a minute. Neither seemed

to like each other. She wasn't too experienced at reading testosterone levels, but if they could be measured on a Richter scale, they'd probably just jumped to a five. Not devastation level, but high enough to get your attention.

The sheriff folded his arms in front of him. "Bobby volunteered to help Cleetus with the report for tonight's meeting. You didn't need to come get it. I'd planned to bring it with me, Tobias. Was there something else you needed?"

The other man stepped backward. "I heard someone was prowling around out behind the bank today. Did you find out who it was?"

Great. This was Gage's chance to inform the mayor he'd arrested her.

"Far as I could tell it was just someone who should've been in school messing around," he said instead.

Bobby bristled at the veiled insult. She resisted the urge to take the pencil on the desk and poke Gage in the back with it—hard.

"Okay. I'll see you tonight at the town-council meeting." Tobias turned to leave, pausing to hold the door open. "It was a pleasure meeting you, Bobby Roberts. I hope to see more of you around town."

"I'm sure you will, sir. And it was very nice to meet you, too." She smiled and waved at him.

Once the door closed, Gage glanced over his shoulder. "You can cut the charm, Ms. Roberts. You're not staying in town long enough to win the Mayor's attention." Ice filled the sheriff's voice. He turned and placed both hands flat on the desk and leaned toward her. "You need to go home before you get into some real trouble."

Okay, she'd had enough of his boorish treatment today. She hit save and print on the computer.

The man had some nerve. He might not take her detective work seriously, but she was tired of him using his size to intimidate her. Slowly, she pushed the rolling chair back and stood. She placed both her hands flat on the other side of the desk, straightened both her arms and leaned forward, meeting him nose to nose.

"No, Sheriff Justice, I don't. I came to town to do a job. And just like you, I keep my promises. When I find the information my client needs I'll leave. And not a moment sooner."

The second hand on the wall clock ticked by a full minute. They stood there, nearly touching, each measuring the other's determination.

Damn, the woman had backbone. Gage would give her that. He hadn't been this intrigued or exasperated by a woman, ever. He owed her some slack after manhandling her today.

Slowly, Gage backed away from the desk. "I can't make you leave, but I don't want you digging around anymore in people's trash. Be here tomorrow morning and we'll discuss your case."

"Really?"

He almost laughed at her surprise. She hadn't expected to win their little battle of wills. He'd hate to burst her bubble that she really hadn't. The sooner he solved her case for her, the sooner he could get her out of town and out of his mind.

"My gun?" She held out her hand.

"For now I'll just hold onto it." Her eyes narrowed and he held up his hand to stall her argument. "You can have it back tomorrow after we talk. Get the rest of your things and I'll give you a lift over to your car."

"You don't have to do that. I can find my way back over to the bank." She got her keys out of her purse and started for the door.

"That's nice to know, but your car isn't parked in the alley behind the bank anymore."

That stopped her escape mid-stride. "What? You told me it would be safe there."

"No, I told you no one would break into it and steal your things." He opened the door and held it for her. "Your vehicle was blocking the alleyway, so I had Bill Johnson tow it over to his garage for everyone's safety."

She shoved one hand onto her hip and fixed him with a very angry stare. "Great. And how much is this going to cost me?"

"Nothing. You can think of it as an added feature of spending time in Westen's jail. A room for you and boarding for your car."

Her eyes narrowed. "If that was a joke, it wasn't the least bit funny."

"Come on. I'll give you a ride over to Bill's. It's about four miles out of town."

She considered his offer a moment longer. With a nod, she pulled her purse strap tighter on her shoulder and walked past him. The soft scent he'd smelled this afternoon when he'd held her tickled his nose as she passed by. He resisted the urge to pull her back and into his arms. Something as soft and no doubt innocent as Bobby Roberts had no place in his life.

"Where's your car?" she asked as he pulled the office door shut and locked it.

"Right there." He pointed behind her.

She turned, stared at the big black-and-chrome motorcycle and took a step backward as if it would jump the curb and bite her. "You've got to be kidding."

"Lady, when it comes to my Harley, I'm deadly serious." He straddled the machine, started the engine and held out his helmet to her. When she stood frozen in place he grinned at her. "Don't tell me the big, bad private detective is a coward?"

When her eyes narrowed again, she resembled one pissed-off kitten ready to hiss or scratch his eyes out. Instead she lifted her purse, slipped the strap over her head so the leather crossed her chest between her breasts. The action pulled the sweater blouse tight across them and gave him a good idea how they'd fill his hands without being too much to handle. He shook off the image as she took his helmet and pulled it on. She straddled the bike behind him, sitting as far from him as she could, trying not to touch him except where her thighs rested against the outside of his.

He glanced back over his shoulder. "You might want to hold on to something."

"That's okay. I'm just fine."

Fine, his ass.

Her back straight, her hands in her lap, once again she looked like a prim and proper schoolteacher. Given her new career choice—and there was no way she'd convince him she'd been a detective for very long—he wondered if she might have a wild side hidden beneath the surface. Time to put her to the test.

He gunned the engine and peeled away from the curb.

"Oh crap…" she shrieked behind him and clutched at his shirt.

With one hand, he pried her fingers loose and pulled her forward, until her chest pressed the entire length of his back, and she had both arms wrapped securely around him.

"You did that on purpose," she yelled over the motorcycle's roar.

"You were being stubborn," he yelled back and sped down Main Street.

The cool spring air whipping past them and the engine's rumble beneath them blocked any further conversation. At the last traffic light, he turned left to head toward the highway that passed just north of town. As he leaned the bike into the turn Bobby's arms tightened around him. He grinned more. He'd lay money that she'd never been on a chopper in her life.

As they flew across the highway, an eighteen-wheeler passed them going the opposite way. The gust of wind blew the bike sideways, but years of practice let him control it with ease. Behind him, Bobby clutched him tighter. He grinned with satisfaction when she buried her head against his shoulder. He'd swear he heard her cussing, but the words were muffled. After a minute she lifted her head and relaxed a little. He missed the warmth of her pressed tight to his body.

All too soon, Bill's service station and auto repair came into view. Gage let up on the gas, slowing the bike before pulling onto the semi-broken asphalt on the shoulder of the road. He maneuvered onto the pothole-riddled drive into Bill's place. All the lights were out, signaling that Bill had closed shop for the night. Gage drove right up beside Bobby's car and turned off his engine.

"Jail-to-car service," he said, just to get a rise out of

her.

"Don't quit your day job, comedian."

The censure in her voice almost made him laugh. She wiggled back on the bike and climbed out from behind him. For a second her legs wobbled, and he reached out to steady her. "Whoa there."

Her body swayed toward him, and he instinctively wrapped his arms around her. Her hand rested on his shoulder, her head bent. "I'm sorry," she whispered. "I've never been on a motorcycle before. It was..."

He grinned at her. "Frightening?"

She lifted her head, her eyes sparkling. "No, exhilarating. I'd love to do it again sometime."

He drew back a little, surprised.

She pulled off the helmet and shook out her hair. Blood surged right down to his groin and he tightened behind his zipper. She was too tempting.

With a saucy wink, she patted his shoulder and stepped out of his arms, which suddenly felt empty. To keep from reaching for her, he dropped his hands to his thighs and gripped them while he watched as she walked around the bike to her car. Despite her bravado, he couldn't help noticing her gait was just a little bit on the shaky side.

He waited for her to pull out, noting her rear vehicle tag was from Hamilton County in southern Ohio.

Wonder where she's staying?

She headed farther down the highway, away from Westen and the Inn. Dread tickled his mind. Surely she wasn't headed to the local motel two exits down, but staying in Columbus at a safer one. It was only about an hour's drive.

He started his bike once more, pulled out and

followed her at a safe distance. He'd just make sure she'd had sense enough to stay in the city in a big hotel.

Two minutes later her car turned off the highway into the motel's parking lot. Gage cursed a blue streak. He pulled into the lot in just enough time to see her close her room door behind her.

For a moment he sat in the parking lot, studying the layout, the engine still purring beneath him. The motel itself was clean and well maintained. He knew the owner personally. His dad had even gone to church with Walt and Mary Lou. Problem was, the motel sat next to a gas station and all-night diner, which made their clientele mostly truckers and strangers passing through town. Even with the best security, a woman staying in an isolated area with who knew what kind of men in nearby rooms had the potential for disaster.

He revved the engine, turned his bike and headed back to Westen. The town council meeting started in thirty minutes.

So much for dinner.

The town was his responsibility, not Bobby Roberts, PI. Besides, it was only for one night. Tomorrow he'd see that she finished her business in town. Then he'd ship the little lady back to whatever suburb she'd wandered out of— safe, sound and with all her body parts still intact.

Bobby let the corner of the curtain fall back over the window ledge once the sheriff's motorcycle turned out of the parking lot onto the highway.

Pacing the short length of the motel room she slapped her hands against her thighs and let her anger surge.

"Who does he think he is? The man had some nerve

following me to my motel."

What did he think she was going to do, break into the bank in the middle of the night? She was a private investigator, not a criminal. Although by the way he treated her, you'd think she was kin to Bonnie and Clyde.

"Ugh." She slumped down on the bed and threw her arm over her eyes.

Her first day as a PI and things hadn't gone nearly as smoothly as she'd expected. She'd believed the easiest way to find some bank information would be to search through the trash. Well, she really hadn't found more than rotted produce from the grocery on the other side of the alley.

But she had landed in the arms of a very solid man.

Suddenly, the whole thing turned funny. A giggle escaped her. The look on his face when she'd landed in his arms had been so sexy, and the next moment he'd been as cold as a human ice sculpture.

"Oh, God!" She started laughing harder, tears filling her eyes. She'd even managed to pick a banana peel off his shoulder.

The muffled sound of her cell phone's ringtone sounded from her purse. Drying her eyes, she retrieved it halfway through the second round of "Wild Thing". She looked at the caller ID.

Great. Chloe. Just the person she didn't need to talk to right now.

"Hello."

"Hey, Sis. How's it going?"

Disastrously. I'm getting nowhere fast.

"Good," Bobby lied. "I'm in Westen and have met with the local sheriff." Well, technically she'd met him, and she did have a meeting set up for tomorrow.

"Anything interesting happen on the case today?"

Let's see, first I went dumpster diving. Then I fell on top of six feet, three inches of solid man, who handcuffed me and dragged me off to jail. Next, I decoded a secret filing system the Nazis would've envied. And finally had my first ride on a motorcycle straddled on behind the most infuriating and delicious man I've ever been near.

"Nope, nothing really interesting happened today."

"Any luck with the bank finding those letters?" Chloe munched onto something hard on the other end of the line.

"Are you eating Doritos?"

"Um, yes."

"Is that dinner? How can anyone stay as thin as you, eating nothing but junk food all the time?"

"Lucky genes, I guess."

"Rub it in."

It did help that her sister was nearly five feet, ten inches tall. Both Chloe and Dylan were. She, on the other hand, had been *blessed* with their mother's height of almost five-five if she teased her hair, and had to watch everything that went into her mouth.

"Besides, it's not dinner. Just something to tie me over. I've been in court all day and I need something before I drive home. My blood sugar is probably nil at the moment." Chloe slurped into a straw in her ear. "Didn't I move out of your house four years ago? You aren't supposed to be playing mom anymore. Wasn't that the whole point of you doing this PI thing for me? So you could finally live a life with some fun and adventure?"

Bobby lay back on the bed again. Chloe had a point. She'd put her life on hold for eighteen years to raise her two sisters. "You're right. It's not my responsibility anymore to be your mother. If you want to eat junk food night and day, it's not my problem. Just don't come crying to me when your metabolism slows down."

"You can't guilt me out of it either." Chloe munched in her ear again. "So, what have you learned about Mr. Byrd's bank loan?"

"Today I mostly got some background information from the local deputy. He confirmed what your Norman Byrd told us. Mr. Byrd was a loner and lived all his life on his farm outside of town. As for the letters, I'll try to find them tomorrow."

"Mm-hmm. My client is Mr. Byrd's only blood relative, but he hadn't seen him since he was a small child. Did the deputy know anything about the supposed bank loan? Norman swears his uncle won't have anything to do with banks."

That was the whole crux of her case. Norman Byrd swore there was no way his uncle would get a bank loan with his land as collateral and he'd hired Chloe's firm to prove the fact. Bobby was sure Cleetus had no idea what kind of loans or business the elder Mr. Byrd had participated in.

"No. He didn't strike me as one who'd pry into people's financial records. I'll stop by the bank tomorrow and see what I can find out from them."

"I suppose I can subpoena the bank records."

"Not yet, Chloe. If those letters disappeared, a subpoena won't make them reappear. Let me see what I can find out." Bobby tried not to sound panicked. She'd convinced Chloe she could get the information and she would. Besides, she wasn't ready to leave Westen and its arrogant sheriff just yet.

"I don't know, Bobby. I hate to have you wasting your time and money…" The hesitation on the other end of the line gave her an opening.

"I'm not wasting my time. As far as money goes, believe me I've hardly spent more than gas money." Staying locked in the jail she hadn't even spent money on food today. "If nothing else, after tomorrow I'll be able to tell you the Loan Officer's name to put on the subpoena."

"Okay. Jeez, I wish you'd decided to go on a cruise for adventure. I never should've let you talk me into investigating this case for me."

Bobby rolled her eyes and stuck her tongue out at the cell phone. Dammit, her sisters owed her this time. "You know Chloe, I didn't complain when you wanted to follow your dream to go to law school."

"Oh no, don't you start telling me how you worked summer school every year to supplement my law school scholarship." Chloe laughed into the phone. "I know I owe you for that and so many more things. Why do you think I gave into this harebrained scheme of yours?"

It was Bobby's turn to laugh. Both Chloe and Dylan had outgrown her guilt-complex lectures. "So I'm still on the case?"

"Sure, Sis. Just keep me posted if you find out anything I can use. The case doesn't go to court for another two months."

They talked a few more minutes about Chloe's other cases and their sister's upcoming graduation. Bobby promised that no matter what she'd meet Chloe in Columbus for Dylan's Med-school graduation ceremony.

It was what her parents would have expected of them. All three daughters graduating from school and with professional jobs. Well, okay, two out of three had professions they liked.

Bobby sighed as she closed her cell phone. Chloe had thrown her this bone of a case to let her "play" detective. It was up to her to do a good job. The idea of being trapped teaching class one more year made her cringe with sick dread.

Her stomach growled loud enough to be heard three miles away. The snack bar she'd eaten earlier wouldn't get her through the night. Unlike her younger siblings, she couldn't survive simply on junk food. She needed some all-American protein, in the form of a cheeseburger. She glanced at her watch. Nearly nine. That little café in the center of Westen was probably closed by now.

Okay, she had two options. She could climb into her car and drive down the highway until she found a fast-food place, get a burger and some fries, bring them back and eat in her room, which would mean her food would be cold and congealed. Or she could take a chance and eat at the greasy-spoon diner less than a hundred yards from her room.

A glance out her window showed the light on at the café on the near side of the parking lot. A man stood behind the counter serving people. Her stomach growled again followed by a hollow pain deep inside. Okay. Greasy-spoon diner it was. She grabbed her purse and room key.

Chapter Four

Assistant District Attorney Moira Dudson stalked back into her office, clicked on the florescent lights and slammed the door behind her. Today's verdict was her third loss in as many months. If she wanted her party's political backers to support her bid for District Attorney this fall, she needed to make some headlines—fast. Her political career was going to hell faster than a serial killer in the electric chair.

She slumped down into her leather chair, kicked off her Carmen Ho linen stilettos and turned to stare at the photos on the wall beside her. There was a picture of her shaking hands with the chief of police. The headline read, "Assistant DA Instrumental in Cracking Cocaine Ring". Another photo showed her at a political fundraiser, arm-in-arm with both the Mayor and Governor. Those photos were nearly three years old.

It was supposed to be so easy. As a junior assistant,

she'd managed to catapult herself into the limelight three years ago with that high-profile drug bust. There should've been more of those. After all, she'd had an inside man undercover in the drug scene.

Gage. The greatest disappointment in her life.

Frustration rumbled through her like the beginning of a late-spring thunderstorm. They should've been the dynamic duo. Him busting the criminals and she prosecuting them, making a name for herself and moving them both into the state's political realm. Instead he spent the first three years of their marriage undercover following a cocaine trail. Just when the major raid took place and they should've been soaring into the limelight, he managed to get himself shot.

Not just once.

Not just twice.

But three damn times.

A tentative knock sounded on her door.

She swallowed the urge to yell at the intruder. What little patience she had today had been used up kissing her boss's ass tonight at dinner. But gossip traveled fast in this office and she had an image to maintain. Screaming like a fishwife at the door wouldn't help her get anywhere.

The knock sounded a second time, this time a little stronger.

Exhaling, she kicked her shoes under the desk, opened a file and pulled out a pen.

Always give the illusion of being busy.

"Come in."

The door opened and her secretary—plain, efficient, the nondescript type of helper she preferred to make her stand out whenever they were seen together—stepped inside.

"Sorry to disturb you, Ms. Dudson, but I wanted to give you your phone messages before I left for the night."

"Thank you, Lisa." She held out her hand and took the slips of paper from the mousy blonde, who waited while she flipped through them.

Damn. Gage hadn't returned her call. The man was impossible.

She clenched her teeth to keep from grinding on the expensive orthodontic work she'd paid for to give her a million-dollar smile. Pressure built inside her chest and she stared at the slips in her hands as if thinking, all the while forcing air slowly into and out of her lungs.

"No message from Sheriff Justice over in Westen?" She never referred to Gage as her ex-husband within earshot of subordinates. That part of her life was in the past. She refused to admit to a failure.

"No, ma'am."

"Thank you. Be here bright and early tomorrow, I'd like to get a head start on the Smith-Johnson case." She glanced at Lisa, who had edged out of the office and started to close the door. "Leave it open."

"Yes, ma'am."

Focusing on the papers in front of her, Moira listened for the elevator bell signaling she was alone in the office. She tossed her pen onto the desk and leaned back in her chair once more.

Gage wasn't calling her back just to piss her off. The man gave stubborn a whole new meaning. After three years you'd think he'd have forgiven her at least enough to take a phone call. He'd answered her first call to his cell this morning, but hung up immediately. The next three calls had gone directly to his voicemail, which he apparently planned to ignore.

She opened her phone book and dialed his home number, the one his father had originally given her. It rang and rang. The clock on the shelves lining her office read eight. Lord knows that small town closed its doors early. Where else would he be?

Suddenly the phone clicked over.

"This is Gage. Hear the beep. Leave a message."

Abrupt and to the point. He'd gotten almost sullen since his little accident.

The phone beeped.

"Gage, it's Moira. Look, I have some interesting intel I need to talk with you about." She lowered her voice to sound huskily seductive, just the way he'd always liked. "Call me."

After hanging up, she opened her bottom file drawer and lifted out the file the narcotics detective she'd been sleeping with had given her. He'd told her the State meth taskforce was looking at the northeastern to central area of the state, right where Westen was located, as a possible new source of the drug. They also had major drug raids scheduled to get the current supplies off the streets. When they'd done so, they planned to concentrate efforts to close down the rural labs.

If she moved quickly, she could position herself to not only tip off the taskforce, but get credit for the bust and possibly maneuver herself out of local politics into the state arena.

All she needed was Gage's cooperation. And she'd get it no matter how dirty she had to play.

***

Gage cursed himself for a fool as he rode back down

the highway to the one-stop motel and diner again. The lady detective was safe and sound behind her locked door. She was probably sound asleep in her bed.

The idea of her in bed had the vision of the first moment he saw her popping into his mind once more. Okay, the first moment he'd seen her ass. He wondered if it looked as good in the flesh as it had with those jeans stretched across those round curves. He'd love to see her on her hands and knees in front of him, his hands cupping those firm round cheeks in his palms as he...

"What the hell?" His erotic dream burst as he pulled into the parking lot and found it missing one thing. Her car. "Where the hell has she gone at this time of night?"

He stopped the bike in front of room number six and stomped to the door. No sign of forced entry. He tried the knob.

Locked.

He pounded on it. "Bobby?"

No answer.

Was she inside? Hurt? Had someone attacked her? Stolen her car? Left her for dead?

"Something I can help you with, Sheriff?"

Gage swung around to see Walt Sanders strolling out the diner's door. He met him halfway. "Do you know where the lady who's staying in this room might have gone?"

"Ms. Roberts?" The motel owner's head shook as he spoke, his white hair bobbing with the effort.

Gage nodded.

"Nice lady. She came in a little while ago wanting something to eat. I hated having to tell her the grill was busted. All I'm serving tonight is coffee and dessert. She said she needed something with more meat on it."

"Did she head toward the McDonald's over near the interstate?" Gage started for his bike.

"Nope. I sent her on over to the Wagon Wheel. She was looking for a big thick burger and onion rings. You know they make the best in town, even if they are my competitors."

"Thanks, Walt." Gage straddled the bike and kicked the starter. "Hey, Walt, is room five or seven open tonight?"

"Seven is. Why?"

"Hold it for me, okay?"

"Sure thing, Sheriff." Walt gave him a puzzled look.

Gage gunned the engine and headed back toward town and the tavern on the other side. He didn't want to take the time to explain he'd be staying in the room to keep an eye on the lady PI tonight. He just prayed she hadn't gotten into any more trouble over at the Wagon Wheel.

What had Walt been thinking to send her there? As much as Gage liked hanging out at the tavern, drinking a whiskey and trying to forget his problems, it wasn't exactly a place a lady like Bobby should be visiting. Westen didn't have a lot of troublemakers or delinquent types. But what few there were called the Wagon Wheel home.

With every mile his bike covered he cussed a blue streak. He should've tossed her back in the jail cell for the night. Nothing good came from private investigators, especially women who played at being one.

Damn, damn, damn.

The Wagon Wheel's parking lot was filled with a couple of eighteen wheelers and cars that had mostly seen better days. No Lexuses or BMWs among the bunch. In fact, the only vehicle that had any street value was Bobby's little Toyota. He maneuvered his bike next to it, so he wouldn't have far to go after he hauled her fanny out of the tavern.

The twangy sound of a steel guitar playing the bridge to an old Conway Twitty song blasted Gage's ears as he entered. It was the kind of place where a man could down a few drinks with the guys without some tight-assed woman whining at him. The tables were covered with red-and-white plastic tablecloths. Dartboards and neon-trimmed beer signs hung on the walls and over the bar. If a fight broke out or the toilets overflowed, well, it just added to the place's ambiance.

In one half of the tavern sat felt-covered pool tables where three guys decked out in biker leathers and worn jeans held pool cues while a fourth took his shot. Half-drunk beers sat in clear mugs on the tables lining the poolroom. Two women he knew were the area's working prostitutes sat on barstools flirting with the men watching the game. Tonight was their lucky night. There was only one woman he planned on taking out of here.

At the bar sat two regulars, Harv and Mac. The two men must be near eighty. They'd served in Korea together, were widowed and spent every night at the bar just to keep from going home to their empty houses. Luckily they only drank a couple of beers while they reminisced and he'd never had to arrest either for DUI.

As Gage scanned the room it took a moment for him to find Bobby, but that was only because she'd managed to get herself caught at a corner table with two burly men who blocked his view.

Her gaze met his and she barely hid the slight look of panic in them. Something hot and feral leapt inside him.

No one was going to hurt her, not on his watch. His first instinct was to pummel both men, then carry Bobby, over his shoulder if necessary, out of the tavern.

For a moment he studied her and the two men. She didn't seem to be in any *real* trouble. She took a bite of her cheeseburger and smiled at one of the men. The same kind smile she'd given Cleetus, but not him. Most women would be nervous being cornered by two strange men, whom he'd bet were truckers staying at the same motel she was. The naïve woman seemed to be trying to sweet-talk them.

What was the matter with him? Not like she was his responsibility. Last he checked America was still a free country and the woman had the right to get herself raped or killed if she wanted to. He ought to just turn around and head home.

Wait a minute. Why should he be the one to go home? He was here. The food was good. A bottle of Jack was behind the bar. Might as well have a shot. It might be fun to watch the lady detective get herself out of this mess.

He sauntered over to the bar.

"Evening, Sheriff." Ralph, the Wagon Wheel's owner and chief bartender greeted him, setting a shot glass in front of him and filling it with the fine amber whiskey. "You're a little late tonight, aren't you?"

Did Ralph really know his habits so well? He didn't come in every night to drink. Or did he? He certainly had when he'd first come back to Westen last year. He'd needed something to chase away the nightmares so he could sleep. Dad had been patient with him, even driving by to take him home on those first nights when he'd nearly drunk himself into a stupor. But after a few months at home his nightmares had eased. Subsequently, he'd had to deal with his father's cancer and death. Now he only had one drink. Something else he'd promised his dad.

"Had a council meeting tonight." Gage straddled a barstool at an angle that let him easily observe the corner table behind him through the bar's mirror.

"Maybe I ought to pour you a double," the bartender laughed.

"No thanks, Ralph." As tempting as the idea was, Gage had a feeling he'd better keep his wits about him. Who knew what trouble Ms. Roberts could get herself into? "Although, just listening to Mayor Rawlins drone on about his plans for the town would make a Baptist minister drink."

Ralph laughed again. "That it would, Sheriff."

The crowd by the pool tables called for more beer and Ralph went to pour another pitcher. Gage sipped his whiskey, his back to the corner Bobby sat in, but he could see every detail in the mirror across from him.

The little brunette nodded at something one of the men said, picking up her burger and sinking her perfectly straight white teeth into the bread and meat. Wonder what it would feel like having those pearly whites nibble their way over his skin. Heat surged to his groin and he swallowed hard, nearly choking on the whiskey.

What was it about this woman that had him thinking like some hormone-crazed teenager? The last time he'd had this problem was when he'd seen Maureen Yoder in her bikini at the high school swim meet his freshman year. Now, getting all hot and bothered over Maureen he could understand. The girl had the figure of a Playboy pinup.

He glanced in the mirror. But Ms. Roberts? She looked more like the pinup of the year for the National Education Association. Wholesome. Sweet. Nothing to really stand her out in a crowd. Well, nothing if you didn't include that nice ass.

"Ralph." He called the other man over as he stepped behind the bar once more. "How about asking Margie to throw me a burger on the grill?"

"Sure thing, Sheriff. Fries, too?"

Gage glanced at the mirror where his little detective still held court. He was pretty sure only one of his hungers was getting eased tonight. "Might as well."

Since laughter emitted from the corner booth and neither man had made an unwanted move on Bobby, Gage leaned over the bar and sipped his whiskey while he watched the sports channel on the bar's TV. Once his food arrived, he split his attention between watching Bobby and catching up on the day's baseball scores as he ate. Every so often he'd glance into the mirror to find Bobby's gaze on him. For a moment he'd watch her, always waiting until she looked away.

Three more bites and he'd be finished. Afterward he'd have to convince her it was time to return to the hotel. He just had to remember they were getting separate rooms.

A movement in the mirror caught his attention. She'd stood, slipped her purse on her shoulder and was moving his way.

Great. He didn't want to leave his dinner unfinished, but there was no way he wasn't following her back to the motel.

"Hope your dinner was as good as mine, Sheriff," she said right behind him just as he took half of his remaining burger in one big bite. She sauntered away, only she didn't head for the exit. Oh no, not her.

Instead she went through the hallway to the restrooms.

Dammit. Of course she wouldn't do the sensible thing and head for home. No, she'd hang around and give the men who'd been eyeing her all night time to muster up their courage to do something stupid. He glanced in the mirror. The beefier guy, dressed in a plaid shirt, faded jeans and the Gone Fishin' baseball cap leaned across to his buddy and whispered something. Tall and skinny, with the stocking cap on, grinned and nodded in the direction Bobby had just headed.

Yep. They were going to do something stupid.

He ate one last fry, looked at his bill and fished the money out of his wallet. He laid them both on the bar next to his plate and fixed his sheriff's badge onto his front shirt pocket once more. Leaning back in his chair, gaze fixed on the hallway, he waited.

Bobby took a deep breath before opening the restroom door. Despite what her dinner companions suggested, she wasn't going to dance tonight. Maybe if she were lucky, they got tired of waiting and left the tavern. If she were going to wish for the impossible, she might as well wish the sheriff gone, too.

She couldn't believe it when he'd walked into the tavern. For a moment she'd been relieved that he'd come and rescue her from the two truckers who'd cornered her. But no, he planted himself at the bar instead. At first she thought she'd been mistaken and he hadn't really seen her, except she'd caught him watching her in the mirror. He'd seemed rather pleased by her dilemma.

So much for a knight in shining armor. She hadn't needed a man's help since her father died, and she could get herself out of this pickle without one now.

Okay, what's the plan?

Make a beeline straight for the door. Don't talk to anyone. Don't look around to see if the sheriff is watching. Once outside, get in the car. Lock the car doors. Head back to the motel.

Right. Simple.

She pulled the door open, clutched her purse by the strap on her shoulder, and headed toward the tavern door.

Another country song suddenly blared from the jukebox.

"Hey there, little lady," someone grabbed her by the arm.

She looked up to see Carl—at least she was pretty sure that's what the bigger of the two men had called himself—grinning down at her.

"How about we have us a little dance?"

"Um," she tried to pull away from the grip he had on her arm, at the same time keeping a smile plastered on her face. "I don't really know how to do country dancing."

"That's okay, sweetheart." He pulled her up against his body, and grabbed hold of her other hand. "I can teach ya everything ya need to know."

"Carl, I really need to head home." She straightened her arms to put some much-needed breathing room between her and her dance partner. The combination of body odor and too many beers threatened to have her revisiting her dinner.

"The night ain't over, yet. Me and Slim want to dance 'til dawn."

"Um, don't you have to get your cargo to California?" She closed her eyes as he whirled her around. She wasn't going to fall and cause a scene. Especially with the sheriff sitting at the bar watching them. Once Carl had stopped trying to twirl her like a top, she opened her eyes, meeting Gage's amused gaze in the bar's mirror.

The big lug still wasn't going to help her. Okay. She didn't need his help. She could get herself out of this. Things weren't that bad. The two truckers simply wanted a dance.

"We ain't got nothin' perishable in our trucks this time, so we can be a day later if we want." Carl tried to pull her closer again.

This time she was ready for him. She straightened her arm and at the same time brought her shoe down hard on his foot. Which immediately gained her another inch of space. "Oh, I'm sorry. I never was good at dancing."

"That's okay. We'll just slow down a little." With those words, he slowed to a short step of a waltz, released his hold on her waist and slipped his hand down to cup her butt.

No way was she going to let him maul her in a public place. "Now, Carl, I agreed to a dance." Actually she hadn't but couldn't see that argument getting her any closer to the door. She slipped her free hand down, pried his fingers loose and attached his beefy hand back to her waist. She smiled to ease the message. "But only if you're a gentleman."

When he turned her once more, she glanced at the sheriff. He'd turned on his barstool and sat watching them. The brim of his baseball cap and the bar's dim lighting prevented her from really seeing his eyes, but it looked like all traces of humor had left his face.

Interesting. Wonder what caused that reaction?

"Didn't you say you had a girlfriend in California?" She smiled up at Carl again. No reaction from Gage.

"Yeah. I got one there and in South Carolina, too. I just got too much lovin' not to spread it around." He leered at her once more and slipped his hand down to her butt again.

This time she hesitated a moment before moving the man's hand back to her waist. A movement from the bar caught her attention. Gage had left his seat, his attention focused on the dance area. For some reason she couldn't fathom, he didn't want the trucker groping her butt any more than she did, which was odd. Nearing forty she'd given up hope of having buns of steel some time ago. And wasn't that what all men wanted? At least TV and magazines said so.

After a moment, Gage made a beeline straight for them, a scowl on his face. Apparently he'd decided to intervene. Too little, too late. No way was she going to let him think he'd rescued her.

"Now, Carl. As much as those two ladies don't mind sharing you, I'm not really looking for a new friend." She pushed back as the song came to an end and pulled her hand out of his. "It's time for me to go now."

"But little lady, Slim needs a dance, too. Don't ya', Slim?" Carl stepped forward, corralling her toward his buddy.

Bobby held her ground. "I said, I'm done, now let me go!" She shoved him back, at the same time keeping an eye on Gage's approaching form.

"The lady said she wants to leave," he said in that deep, I'm-in-charge-here voice of his. "I suggest you let her leave."

"Look, buddy, this little lady's ours. Go find your own..." Carl stopped mid-sentence as he turned. Beads of sweat suddenly popped out on his forehead and all the blood rushed out of his face, leaving him a large mass of pale, quivering flesh looking into the face of imminent death. "Uh, hey, Sheriff. We wasn't causing no trouble."

"If that's the case, I suggest you move away and let the lady leave." The command had Carl stumbling two steps out of the path between Gage and Bobby.

Gage reached over and grasped her elbow, pulling her toward him and the door. "It's time to leave, Bobby."

"Now look here, Sheriff." She tried to pull her arm away. "You can't order me about. I'll leave when I'm ready."

"Now." He gave her a little shove toward the door, releasing her arm. "Before I have to cite you for disturbing the peace."

She wanted to ask him whose peace he thought she was disturbing, but the threat of the small jail cell in her future stopped the retort on the tip of her tongue.

Except for the new song playing on the jukebox the tavern fell silent. The pool players moved closer, leaning on their cues, waiting to see what would happen next.

Bobby glanced around then back at Gage. She could stand and argue with him and cause a bigger scene, but the intense anger rolling off him suggested she pick her battles with this man very carefully. Tonight, retreat seemed her best option. Straightening her back and holding her head high, she turned and marched out the door, heading to her car with all the dignity she could muster.

Stupid man.

Despite what he thought, she could've handled the situation just fine on her own. She slammed her car door shut and started the engine. For a split second she considered driving right over his motorcycle as she pulled out, but she'd enjoyed riding on it so much she hated punishing it for its owner's overbearing treatment.

She did let a little gravel spin out beneath her tires as she left the parking lot onto the county road once more. With a quick glance in her rearview mirror she saw Gage leave the bar and climb on his Harley. At least he left the bar before anyone got hurt. Well, almost anyone. Humiliation was never her strong suit.

How dare he treat her like some inane child who'd been caught drinking in a bar by her daddy? She'd been on her own since she was nineteen and raised her younger sisters without his or anyone else's help.

The streets of Westen were deserted as she drove through them. Good thing. Her mind swirling in a jetty of anger, she wasn't quite sure when she pulled onto the highway and headed west toward her motel room.

Just as she turned into the parking lot, the rumble of a motor sounded behind her. She looked in her rearview mirror once more to see Gage's motorcycle arriving right behind her.

Now what?

Why was the man following her? She certainly didn't need an escort to her motel. Didn't he trust her to go there? The man's arrogance knew no bounds.

She pulled to a stop in front of her room door, grabbed her purse and climbed out of the car. She slammed the car door and stalked around the rear just as Gage pulled the motorcycle to a stop.

"What do you think you're doing?" she said,

punching him on his shoulder with her finger.

"I'm making sure you weren't followed from the tavern." He twisted around, dismounting and forcing her to take a step back or get knocked to the ground.

Crossing her arms over her chest she waited for him to turn and face her. "Exactly who did you think was going to follow me?"

"Your dinner buddies for one." He grasped her by the elbow and tried to turn her toward her room. "And any crazy out on the road this late at night for another."

She dug her heels in and jerked her arm free. "Quit that. You've been manhandling me all day. And quite frankly I'm a little tired of it."

He turned and took a step forward, pinning her between her car and his body. "Look, I know you've come from the big city to a small town and think nothing bad can happen to you. Open your eyes and look around you." He waved his arm toward the parking lot filled with big rigs. "You're in a dark and secluded area. Most of these truckers are hardworking guys who won't bother you. But there may be someone like the two guys back at the tavern who might just decide to take more than you're willing to give."

"I don't think they meant to harm me." She leaned back, the feral look in his eyes warning her she'd crossed the line with his patience.

"You don't think so?" He loomed closer. "His hands all over your ass seemed harmless to you? You didn't mind him forcing you up against him? Or maybe you'd rather he'd done something like this?"

Gage grabbed her by the shoulders and pulled her hard against his body. He hesitated a moment. "Oh hell," he growled out before capturing her lips with his.

The fierceness of his embrace and kiss startled her. She gripped his arms and tried to push him away. What happened next completely confused her. He changed tactics. His lips softened against hers, his tongue slipping out to tease her. He slid one hand down her back to press her closer, while he let the other slide into her hair to hold her head still.

Heat started in her chest and spread outwards. She clutched his denim jacket to pull him closer. Never in her life had she wanted a man as much as she suddenly wanted this man. She wanted him to claim her and keep her. She wanted to strip him naked, and taste every inch of him.

"Yes, baby," he moaned against her mouth. Slowly he slid his lips to her jaw and over to nibble on her ear. The grip in her hair tightened as he turned her head to the side, arching her neck and skimming his teeth against the sensitive flesh he'd exposed.

She bent one leg and curled it around his jean-clad thigh, pulling him in tighter. Was it possible to get any closer? She didn't know, but the hard bulge in his jeans felt delicious rubbing against her. A moan escaped her.

He released his hold on her hair and reached down with both hands to cup both her butt cheeks. As he pulled her in tighter, he sank his lips into the juncture of her neck and shoulder. For a minute he ground himself against her as he nipped at her pulse, sending wave after wave of heat coursing through her.

Slowly he eased his mouth from her sensitive flesh. Her heart pounded so hard in her chest the people in the next county could probably hear it. She gulped in air and turned to stare at him. Passion filled his eyes and he seemed to be having trouble controlling his breathing, too. He hadn't released his grip on her bottom. In fact, he'd begun kneading each cheek with his hands.

"I wanted to knock that trucker on his ass when he grabbed you here. I didn't want to see another man's hands holding you like this."

The anger and possessiveness he implied with those words both thrilled and surprised her. No man had ever shown any jealousy over her, especially not one she'd known less than twenty-four hours. The reality of the situation hit her. She was standing in a motel parking lot, making out with a man she barely knew, and he was mauling her like some common streetwalker. Worse, she was enjoying every second of it.

She dropped her leg, and pushed with all her might against his shoulders. "Let me go."

He released his hold on her and braced both hands on either side of her against her car, virtually trapping her between them. He leaned in until they were practically eye-to-eye. "Scared, aren't you?"

All she could manage was a swallow and a nod.

"And you should be. You don't know me any better than those truckers in the tavern tonight." He reached up and smoothed a loose strand of her hair from her cheek. "This isn't the safe little classroom, Bobby. There are all kinds of dangers out here in the real world. You'd better open your eyes and pay attention before you get hurt."

Before she could say anything else, he pushed himself away from her, waving his hand at the parking lot filled with both cars and big-rig trucks. "See all these vehicles? Every one of them belongs to a stranger. Most of them are innocent people just looking for a place to rest before continuing on their journey, but any one of them could be a potential killer traveling the back roads looking for an easy victim to prey upon. You picked a spot where no one knows you, no one knows the people here and it's isolated from any sort of help. This is the worst place for a woman alone to spend the night."

Okay. He'd already made his point. He didn't have to make her feel more stupid. She stepped to the side and fished her keys from her purse. "Well, it's a little late to get a room in town, isn't it?"

She looked around a minute before trying to unlock her door. Her hand shook so badly she couldn't fit the key in the lock.

"Here, let me." Gage took the key, unlocked the door and opened it. Then he walked in and checked out the bathroom and the small closet. "No one's here."

Still scared, she stood just inside the doorway. She should be angry he'd frightened her, but was glad he'd checked the room out anyway. "Thank you," she managed when he handed her back her key.

"Hey. You're going to be okay tonight. I won't let anything happen to you."

Whoa. Wait a minute. She hadn't invited him to stay. "You aren't staying with me."

The corners of his lips turned up in a slow smile and he swept his gaze from her eyes down to her toes and back up again, sending sexual awareness sizzling over her once more. "Tempting as that might be, you're right. I'm not. I've got the room next door." He pointed to the wall behind her bed. "You need anything, or hear anything, you pound on that wall. I'll be here in a flash."

He started out the door, then paused. "And Bobby?"

"Yes?"

"Don't forget, my office first thing tomorrow morning. Sleep tight." He winked at her and closed the door behind him.

She hurried over, clicked the dead bolt and slipped the chain in place. Pressing her back against the door, she breathed deeply. Sleep tight? The man just kissed her senseless, scared the living daylights out of her and he expected her to sleep at all? And he thought *she* was delusional.

***

The lights off and the engine as quiet as fog rolling through the low Ohio hills, the black sedan pulled out of the motel's parking lot without disturbing even the gravel on the semi-paved surface and headed back toward town.

Damn that man. With the sheriff in the next room it would be impossible to get to the snooping woman. For some reason she'd been rifling through the bank's trash today. Her curiosity could ruin everything.

For months the sheriff's apathy for his job had played right into his plans. One wrong move or one slip of the tongue and everything could collapse. He'd have nothing. And worse, his partners would demand payment—in either cash or his blood.

He needed to find out just what she knew and silence her. He also needed to tie up some loose ends to be sure she didn't get any answers to her questions. Starting tonight.

Miles from the motel, the sedan's lights came on, resembling a dark predator prowling the lonesome highway.

Chapter Five

Footsteps sounded hard and fast behind him. His warm breath puffed into the winter air as he ran.

The corner. Turn the corner. Find a spot to hide.

One step.

Two.

Just a little farther.

Pain seared into his chest like a bolt of lightning as he cleared the brick wall. The impact swung him around.

Bells rang.

A second wave of pain hit him in the belly. A third, in the other side of his chest. He fell to the ground, his face pressed into the snow. The smell of his own blood mixed with the leftover remains of someone's fish dinner.

Bells rang.

Gage came awake with a lurch, sweat pouring off his body. He landed back onto his pillow, wiping one hand over his face. The nightmare again. Hadn't had one in a month. Three years ago in the hospital, he'd had them nightly. The doc said the culprit was post-traumatic stress.

The phone by the bedside rang again.

Gage grabbed it. "Yeah?"

"Sheriff, you wanted a wake-up call?"

He rolled over and squinted at the glowing red numbers on the clock. Six-forty-five in the friggin' morning. No sane person woke up voluntarily at this hour of the day. He looked around the room. He wasn't home.

The motel. Walt was on the phone.

"I'm up. Thanks, Walt."

After he'd left Bobby for the night, he'd walked over and paid for his room and asked the motel owner to make sure he was up this morning. It had taken him a while to calm down the erection kissing her had caused. Now he was awake before the crack of dawn.

He grabbed his jeans, pulled them on, stepped into his boots and headed out the door. Passing Bobby's door, he knocked once, loudly.

"Don't forget. My office, first thing," he said through the door.

Climbing on his bike, he gunned the engine. He needed to get home to shower and shave before his meeting with Bobby. Coffee. He'd need lots of it if he meant to be civil with the woman this morning.

At his house, he threw his keys onto the kitchen table and shoved his hands through his freshly cut hair. He hated keeping it this short, but it was part of the image he now had to display—clean-cut, all-American town sheriff. What he wouldn't give for a cigarette right now. Tasting the woody, sweet tobacco on the tip of his tongue. Inhaling deep to let the smoke fill his lungs, exhaling slowly as the nicotine calmed his nerves, woke his senses and allowed him to think clearly. Every morning for the past six months he'd craved that first smoke of the day, and mornings like this were the worst.

Lying in the hospital gasping in his last breath, his dying father had asked only two things of him. He'd sworn to the old man he'd stay in this rinky-dink little town to finish out his dad's last term as sheriff, and he'd promised to quit smoking so he wouldn't die of lung cancer, too. So no matter how much he craved a cigarette, he hadn't touched another from that moment on. He wouldn't break either promise.

"Damn, this is going to be a long day."

Upstairs, he stripped down to his boxers then saw the blinds in the house next door close.

Dammit! He'd forgotten his voyeur neighbor.

The first morning he'd come home to stay with his dad, nearly two years ago, he'd gotten a rather rude reminder of small-town etiquette. If you didn't want your neighbor, the widow Munroe, getting a bird's eye view of you in the buff, you closed your shades at night before taking off your clothes. You didn't open them again until at least your underwear was on in the morning.

He smiled and shook his head at the memory. Dad had gotten quite a kick out of that, especially since every time he saw Mrs. Munroe from then on, the elderly lady blushed and gave him a sly smile.

That was one thing he missed about living in the city—anonymity. Your neighbors didn't try to get to know you, didn't want to know you. And they certainly didn't get a good look at you completely naked, unless you wanted them to.

He stalked across to the bathroom and turned on the shower. He stood beneath the hot water, letting it run over his body. The hot-water heater in this old house gave out quick. Pretty soon the water temperature would turn cold, so he enjoyed the few minutes of near-scalding water pounding over his muscles.

When he finished showering, he wiped the steam off the glass and studied himself a moment. The three round, puckered scars on his torso stuck out like neon lights. He fingered the one on his upper left chest. When he'd awakened in the ICU, the surgeon had told him that if that bullet had been just a fraction of an inch lower it would've hit his aorta, and there wouldn't have been a chance in hell of saving him.

He slid his finger lower to the one on his left abdomen. That one had cost him his spleen, but at least that was an organ you could live without, if you didn't bleed to death before help got there. That was the only thing he'd managed to do right that winter night three years ago. The cold kept him from completely bleeding out.

Finally, he slid his finger back up to the midsection of his right ribcage. That one had been the worst of the three. Broke three ribs while it bounced around inside his lung. He still had two thin scars from where the chest tubes sucked the blood out of his lung for nearly a week, trying to re-inflate his collapsed lung. Every time he got a cold and coughed, it still hurt like a son-of-a-bitch.

He stared at all three wounds in the mirror. The betrayal that caused his injuries and his near death hurt worse than any of the bullets had. Most days he tried not to think about it and most nights he tried not to let a bottle of Jack drown out the pain.

Opening the medicine cabinet, he looked for his shaving cream. As he lifted it out, he saw the small glass bottle behind it. He picked it up and stared at the contents. One mangled bullet and a plain gold wedding band—souvenirs to remind him of his own stupidity. He shoved the bottle back into the farthest corner of the cabinet. He couldn't change what happened in the past, and it had little to do with hurrying Bobby Roberts out of his life and town today.

After receiving Gage's rude pounding on her door before dawn, Bobby decided to delay her meeting with him and pursue her case with a visit to the bank. Outside the brick building, she tugged her sweater shell and cardigan set down over the top of her slacks, moistened her lips, took a deep breath and entered as if in a hurry. She stepped past the line of patrons and tellers to the office nearest the door.

"May I help you?" The platinum blonde—Geraldine Taylor, New Account Representative, her name plaque boldly proclaimed—looked up from her desk. Lips the color of Pepto Bismol, sky-blue eye shadow applied with a trowel and cheekbones sculpted from three shades of blush suggested she hadn't had an updated look since the early seventies.

Bobby schooled her attitude, plastered an embarrassed smile on her face and held out her hand. "Oh, I do hope you can. I have a bit of a problem."

The female bank officer, dressed in a navy gabardine suit tailored to fit the curves of her waist and hips, and a white blouse with a plunging neckline to show off her well-endowed chest, stood to shake her hand. She motioned for Bobby to take one of the two straight-back chairs in front of her desk. "Please tell me what seems to be the problem?"

"I am so embarrassed." Bobby lowered her eyes and forced herself to swallow hard in order to appear flustered. "I'm traveling through town, and somehow I managed to lose my ATM card. I've run out of cash, and frankly I hate putting items on my credit card. The interest is so overwhelming sometimes."

"There shouldn't be a problem, ma'am. If you have an account with one of our branches, you can simply cash a check here."

"I feel so stupid." Bobby let out a long sigh, twisting the strap to her purse in nervous agitation. "When I left my house yesterday, I managed to only bring one check with me, which I already used. You must think me a complete ninny."

"Oh, no. Think nothing of it," the woman reassured her with a gentle smile and a pat on the hand. Only her eyes seemed to say *yes, you're a complete moron.* "People do things like this all the time."

"Since I'll be doing a lot of traveling in this area for my work, I'd hoped you could wire money from my other bank into a new account here at your bank."

"Why certainly. Do you know your banking information?" Ms. Taylor pulled open her desk drawer faster than a mechanical rabbit out of the gate at a greyhound race and withdrew several papers. Realizing she was about to get a new account for her bank seemed to take all the cynicism out of her demeanor.

"Yes, it's all right here." Bobby fished out the paper she'd written her banking information on early this morning. Knowing Gage slept on the other side of her motel room's wall, she'd given up on trying to get any semblance of sleep around four. She'd spent the rest of the time before the bank opened deciding on her next plan to find out information about the bank and its employees. Dumpster diving had done little more than make her a walking bulls-eye for the sheriff. "I'd like to deposit two-thousand today and get a little cash, too?"

"It will be ten days before you will have an ATM card to make withdrawals," Ms. Taylor explained as she happily filled all the little spaces on the paper in front of her.

"Oh, I won't need a card. I'll just come in and fill out a form whenever I need a little cash and I'm in the area. If that won't be too much trouble." Bobby gave her a little smile. God, she hoped she wasn't sounding too inane. If her sisters could hear her now they'd be convinced she needed to visit the little men with white jackets and padded room for an unscheduled vacation.

"If you're sure." The woman gave her a look that said she thought she was crazy, as well as stupid.

After handing over her driver's license, Bobby reassured her it would be no inconvenience to come into the bank for her cash, which was true considering she wanted to have a legitimate reason for being inside it and observing the workers. She sat back and waited as the woman finished filling out all the necessary paperwork. With the signatures on the appropriate lines, Ms. Taylor shimmied her way into the next office to get approval from the bank's manager for the money wire.

Taking out her pad of paper, Bobby made notes as she surveyed the bank's layout and personnel. Her PI manual taught that even the smallest observation could have meaning in an investigation. Observing people came easily to her as years ago, when she and her mother went to the mall to shop, she'd developed a passion for people watching.

Behind the long counter sat three female tellers of various ages. They handled the business of the few customers who entered the bank this morning and conversed among themselves. An aged security guard sat near the entrance, flipping through a magazine. Besides the office she sat in, there were two others located far from the tellers on the bank's opposite side. One was dark, as if its owner had taken the day off.

It was the other office her new best friend, Ms. Taylor, disappeared into. The manager, an older gentleman, nearing retirement age if Bobby had to guess from his white hair and slightly hunched posture, sat at his desk as the new account officer presented him with her paperwork. The man briefly glanced at the papers, but spent the rest of the time leering down his co-worker's exposed cleavage.

Bobby chuckled softly and wrote his description down in her notebook—near retirement, but apparently not feeling it.

A few moments later, Ms. Taylor returned, a smile lighting up her face. "We have you all set, Ms. Roberts. Your checks should arrive at your home in a week or two. In the meantime if you need any cash, just fill out a form and show the teller your ID to make a withdrawal."

"That will be just wonderful." Bobby stood and took the papers Ms. Taylor handed her. "You have been so helpful. Might I ask one more question?"

"Of course."

"The scenery around Westen is so lovely. If I wanted to buy some property, say in the next six months or so, could you help me with a loan?"

Ms. Taylor shook her head and gave her another placating smile. "I'm sorry. I don't handle that kind of transaction. That would be done by our loan officer, Mr. Evans."

"Oh. Would that be the gentleman you were speaking with just now?"

Ms. Taylor laughed. "No, that's Mr. Peters, the bank manager. Mr. Evans is out of the office today. He should be back next Monday."

"Well I'm sure I won't find any property to buy before then." Bobby laughed and thanked the bank officer once more before leaving.

Out on the street, she paused to write the names of the bank managers into her notepad. Mr. Evans was in charge of loans. He was the most likely candidate to file a lien on the Byrd property. Now she had a name to put in her report to Chloe.

"What are you doing?"

Gage's voice startled her from behind. She would've jumped into the path of a passing pickup had he not grabbed her firmly by the elbow and held her in place.

"Do you *have* to keep doing that?" For a big man, he moved with great stealth. She narrowed her eyes at him. His reflective sunglasses blocked her view of his eyes, but she'd just bet he'd enjoyed scaring her out of another few minutes of life.

"If you'd stop snooping around where you have no business, I wouldn't have to question you, now would I?" He kept his grip on her elbow and steered her down the sidewalk toward his office...and the very small, confining, suffocating jail cell.

She dug her heels in, ignoring the stares of the few pedestrians on the sidewalk on a Friday morning. "I wasn't snooping and I wasn't doing anything wrong. You can't arrest me."

"You were supposed to meet me at my office first thing this morning, Bobby. Instead I find you in the bank. The same bank where I hauled you out of the trash yesterday. We're going to my office to have that discussion about your case. I'm not going to arrest you." His voice was low, but the intensity suggested he barely had a leash on his temper. He gave her arm a small, firm tug.

The message was clear. Follow or risk causing a public scene. Without further protest she let him lead her down the block. With her luck he'd probably use an altercation as an excuse for arresting her for disturbing the peace or causing a public nuisance.

She really needed to sit down with Chloe and figure out all the ways she could avoid getting locked up while she tried to work this case. Of course, with a more ordinary and reasonable lawman she wouldn't have to worry about spending time in jail. However, in the brief time she'd known Gage Justice she'd learned one thing. Ordinary and reasonable weren't part of his makeup.

At his office, the sheriff released his hold on her and opened the door. For a moment she considered fleeing, but didn't doubt for a second he'd tackle her, haul her back over his shoulder like some caveman and shove her into the cell once more. She was more scared of the jail cell than she was him. One eyebrow lifting in question above his sunglasses, he stood almost patiently waiting for her to enter as if he knew what she contemplated.

Crap. She might as well get this over with. With a huff, she straightened her shoulders, lifted her chin and marched through the door.

"Mornin', Miz Roberts." Cleetus stood from his position behind the computer. "Pleasure to see you here again this morning."

"Good morning, Cleetus. Please call me Bobby."

Gage humphed as he strode over to his desk.

He didn't want her being nice to his deputy? Well too damn bad.

She smiled at the kind deputy. "How was Ruby last night?"

"The doctors have her on a lot of pain medicine right now, but she's ordering everyone around already, so she must be feeling okay." He grinned at the idea.

"I'm glad she's doing well."

"Thank you for asking, ma'am."

"Ahem." Gage cleared his throat, drawing both their attention. He pointed to the chair beside his desk. "Ms. Roberts, if you're done catching up on the day's gossip, perhaps we could get on with our conversation? Cleetus, you want to take the cruiser around town before lunch?"

"Sure thing, Sheriff." Cleetus grabbed his keys and hat from the desk. "Nice to see you again, Miz. Bobby, ma'am."

Bobby narrowed her eyes at Gage for a moment. The man gave insufferable a whole new definition.

"Nice to see you, too, deputy." She patted Cleetus on the arm and walked to the seat Gage had indicated. She plopped down on the wooden seat, crossed her legs, leaning one elbow on the desk and propping her chin in her hand. "Now, Sheriff, what is it you wanted with little ole' me?" she asked in her best Scarlett O'Hara impression.

Gage leaned back in his chair and studied her. Her

flippant question caught him off guard and sent heat straight to his groin. If he told her what he really wanted from her, she'd probably run out of town as fast as her legs could carry her. Which is what he wanted, right? Otherwise, why did he have this desire to keep her around until he could fulfill at least one of the fantasies he'd been having since he'd sat in the cruiser watching her jean-clad ass yesterday?

Holding her in his arms and kissing her last night had been a bad idea. He'd thought it would cure the ache inside him. Only instead of quenching the thirst, it had heightened it like a cold beer after a day of hard work in the blistering sun. All he'd wanted was another.

He'd spent a nearly sleepless night thinking about Bobby lying in the bed on the other side of the wall. He'd wondered if she slept naked or in one of those short little nightie things women liked to wear. Between that image and the nightmare that woke him, it had taken four cups of coffee to get his mind in working order today.

To top it off, she hadn't come straight to his office this morning like he'd ordered her to do. He'd waited until after ten for her to show up. When she hadn't, he'd gotten concerned something had happened to her and called Walt over at the motel to see if she was still there. Walt told him she'd left the motel nearly an hour earlier. That had him wondering where she'd gone. He hadn't believed for a moment that she'd left town. She was here for a reason and wouldn't leave until she had some answers. That he was sure of.

Determined to find her, he'd started over at The Peaches 'N Cream Café. Lorna, who hadn't seen her yet that morning, offered him some of her special blueberry pancakes and ham, which normally he'd eat double helpings of, but he'd refused. Until he found Bobby, assured himself she wasn't hurt and gave her a piece of his mind, he knew he couldn't enjoy breakfast.

His anger simmering on a low boil, he'd just left the café when he saw the little brunette exit the bank. Instead of feeling some relief at finding her—the fact that he'd worried about her in the first place wasn't something he wanted to think about anyway—his temper soared and he simply wanted to shake some sense into the woman. He'd settled for scaring her once again. He had to admit it was fun to watch her jump and see that startled, wide-eyed deer look she gave him. The blush that filled her cheeks and her offended tone when she scolded him only added to the fun.

Now here she sat next to his desk looking all sassy and asking him what he wanted with her.

"What I'd like, Bobby..." he leaned forward and set both his elbows on his desk, folding his fingers together like a church steeple just like he'd seen his father do a hundred times before when questioning someone, "is for you to fill me in on this case of yours. I'd also like you to explain to me what you were doing in the bank this morning, instead of meeting me here."

She stared straight at him. Didn't blink or hesitate one second. "Why Sheriff, I was simply opening a checking account."

He opened his desk drawer and took out his ace card. "I'm not in the mood for twenty questions, today. So let's just cut to the chase."

He watched her face as he unfolded the letter. She inhaled a little deeper, the smile on her lips fading just a hint. Oh yeah, she hid her tell well, but not completely. "What I don't get is why you sent this letter to my office stating you had a case to discuss with me, instead of just sending one to the bank?"

Now he had her and she knew it. The game had ended and he'd won.

Her smile disappeared completely. Her eyes widened then narrowed. "You knew I was a private detective yesterday?"

What was she getting her panties in a twist about? He wasn't the one lying. "I'd like some answers about your case and what it has to do with Westen's bank."

Her lips pressed into a thin line and she swallowed several times. "When you were frisking me, and cuffing me, and treating me like a criminal, and locking me up in that minuscule jail cell," she propped both her elbows on his desk and leaned closer, "all that time you *knew* I was a detective?"

Before he could defend his actions, the back hall door opened and Jason Clarke, the youngest of his eight deputies entered. He stopped in the doorway and looked from Bobby to Gage, his eyebrows lifted in question. "Sheriff, I hate to interrupt…"

"What is it, Jason?" Gage continued to return Bobby's glare for a moment before pushing back in his seat to focus on his deputy, who'd stopped mid-sentence and smiled at Bobby with interest. For some reason the look on the younger man's face irritated him. "And why aren't you home sleeping after class?"

Jason blinked then focused back on him. "Oh, yeah. I'm headed home in a second, but I forgot to give you a message from Chief Reynolds when I finished my shift this morning." He hurried to his desk, rifled through some papers. He returned with a sticky note in his hand. "He said there was something suspicious about yesterday's fire and he wants to meet you out at the crime scene. Says he'll be there most of the morning."

Gage took the note from Jason, recognized Deke's phone number on it. He glanced at the clock. Nearly eleven. Great. He wanted to get some concrete information out of Bobby about her supposed case, but no matter what the little detective was mixed up in, no way could it take priority over Deke's fire investigation.

He fixed Bobby with his gaze and dialed Deke's number.

"'Bout time you called, Gunslinger," Deke muttered in way of greeting.

"I've been a little preoccupied."

"I wanted to keep this between the two of us, but I tried your home and cell phone with no answer."

He glanced at the corner of his desk where his cell phone lay in its charger. His gaze met Bobby's across his desk. "Yeah, I didn't have my charger last night."

"Oh? What was her name?" Deke's deep chuckle rumbled over the phone.

"Don't worry, she's not your type." A week ago he wouldn't have said a schoolteacher was his type, either. Something stirred in Gage's gut. As close a friend as Deke was, he didn't want to discuss his serious case of the hots for Bobby with him. Certainly not with her watching him with those big brown eyes. Time to change the subject. "Jason said you had information about yesterday's fire? Yesterday you said it wasn't a meth lab."

"It wasn't. And it wasn't some kids fooling around with weed like we thought, either."

Gage sat straight up in his chair. "You're sure?" Stupid question. Of course he was sure. It was Deke's job to investigate fires, and Deke was very good at it. If he said it wasn't an accident, then he meant just that.

"Why don't you drive out here and I'll show you."

Damn. As much as he wanted to interrogate Bobby and get to the bottom of her reason for being in Westen, arson took precedence. "I can be there in fifteen minutes, as soon as I get Cleetus back in the office."

Deke agreed to wait for him and disconnected. Gage set the phone back in the receiver.

Bobby relaxed. The interrogation was over. If Gage was going out to that fire scene she'd be free to drive over to the county seat in Newark and check on any property claims made by the bank. She'd be free of his scrutiny and his physical presence, which she had to admit reminded her much too clearly of how he'd held her and kissed her last night.

She uncrossed her legs, picked up her bag and stood. "Seems your duty calls, so I'll just be on my way."

"Sit."

She sat, but only because the narrow jail cell was visible through the room's back door.

He went to the station's dispatch microphone and clicked it on. "Cleetus? Where are you? Come in?"

"I'm over on Portis Street, Sheriff. Over."

"Good. I need you back here for a while."

"Yes, sir. I'm 10-19 to the station."

"Cleetus. It's not an emergency, no sirens."

"Roger, Sheriff."

Gage's lips lifted in a small grin and he shook his head. He leaned one hip onto the desk, his arms folded over his chest and turned his attention on her once more, his momentary humor at his deputy apparently over .

"We aren't finished with this conversation."

She hadn't doubted it for a moment. The man went after information like a pointer after a duck. He wouldn't stop until he'd gotten the answers he wanted. She just needed some time to find her own facts then decide how much she wanted him to know. If he took over her investigation, Chloe would have no reason to keep her on the case. And she wasn't ready to leave just yet.

"What is this case you're working on?"

Not a question, a demand. Oh crap, it probably was time to bring him in on the problem. "Did you know a Mr. Gilbert Byrd?"

Gage blinked. "Dad knew him. He's been dead about six months now. Why?"

"His will is going to probate and I'm investigating the bank's claim of a lien against the property."

"That's all? You could've found out all you needed to know by talking to Harley Evans over at the bank. No need to climb into the trash."

His ridicule at her first foray into investigating irritated her. Besides, despite what he thought, he didn't know everything. "There's a bit more to it than that."

"Okay. We'll talk when I get back."

"I'm free to go?" She reached for her purse.

"Actually, I'd like you to stay here until I get back."

The cell was still visible just over his left shoulder. She put her bag back on the floor. "You can't force me to stay."

He shoved his hands through his short hair, the sunlight filtering in through the blinds picking up the glints of red scattered amongst the blonde. If he weren't so infuriating she'd probably offer to climb on his desk and beg him to fulfill every one of her fantasies.

"You're right. I can't force you to stay. It was a request, not an order."

It was her turn to blink. What? He was agreeing with her?

"I'd like to find out more about this case you're investigating. I've been back in town not quite a year, but I'm sure I can help you get whatever information you need." He stalked over to his desk, grabbed his keys, shoved his baseball hat on his head once more and picked up his sunglasses. "I don't have time to argue with you. If you wouldn't mind, I'd really like you to wait here until I get back."

He sounded sincere.

She narrowed her eyes and hesitated a moment. This had to be a trick. He hadn't been nice to her from the minute he'd learned her name. "How long will this take? I do have things to do today."

"I should be back within the hour."

He flashed her a grin, the same one he'd given her when she landed in his arms. It was the kind of grin she'd seen daily in her classroom. The kind of grin that the class charmer always gave her when he turned in his late homework.

"I'll buy you lunch when I get back."

"Ah, a bribe." Should've seen that coming. The charmer always followed his request with a bribe. She sat back in the wooden chair. She'd always been a sucker for the class charmer, but she'd let him know she had limits. "In that case, I'll give you one hour. After that, I'm free to go about my own business."

His countenance sobered and for a moment he simply stared at her. Would he renege on his request and lock her up again? She licked her lips in nervous agitation.

Something must've convinced him she meant to keep her word, because he nodded and slipped his sunglasses back in place. "It's a deal. Just keep Cleetus out of trouble while I'm gone."

As he opened the front door, she hurried after him. "What am I supposed to do with him while I wait for you?"

He stuck his head back in the door and glanced around the room at all the half-opened drawers and manila folders sticking out at odd angles. "You might try filing." Then he disappeared out the door.

"Filing?" She glanced around. He couldn't be serious? He wanted her to spend the hour trying to straighten up his filing system? She didn't even live in this town, much less work for the man.

"I'm not going through this mess he made," she muttered as she stared at the disaster. Besides, yesterday she learned it was difficult to make sense of Ruby's filing system and only God knew what kind of information the woman had hidden in what folder over the years.

Wait. Perhaps this wouldn't be a waste of time after all.

Bobby looked around her once more. She picked up a pile of folders, carried them to the computer desk and sat down in the seat. She smiled and wiggled her eyebrows. No one knew what facts Ruby had stashed in her bizarre filing system. Maybe even some reference to the Byrd property.

Shoving Bobby out of his mind, Gage focused on his brief conversation with Deke as he drove his dad's old truck up to the fire scene at the MacPherson's abandoned place once more. Deke wasn't one to jump to conclusions. His attention to details and ability to ferret out the facts in a case was ingrained as if by some magical DNA code. Gage's own internal alarm gauges hit the warning level. If Deke wanted to show him something out here, it couldn't be good. And in fireman's terms, that meant arson.

But who'd want to torch a dilapidated barn on equally neglected and abandoned farmland? The place had sat empty since he took over the sheriff position from Dad six months ago and as far as he knew it had been empty the six months before that when he'd returned to Westen to recuperate.

He parked the Ford by where Deke stood leaning against the hood of his own pickup. A second pickup sat parked next to it. "So what's up?" he asked his friend as he hopped out and walked around the vehicle.

"Arson."

Damn. He knew it. "Any clue as to why?"

Deke rubbed the back of his neck. "Not that I can figure out. That's why I called you. Let me show you what I found and you see if you can come up with one."

They walked past the dead grass and scorched earth surrounding the barn's charred remains. The fire teams had pulled the more dangerous pieces down and away from the structure to hopefully prevent any curiosity seekers from getting injured by falling debris. Now the black, roofless shell resembled a building he'd seen in old World War II photos his Dad had taken while serving in the army in Germany. The campfire smell still emanated from the burnt wood.

"Watch your step," Deke warned as they stepped through what used to be the barn's door.

Here the wood seemed blistered and not burned completely through, but as they moved further into the charred remains, the wood was blackened like charcoal. Near the back of the barn, the damage appeared to be the worst. A metal sign, which once advertised the local farmers' favorite chewing tobacco, lay on the ground, twisted and blistered from the fire's intensity.

A man stood among the debris. It was Mike Feeney, the county arson investigator. Gage had met him once before, about six months earlier, just as his Dad had gone into the hospital for the last time and he'd assumed the position of sheriff in his stead.

"Gage."

"Mike."

They shook hands.

"So, Deke called you, too?" Gage studied the other man's serious countenance.

"We've been out here since first light sorting through this mess. At first Deke was sure it was a case of kids getting carried away and causing an accidental fire."

Gage nodded. "That's what I figured, too, based on the beer cans, tire tracks and leftover doobies scattered around outside."

"Except the fire didn't start out there." Mike dug his knife into the charred wood, pulled off a piece and held it to his nose. "The accelerant was gasoline."

He passed the piece to Gage who sniffed and could still smell the faint pungent smell of gas.

"And this," Mike lifted a wad of fused plastic and metal wires from the pile of wood, "is a delayed timer. This was a planned fire."

"So someone wanted to set this place off. Why? As far as I know this place has been abandoned for more than a year."

"I checked with the bank this morning while I waited for you to return my call," Deke said. "Seems this property went into default two years ago, so I doubt it was arson for profit."

They made their way outside. Clouds dotted the blue sky above and in a few days they would have rain once more.

"Good thing it's been a rainy spring, otherwise the fire might've spread to the Turnbill place next door." Gage nodded to the freshly planted fields not a hundred yards to the west.

"How's Aaron doing these days?" Deke asked as they wandered the fire scene's perimeter.

"We talked last night at the council meeting. Said he's been behind a little with last year's bad crop, but if the weather holds, he should be able to make up the difference and then some this year."

"Good thing we managed to get this blaze under control," Deke said as they studied the burn pattern from outside. "I'd hate to have seen him lose his home and land. Aaron's a good man."

The trio stood silent for a few moments. Gage glanced at Mike who seemed to be calculating the surrounding area. "What are the usual reasons for arson?"

"There's a number of reasons. Arson for profit. The owner of a property sets it on fire to collect on the fire insurance."

Deke nodded in the direction of the half-standing, burned barn. "We're pretty sure that's not the case here."

"There's arson to hide a crime. Say you've murdered someone. The arsonist sets the building ablaze to conceal the actual cause of death. Sometimes it works, sometimes it doesn't."

Gage shook his head, remembering a case he'd worked years ago in Columbus. "Yeah, not even a fire can hide a bullet still inside the body."

"Then there's the firebug. Someone who just loves fire."

The trio grew silent once more. A chill seemed to fill the air despite the late spring day. No one wanted to believe they had a psychotic firebug in their midst. If so, more of these fires could spring up in the area and someone could get hurt. Or worse, die.

Chapter Six

"That's all the restraining orders issued for the past ten years, Ms. Roberts," Cleetus said as he set the files down next to the computer and resumed his seat beside Bobby.

She smiled at him. "Good. We'll enter each one by the date it was filed, then by the last name of the person it was filed against."

As she instructed Cleetus, she let him type each statistic into the columns she'd had him make before. His hunt-and-peck style of typing drove her crazy. She nearly had to sit on her hands to keep from helping him. Over the years, she'd taught many students how to make tables like this on the computer. It was her firm belief that people learned better by doing than watching. Despite her misgivings at first, Cleetus proved to be an excellent student and seemed to enjoy using the new tool.

"You're doing fine." Patting his shoulder, she

scooted her chair back and stood. "You go ahead and fill in all that data and I'll start on the next files. What's next on the list?"

Cleetus handed her the legal pad of categories they'd brainstormed earlier. "Fires and arson. But I don't think you'll find many of those in these files."

"Why?"

"I've worked for the sheriff's department almost twenty years, and I don't recall too many fires that weren't an accident."

Bobby grinned at him. "Good. Then it won't take me long to look through the files for them."

"It might not take long if you can figure out what Ruby called them. I'm figurin' that'll take longer than picking out the cases."

Bobby chuckled. "You're right. What do you think she might've called them? Burning problems?"

"Hot stuff?" Cleetus grinned at her from beside the computer and they both laughed.

"No such luck," Bobby held up a one-inch-thick folder. "Ruby wasn't as creative. She just called them fires." She leaned one hip on the corner of the desk and flipped through the file. "Nothing too unusual here. One fire a year, for the past ten years. Until…"

The front door opened. Bobby turned around to see the handsome mayor enter, followed by an older gentleman.

"Miss Roberts." The mayor oozed charm once more, extending his hand to her. "Funny we should meet here again. Are you working here now?"

"Mayor…Rawlins, isn't it?" Bobby shook his hand and had to pry her fingers loose from his when he held them a little longer than necessary. "The sheriff asked me to help with the filing for today." *File something* was sort of a request, wasn't it?

"Please call me Tobias and this is Richard Davis," the mayor nodded for the other man to step forward. "He owns the local newspaper."

"Hello, ma'am," the newspaperman gave her a weak handshake.

Ick. It was like shaking hands with a cold, wet fish. Bobby suppressed a shudder and plastered a smile on her face. "Was there something I could help you gentlemen with?" she asked, looking from Mr. Davis to the mayor once more.

"We had hoped to talk with Gage about yesterday's fire."

"He's not here right now..." Bobby started to explain.

"The sheriff's out on rounds right now, Mayor," Cleetus interrupted, coming around the desk to stand next to Bobby. He'd sucked in his stomach, puffed out his chest and for the first time resembled an imposing law enforcement officer. "I'm sure he'd be real happy to give you a call when he gets back in the office."

"Now Cleetus, you just go back to what you were doing. We'll just talk with Ms. Roberts." Mayor Rawlins smiled at the deputy and patted his arm as if he were talking to a child.

Tension radiated off the usually easygoing giant next to her. He'd crossed his arms over his ample chest and set his jaw in a show of stubbornness. Whether or not he was putting on this show of male prowess to keep the mayor's nose out of the sheriff's department's business or to protect her, she wasn't sure. The last thing she wanted was for Cleetus to get into trouble because of some misplaced sense of chivalry on his part.

Time to defuse the situation.

She stepped between the two men and used her most sanguine smile—the one she'd honed on belligerent parents over the years—on the small-town politician and his minion. "I'm not really sure how I can be of help, gentlemen. I'm simply helping revamp the sheriff's department's filing system while Ruby is in the hospital."

She lay the fire file facedown on the desk to hide the title. Stepping around the computer, she opened the table of information she'd compiled the previous day. "We've been working on the traffic violations for the past year. As you can see, Cleetus and I have a great deal of menial work to do, what with tickets and fines to list, as well as the number of stray dogs picked up by the deputies for the county animal control people." She leaned to the side and picked up a pile of yellowed paper. "Speaking of which, we've unearthed a fascinating report from the nineteen thirties on the local skunk population. Would any of that information be helpful?"

For a moment both men appeared stunned by her prattle. She almost laughed at their expressions, but her years as a teacher kept her from even cracking a grin.

Mayor Rawlins recovered first. Plastering his politician's smile on his face once more, he backed up a step as if she actually held a skunk in her hands. "No, we wouldn't want to stop you from your work. We'll just catch Gage when he's back in the office."

The two men couldn't get out fast enough, bumping into each other trying to get through the door first.

Bobby glanced at Cleetus, who looked at her. They both cracked up.

"I'm glad you two have something to laugh about,"

Gage said as he entered from the back hallway. The tense set of his jaw suggested he hadn't liked what he'd learned at the fire scene.

"Tobias was just here," Cleetus said, sobering quickly.

"What did that leech want?" Gage asked. He tossed his sunglasses onto the desk and sat in his chair, turning his head to one side then the other as if to relieve the tension there.

"My guess is he wanted to have the newspaper do an article with him grilling you about yesterday's fire." Bobby swallowed as she watched the thick muscles of his neck and shoulders. Right now she'd give anything to walk around behind him and knead his shoulders beneath her hands.

She clenched her fingers into tight fists to keep from doing just that. What was it with her?

"Great. Just what I need today, on top of everything else—a photo-op with the mayor and a politically slanted article for his re-election campaign."

"What did Deke have to say out at the fire?" Cleetus had resumed his seat at the computer, but didn't pay attention to the screen.

"That it wasn't an accident. Someone torched the place on purpose."

"Why? Ain't been anyone living out there for years. Not since Old Man MacPherson went into the nursing home."

"That's what Mike, Deke and I can't figure out. There's no profit from torching the place. And if that's the case, we have a bigger problem on our hands."

Cleetus looked at the computer screen with a puzzled look.

Bobby reached over, pointed to the button to close the screen for him and smiled as he followed her directions. She looked back at Gage. "What kind of problem?"

"A firebug."

That got her attention. "Someone who sets fires just for the fun of it?"

"Yeah. The kind that likes to light a match just to see it burn as a kid, then decides seeing whole buildings go up is more fun as an adult."

Bobby leaned her hip against the computer desk once more, an icy feeling creeping over her skin. "That can't be good."

"Nope. And given the amount of foreclosed or abandoned acreage with dead underbrush in this county, it's even worse that anyone might think." He leaned his elbows on his desk, dropped his face into his hands and rubbed it up and down for a moment as if he was trying to rub away the weariness in his eyes.

His cell phone rang. Muttering a curse, he read the caller ID, hit a button and cut the caller off. He looked around the office. "What have you two been doing?"

"Just what you said. Filing." Bobby replied, wondering whom it was he'd just hung up on. Not that it really was any of her business.

"It looks like the mess is worse than when I left."

She followed his gaze around the room. Folders still lay piled all about. Only now there were even more open drawers and manila folders lay open on every square inch of furniture, except his desk. She chuckled and shrugged. "Sometimes you have to lay out all the pieces in a puzzle before the solution becomes visible."

Gage drew his brows together. "Really?"

"Sure, Sheriff." Cleetus poked his head around the monitor. "Bobby is teaching me to use the computer. We're de...de..."

"Deciphering," Bobby supplied the word.

"Deciphering Ruby's system and getting all the department's records on the computer."

Nodding at his deputy, Gage focused his attention back on Bobby. "You're teaching Cleetus how to use the computer?"

"Actually, he's a very good student."

Gage pushed his chair back and stood. He moved around the desk to stand no more than an inch from her. She had to tilt her head to look up at him. Their gazes held and sparks seemed to snap through the very air about them.

"You know all about students, don't you? I'm thinking I could teach you a few things," he said just loud enough for her to hear. His warm breath fanned her suddenly hot cheeks.

Bobby narrowed her eyes at him. Before she could decide whether to kiss him or smack him, he turned and sauntered over to the computer desk.

"Show me what you've done so far, Cleetus."

"We've been putting together statistics in these tables so they're easy to find when we have to do the monthly reports. We just click a button or two and the information is ready to print." Cleetus clicked on a button. "Some of this stuff goes back near ninety years, Sheriff."

"Looks like you're finding your way around here pretty good, Cleetus."

Cleetus grinned at his boss. "Bobby made it real simple to learn. She's a whiz at this computer. She taught middle school kids how to use computers every day.

She's a real good teacher. I bet she could teach you some things, too."

"Really?" He glanced over at her and winked.

Bobby tried not to gape at the hidden message in that look. She was having trouble enough keeping her mind on what she was doing.

Standing next to the deputy, Gage leaned over to view the screen better. With one hip out, his jeans stretched and accentuated the tight muscles of his butt and thighs. The sudden urge to reach over and caress them shocked Bobby. She hadn't been this hormonal since her first year in college.

Giving herself a mental shake, she grabbed the file she'd been holding before the mayor had interrupted them. She sat in Gage's chair to study the file's contents. The reports were in neither alphabetical nor chronological order. Organizational filing was another thing she'd discovered Ruby didn't believe in. She laid them out, earliest date to the latest so they would be easier to file in the computer.

As she worked, she glanced over to see that Gage had pulled a chair up beside Cleetus and was actively discussing the computer programs with his deputy. He seemed genuinely interested in what Cleetus had to show him. The fact that he treated Cleetus with such respect and patience almost negated his overbearing behavior toward her. Almost, but not quite.

Time to get back to work. She focused on the papers in front of her. The file dated back to the mid-seventies.

"That's odd," she muttered to herself.

"What's odd?" Gage asked from the other desk.

"I found this file on fires. And the timing is odd."

"Fires?" He shoved back his chair and came to read

over her shoulder.

"See?" She pointed to the top right corner of the square she'd made with the papers. "The first fire reported took place in 1976."

"That was the year we moved here and Dad took over as sheriff. No one had really kept records on fires much back then. I remember him saying the sheriff before him only worked two days a week. We had a huge storm that year. Lightning torched a dry field that burned two barns before any fire crews could get to it."

"Not another one was reported for almost two years. After that a fire is listed once every year or two, no pattern to them whatsoever, until about two years ago. All the early ones were weather related."

"Then they started with more frequency." Gage leaned closer. "Last year when Dad was diagnosed with cancer there were two fires, six months apart. Somehow we both missed this."

"I would imagine you both had more important things on your minds."

Their gazes met. A deep sadness filled his green eyes. The pain of losing his father still hurt. It was hard to imagine a man this hard hurting so deeply for someone he loved. Her heart softened a bit more for him.

Bobby blinked. She focused on the papers once more. "Of course, Ruby's super-secret filing system didn't help matters either. I swear she could give the CIA lessons on hiding secret data."

"That she could."

Gage's deep chuckle rumbled next to Bobby's ear and sent shivers over her once more. Oh, she really was in over her head right now. The more time she spent with this man, the closer she came to losing what sense she still had.

"So if I read this information correctly," he said, picking up the five latest reports, "our ratio of fires has nearly tripled in the last two years. Damn."

"Does that mean you do have a firebug operating in the area?"

"It's not a conclusion, but it sure seems possible, which isn't good. Someone who lights fires for fun acts randomly, or can commit a crime of opportunity."

"Where an arson-for-profit crime is planned and more predictable?"

"Right." He gave her a brief nod, his face growing serious again. He picked up the pages in the order she'd laid them out. "I'll have to call Mike, the county arson investigator, and give him the news. He's not going to like it any more than me."

"Why don't you…" She stood and almost slammed into his chest as he turned back around.

"Whoa," he said as he caught her against him with one arm, the other hand clenching the sheaf of papers. He held her there for a moment, her body pressed close to his. "You okay?"

Sure, if not breathing was okay. If wanting to crawl all over his body was okay then she was just zip-a-dee-doo-da-dandy okay. "I'm…I'm fine."

"What were you going to say?" He asked as he eased his grasp on her.

"Um." She took a step back to get some much-needed air between them and collect her thoughts. "Oh, yeah, why don't you let Cleetus or me add those reports to the login file we started, before you call your friend."

"Sounds like a plan. Cleetus," he called over his shoulder, "you want to add these to the program while I take Ms. Roberts to lunch?"

"Lunch?" The man shifted gears faster than a formula-one racer.

"You thought I forgot about our deal, didn't you?"

Before she could answer, the strains of her ringtone sounded from her purse. She grabbed the purse and fished out her phone.

"Wild Thing?" Gage grinned at her.

She shrugged and pressed her phone to her ear. "Hello?"

"Hey, sis. Any news for me?"

Great. Chloe. And she really couldn't talk to her with Gage standing less than a foot away studying her like some hungry wolf. "Can I get back with you on that in a little bit?"

Gage grasped her elbow and moved her around the desk toward the door. She couldn't fight him and Chloe at the same time, so she followed his lead.

"I'll be in court all afternoon and I have a dinner meeting with our client. I really wanted to give him some information."

"Let me call you later and we can talk about it."

"Okay, but if I don't hear something soon, I'll just file the subpoena for the information." Her sister sighed into the phone. "I'm thinking this wasn't a smart idea in the first place."

"Chloe. I said we could talk about it later. I'm still your older sister and I don't intend to discuss my decisions with you out in public." She hated taking the I'm-the-big-sister-and-you'll-do-what-I-say tone with Chloe, but she had tolerated her attitude long enough. "In fact I'm having a luncheon meeting right now."

"Oh. If you're working on the case, I guess that's

something I can tell Mr. Byrd. Can you call me around five?"

"That should work." She was relieved her sister had given up so easily. One of the reasons Chloe was such a good lawyer was her tenacity when it came to arguing.

"Okay. Talk to you then."

She closed her phone and realized Gage had led her down the street to the little café. She read the hand-painted print on the front window. "Peaches 'N Cream, Café?"

"Yeah," he grinned as he opened the door. "Lorna's husband named it after her. Said she had a peaches-n-cream complexion just like on the old TV commercials."

"And I still do," a short, stout lady with hair as yellow as a crayon piled high on her head said from the other side of the counter. Her voice was loud enough to carry over the din of the lunchtime crowd's conversation and several old-timers laughed. "Bring that girl right over here and introduce us, Gage."

"Yes, ma'am." He grasped Bobby's elbow and maneuvered her to the counter. "Bobby Roberts, Lorna Doone, maker of the best blue-plate specials this side of the Mississippi."

"Lorna Doone?" Bobby held out her hand.

Lorna shook it and grinned. "Yep, just like the cookie. My husband Earl wanted me to take his name Smith, but I said, ain't no one gonna remember Lorna Smith. But Lorna Doone? No one's gonna ever forget that."

Bobby instantly liked the jovial woman. "I can see your point."

"You can have that seat back there, Gage." Lorna pointed to the corner booth and winked at Bobby. "Now you don't let that boy con you into buying him lunch. He hasn't brought a pretty girl in here to eat since he was in high school. And make him buy you dessert, too. My pies are to die for. Aren't they?" she asked the dining room in general.

"Yes, ma'am," came the chorus of replies as Gage maneuvered Bobby to the appointed booth. He motioned for her to sit, sliding into the opposite seat with his back against the corner wall of the restaurant.

"So, you have a sister?" he asked once they were seated.

Bobby looked up from her menu. "Two, actually."

"Younger, I assume?"

"Yes, how did you know?"

"The way you told her to mind her own business. Oh yeah, and you reminded her you were the older sister. Sort of hard to miss." He grinned over his menu at her.

She ignored the little extra beat his grin caused in her pulse. "It's a habit. I've been responsible for them both for a long time. Now that they're on their own I have a hard time not being their bossy older sister. Especially when they take an attitude with me."

"What do they do?"

"Chloe's a lawyer. She's been in practice almost three years now. Dylan is graduating from OSU's med school at the end of this month."

"Your parents must be real proud of you all."

"I'm sure they would be. They died nineteen years ago."

There was a pause and she lifted her gaze from the plastic menu to meet his. Tenderness creased the lines at the corners of his eyes, the grin completely gone.

"I'm sorry to hear that. How old were you?"

"Nineteen. I'd just finished my second year of college, but I had enough credits to get my teaching certificate." She shrugged. She wasn't looking for sympathy. Never once in all the years since had she felt sorry for herself. Some things in life you just had to deal with. "So I went to work, applied to get custody of my sisters and the rest is history."

The young waitress came to take their order, saving Bobby any more prying questions. She didn't talk about her parents' death and her subsequent responsibility with anyone, not even her sisters. Doing so with Gage dug at emotions better left buried.

When she ordered a salad, he insisted she add French fries on the side.

"They're the best you've ever eaten," he reassured her.

"I'll hold you to that evaluation."

While they sipped their drinks—hers water and his a glass of southern-style sweet tea—and waited for their food, Bobby relaxed into the overstuffed vinyl booth seat and watched the people in the café. The atmosphere was a cross between a 1940's diner and small town Renaissance restaurants she'd seen cropping up in suburbs throughout the state. Only the people here greeted everyone like they actually knew and cared about each other.

"Different from Cincinnati, isn't it?"

She blinked and focused on Gage only to find him studying her with a quiet intensity. "I was just thinking how comfortable and peaceful it all seems. People saying hello just because you come inside. A real sense of community."

Before he could reply a redheaded woman dressed in

pale-green scrubs approached their table.

"Hey, Gage."

"Afternoon, Emma." He stood and hugged the woman then scooted to the side.

A pang of jealousy knifed through Bobby as she watched him greet the woman with ease and affection, which was stupid. Of course there were other women in his life. Besides, she had no reason to think of him as anything other than a colleague on a case, even if he had nearly kissed the stuffing out of her.

He returned to his seat and grinned at her. "Bobby, this is my cousin, Emma Preston. Emma, Bobby Roberts. Want to join us?"

"Glad to meet you, Bobby." Emma shook her hand before sitting on the edge of Gage's seat. "I'm only staying until our food is ready. Clint is knee-deep in physicals today. Summer baseball starts this week for both the pony league and the industrial teams. So we're having lunch at the clinic. I told him I wasn't hungry, yet, but he insisted I get us all something to eat."

"Aren't pregnant women supposed to eat regularly?" Gage asked.

Emma laughed. "Yes, but my husband seems to think if I'm not eating there is something wrong. That's what I get for marrying the town doctor."

"Is this your first?" Bobby asked.

"Oh, no. I had twins seven years ago. But this baby is my husband's first, and he's turned into a complete worrywart."

"I'm going to tell him you said that." Gage grinned at his cousin as he teased her.

Bobby swallowed hard. When he grinned like that he looked less like the Neanderthal thug who'd trussed her up and put her in a cell yesterday, and more like the small-town hero she'd read and dreamed about in books over the years.

She really was pathetic. Not since she dated the nose tackle on the football team back in high school had she had this much testosterone in her presence. She was succumbing to it like a woman with PMS on a shopping spree in the chocolate store. The more time she spent with Gage, the more she found to indulge.

The waitress brought their food. "Your order will be ready in a few minutes, Em."

"Thanks, Rachel. Can you toss in some gingersnaps for the boys? You know how much they love your mama's cookies."

"Sure thing, Em." Rachel handed the check slip to Gage. "Mama said she expects you to buy pie, so I added two slices on the tab."

Gage didn't argue, just slipped the check far out of Bobby's reach.

The man's take-charge attitude aggravated her. She should insist they split the bill. Technically, this would be the first meal a man had bought her in months. And since it wasn't a date, not paying her own way felt odd.

"So, what brings you to Westen, Bobby?" Emma asked, snatching one of the fries from Gage's plate.

"I'm here to…" she started to explain.

"…fill in for Ruby and fix the filing system," Gage finished staring directly at her, daring her to contradict him.

What game was he playing? Even though she didn't wish to announce her case to the town, he had no reason to keep his cousin from knowing the truth behind her visit.

Emma looked from her cousin to Bobby and back again. "Oh, really? That was quick, wasn't it?"

Gage grinned. "Yep, I had a need, and Bobby just fell right into the position."

Heat filled Bobby's cheeks at the double meaning behind his words, knowing he referred to how they met. Luckily, Rachel waved from the cash register at that exact moment preventing Emma from asking for any more details.

"Food's ready. Gotta go," Emma said taking one more fry. "Nice to meet you, Bobby. Good luck with the filing. Maybe you can get this lug to bring you to dinner some night."

"She seems happy." Bobby watched Emma wave to almost everyone in the room as she left.

"Em's had a hard life. I'm glad she's finally found someone to take care of her." Gage took a big bite out of his burger.

"Is that why you lied to her about me? To protect her?"

Gage winked at her. "I didn't lie."

Bobby stared at him a moment. "You gave her the impression you'd hired me."

"No. I told her you were filling in for Ruby and working on the filing system. Seems to me, that's exactly what you were doing before we came to lunch."

She swallowed the bite of salad in her mouth and pointed her fork at him. "I know, but that's only because you threat—"

He reached across the table and put his finger to her lips. Leaning close, he whispered. "Look around. See everyone is watching us and half the people in here are listening to every word we say. We'll talk about your case after lunch. Right now we're nothing more than a man and a woman enjoying a lunch date. Got it?"

She nodded, trying not to think about how his finger rubbed across her lips as if he were caressing her. It was all a show for their audience.

He winked at her. "Now smile at me like you do when you smile at Cleetus."

She happily obliged him.

***

An hour later, they sat in his truck parked beneath a budding old oak tree, far from the town's prying eyes. The rain promised by the spring storm clouds tapped gently on the truck's hood and windows. The world outside dressed in a cool misty gray made the truck cab's inside seem cozy and secluded. On their laps sat plastic boxes with a slice of pie in each. Cherry for her, apple for him.

"So tell me why you're investigating the lien on Gilbert Byrd's old place." Gage scooped a bite of pie between his lips.

The man was way too distracting. Bobby focused on eating her own pie and staring out the front window a moment before beginning her tale.

"A client came to my sister with this request to look into his uncle's estate. The problem was Mr. Byrd's nephew believed he'd be inheriting the house and land, which he intended to sell for a profit. He was quite surprised when the executor of the estate, a lawyer here in Westen, informed him the local bank had a lien on the estate that had to be paid off before the estate could be settled or he could inherit the land."

"There's nothing unusual about that. People die with outstanding loans all the time."

"True. And I know for a fact Chloe told her client the exact same thing." Bobby scooped up another cherry with her fork and licked it into her mouth.

"Why the big investigation?"

"Because the nephew swears his uncle has never trusted banks, didn't have a bank account of any kind, and hated them so much he'd never stepped foot inside of one. His uncle blamed the banks for his father's death during the depression."

"That should be easy enough to check. Like I said before, we'll just go visit Harley Evans over at the bank. You'll have the answers you need in no time." He forked up the last bite of his pie and ate it. He licked his lips as if he'd settled the matter the way he's just devoured his desert.

"Are you in that much of a hurry to get rid of me?" she asked, only half teasing.

"Oh, I didn't say I wanted you to leave."

Gage's voice deepened and Bobby glanced at him sideways. He'd gone completely still. He watched her with such intensity she shivered. So this was what it was like to have a man's undivided attention.

Suddenly the cool spring air blowing in through the truck's vents wasn't enough to stop the heat between them. What she needed was an arctic burst straight from a blast chiller.

"Come here." He slipped his hand behind her neck and nudged her closer.

The fierce look in his eye and the pressure of his hand on her neck drew her to him. She parted her lips, darting her tongue out to lick them.

"Wait," he commanded and stopped her within inches of his lips. He reached forward with his other hand and ran a finger over the corner of her mouth. "Got it."

Mesmerized, she watched as he pulled his finger away. A dollop of cherry pie filling clung to the tip. His gaze locked on hers, he slowly brought it to his lips and licked the sweet treat off. "Delicious."

Her heart jumped two beats then remembered its job.

The pressure on her neck increased again. This time he didn't stop until his lips were on hers. He tasted like molten cherry pie. Hot. Sweet. Dangerous.

His grip on her neck tightened. He pulled her in closer until she was pressed flush against his chest, his lips demanding in their claiming of hers. She opened her mouth under his assault and he slipped his tongue inside. His hand gripped her hair, holding her still as he devoured her.

She cupped his face in her hand, the skin scratchy from tiny whiskers poking through. She ran her fingers back and forth over them, leaning in closer. More. She wanted...no, *needed* more.

He eased the grip on her hair and the pressure on her lips. Slowly he withdrew. She whimpered, a needy puppy sound, trying to recapture his lips with hers. He refused her, resting his forehead against hers. She opened her eyes and stared at him through her own passion-induced haze. His pupils were so dilated with such need she barely saw the deep green rim of his irises.

"Damn, woman. Is it always going to be like that when we kiss?"

His words and their implication of repeated efforts sent shivers of delight through her. In all her life she'd never had this affect on a man, or he on her, not even the chemistry TA in college she'd considered marrying.

Gage scooted back into the driver's seat.

When had he vacated it?

He started the engine then sat staring out the window at the slow swish of the windshield wipers. He gripped the steering wheel so tight his knuckles blanched white. Bobby wiggled back into her seat, setting the empty pie containers between them.

"To answer your question," he said after a moment, his voice sounding strained and thick with emotion. "I don't want to get rid of you. In fact, I have plans for you."

"Like filing?" She tried to lighten the mood. Things just felt too serious, too intense.

Loosening his grip on the steering wheel, he turned to stare at her. Slowly he smiled, sending her pulse back into overdrive. "Yeah, filing."

He turned the car and headed back to town.

"Where are we going now?"

"To see Harley Evans over at the bank about your case."

"Oh, I just remembered! He isn't there. They told me he called in sick today."

"Harley called in sick?" Gage stared at her. "You're sure?"

"If he's the loan officer, then yes. The blonde lady said he called in sick today."

"That's odd."

"Why?"

"Harley Evans has never missed a day of work in thirty years."

"You're sure?"

Gage nodded once. "He just received the award for it last week. It was in the newspaper."

116

Bobby laughed. "I guess he deserves one."

"He might, but his job at the bank is the center of his life."

Bobby shook her head, a little bewildered. "I don't think I'd ever get used to living in a small town. People know your every move."

"Yep. It's one of the things I love and hate about it. And one of the reasons I can't wait to get back to the city. People know your name and care about you. People also know your routines and if you do anything unusual everyone gossips about it." He turned left at the red light and headed east of town.

"Just the same, let's go check up on Harley. That way we can get back to some serious work." He grinned at her once more. "Like filing."

Chapter Seven

By the time they pulled up in front of Harley's house the rain had stopped. The two-story Victorian sat on a side street nestled on a half-acre lawn among other houses all built about the same time. A flagstone path led through the neatly trimmed lawn, edged with purple and yellow flowers, to the front entrance. Hanging pots of white flowers and standing pots full of red ones decorated the wraparound front porch. A large American flag hung from the flag holder mounted on the side of the house. Two white Adirondack rockers sat off to the side where the owner could sit out on a warm summer evening and visit with their neighbors. The picture-perfect, peaceful, mid-western home.

Gage knocked on the front door. No one answered, so he knocked again. "Harley? It's Gage Justice."

Bobby wandered across the porch to the front window.

Gage opened the screen door and knocked a third time, this time directly on the front door. "Harley. You in there?"

"Gage?" A slight tremor laced Bobby's voice.

"What?" he asked peering at her through the screen.

She continued to look inside. "Is Harley Evans an older man with white hair, glasses and a little on the small side?"

"Yes." A frisson of dread slithered up Gage's spine.

Bobby had grown very still and pale as she stared in the front window. "Then you better come see this."

He stepped to her side and pressed his face against the front window's glass. A man lay sprawled facedown on his floor, glasses off-kilter on his face, a pool of blood beneath him. His chalk-white skin and open, sightless eyes pronounced his death. "Shit. That's Harley."

"He's dead, isn't he?"

For the first time since he'd met her yesterday, Bobby sounded nervous, almost scared. Gage grasped her by both elbows to keep her from falling to her knees. "Sit here," he said as he led her to one of the rockers.

Once she was seated, he pulled her head toward her knees. "Keep your head down. Inhale slowly."

She followed his instructions without arguing, which in itself spoke to how shaken she was. "I've…I've never seen a…a dead body before."

"It's a shock, I know." He pulled her collar away from her neck, kneading her shoulders and neck with his hands. "The first one gets to everyone."

"You're used to this?"

"When I was undercover in Columbus, I saw more than my fair share of dead bodies. Some in the line of duty, others, well, in the drug scene you see way too many overdose victims." He felt her relaxing beneath his hands. He bent sideways and peeked at her. The color had returned to her lips. "Feeling better?"

"Uh huh. As long as you keep doing that."

He kissed her on the nape of her neck. "As much as I'd love to spend the hour massaging you, I need to get inside to see what happened to Harley. If you think you'll be okay."

She straightened in the chair. "I'm fine now. What do you need me to do?"

The woman had grit, he'd give her that. "You don't need to do anything. Sit here and I'll go inside."

She looked up, a determined set to her jaw. "No. I'm a private investigator now. I need to help."

The last thing he needed was her mucking up a potential crime scene. Yet, he wouldn't even be here checking on Harley this early if she hadn't been investigating something that was probably little more than a banking error.

"Okay. First I need a pen and paper." He flipped open his cell phone while she fetched both items from the big black bag she carried. He dialed the station. "Cleetus. I need the number for the county Crime Scene division." Bobby jotted the numbers down as he said them aloud.

"Okay. Got it."

"You got something you need help with, Sheriff?" Cleetus asked.

"No. We're over at Harley Evans' place and he's dead. I don't know if it's an accident or something else, yet. Send Daniel out here. For now you're on overtime at the station and see if you can get Wes or Mike in for the day, too. Send one of them to the bank and find out if Harley actually called in sick today."

He started to hang up then had another idea. "Cleetus?"

"Yes, Sheriff?"

"Until we know exactly what happened out here, our official comment is "no comment". And Ms. Roberts is simply helping at the office, no mention of her PI status. That's to everyone, the paper, the town council, even the Baptist Ladies Association. Got it?"

A soft snort came from Bobby. She was certainly getting a lesson about small-town politics today.

Satisfied with Cleetus' part in the process, he dialed the county CS division and walked over to his truck. When Frank Watson answered, he gave him the details and address. Behind the front seat, Gage grabbed two pairs of powder-free latex gloves from the small box he kept there.

"Okay," he said, pocketing his cell phone once more. "Raise your right hand."

"Why?"

"Because if you're going inside, you're going in official, as my deputy. You'll do what I say, and no one can question your presence in a potential crime scene."

"Oh, okay." She raised her hand, her eyes narrowed. "You're not doing this just so I'll have to obey you as my superior, are you?"

"I could get so lucky."

He swore her into duty. Then he opened the screen door once more. "Let's take a look inside."

"Aren't we supposed to wait for the CSI people?"

"We're not going to remove or disturb anything. Frank won't be here for the better part of half an hour. I just want a better look from the inside." He handed her two gloves. "Put these on."

Grasping the doorknob with his finger and thumb, he turned it. It was unlocked.

He shook his head.

Small towns. No one locked their front doors.

With his foot, he pushed the door gently open. Somewhere in the back of the house came the strains of a classical song. A grandfather clock in the front room clicked off the seconds.

Gage stepped inside. Two odors met his nose. Neither one comforting. Crime shows never told people how dead bodies, especially those that died suddenly, smelled.

"Oh God," Bobby whispered behind him. "Is that what I think it is?"

"You going to be okay?" he asked, looking over his shoulder at her. She was holding her nose. He tried not to laugh.

"I think so. No one ever told me how bad the stench would be."

"That's something you never get used to." He pulled his service revolver out of its holder and held it down at his side.

He ventured farther into the house, stopping them both in the living room's doorway.

The furniture, Victorian-period, velvet-lined couches and chairs, lay in a meticulous rectangular grid. All accept the solid-oak coffee table—askew where Harley's body lay next to it. The far wall was lined floor-to-ceiling with built-in oak bookshelves. Each shelf had the books lined in order, spine out. The wall opposite the window held precisely hung, framed maps. Antiques, if he had to guess.

"You stay here until I'm sure Harley's the only one here. And don't touch anything until I get back. Got it?"

"Yes, sir." She saluted him and leaned against the doorjamb.

A quick tour of the house, both upstairs and down, showed nothing but the same well-cared-for antiques and vintage décor. Assured no one lurked in the shadows of the rooms, he holstered his weapon and headed back downstairs.

Bobby hadn't moved from the living room door but had turned so she couldn't see Harley's lifeless body.

"The rest of the house is clear," Gage said as he joined her. He grasped her by the shoulders, turning her to look in the room once more. "Don't look at the body. Just tell me what you see."

"Okay." She paused, looking carefully around the room. "This was a very neat man. Everything has a place and everything is in its place."

"Good. What else?"

"Our victim likes expensive things. Leather-bound

books, antique furnishings. Probably expensive whiskey in those crystal decanters on that table beside the sofa." She pointed to the maps. "He's also a collector of rare maps I bet."

Gage nodded at her. The woman had a good eye. "Very good. You're a better observer than most rookie cops. Now work your way toward the body. What else do you see?"

"The corner of the Persian rug is flipped up by his feet. The coffee table is crooked. Papers are scattered on the floor and table."

"Any conclusion?"

"It looks like he tripped and hit his head."

"Very good. This could be nothing more than a tragic accident. That's what the crime scene people will let us know. Or it could be something more, like a murder staged to look like an accident."

"Why would someone do that?"

"To throw us off, make us not look any further into the case. They'd probably hope we'd give up quickly. This is a small town with limited funds and resources. In the past two days, since you literally fell into my arms, you've seen me call in the county fire department, the county arson investigator and now the county crime scene unit." He held her gaze. "In fact, you might even say you brought all this crime with you."

"I wouldn't, but obviously you have no problem saying it."

She gave him a scathing look. He felt her bristling beside him, the dead body completely forgotten. The woman might've been shaken by viewing her first dead body, but she certainly knew how to remain calm and focused.

"So what do we do now?"

Suddenly, something darted out of the kitchen and under the piano.

Bobby screamed, nearly jumping onto Gage's back. "Oh my God!"

So much for calm and focused. Maybe she was more shaken than she let on.

"It's okay, sweetheart." He pulled her against his side, his hand stroking her dark hair. "It's just a cat. Look." He pointed to where the long-haired gray Persian crouched beneath the baby grand piano.

She turned her head from his chest. "It scared me to death."

"Your scream probably scared it, too."

She smacked him lightly on the chest before pushing away. "I wasn't expecting anything to move in here except us. How long do you think he…he's been dead?"

Gage moved closer to the grandfather clock in the corner. "See this?"

"The clock?" she asked stepping up beside him.

"It's a three-day clock."

"What's a three-day clock?"

He pointed to the chains with the weights attached. "You pull the weights down and that puts the pendulum in motion. It runs for three days. It's still running now."

"So, he's been dead less than three days."

"Probably less than forty-eight hours."

"Why do you say forty-eight hours?"

125

"Here's one of those bonuses of living in a small town. Harley's a deacon over at the Baptist church. Never misses a Sunday or Wednesday. Since no one seemed concerned about him before you and I showed up, I have to assume he made both Sunday services, morning and evening and the Wednesday evening service. And today's Friday, so I'd say he's been dead less than two days."

She nodded and turned to look at Harley once more. "Did he have any family?"

"I believe he had a sister who lives over in Youngstown." Gage walked over and stooped near the body. "While I can only guess as to the time of death, there are other things that can give us a closer estimate."

"Body temp and amount of stiffness?" She said from right behind him.

He nodded at her over his shoulder, her face inches from his as she stooped beside him. "Very good."

"Thank you. Believe it or not, I have studied. I didn't make this career change out of the blue."

"Okay, what else do you see that could tell us the time of death?"

"The wound must be on the side of his head facing the floor. This side is undamaged." She pointed to flies wiggling out from beneath Harley's head. "Are those blue bottle flies?"

Wow, now he *was* impressed. "Looks like it to me."

"Since they're the first insects to feed off dead tissue, the stages of their egg development or larvae can narrow the time of death closer for us."

"I'm not sure what you need me for, Gage. Looks like the young lady knows her stuff," a thin, middle-aged, African-American man said from the doorway, a smile on his face and a large toolbox in his hand.

"Frank," Gage went over and shook the other man's hand. "Glad you could make it. This is Bobby Roberts, she's…"

"His newest deputy. The Sheriff was just showing me how you can learn about a crime scene without touching anything." She shook the other man's hand. "The rest I have to confess I learned by watching too many crime shows."

A meow sounded below them. All three glanced down to see the Persian rubbing up against Bobby's legs. She knelt and picked it up. "Well, hello. Did you decide to come out of hiding?"

"Seems he likes you," Gage said.

"Who will take care of him now that Mr. Evans is dead?"

"I'll have to take him over to the county animal shelter for safe keeping." Frank said, pulling a small brush out of his toolbox. "Hold him still a minute."

Bobby held the cat close as Frank combed through the long hair. "What are you looking for?"

"Trace evidence. The cat may have brushed up against anyone who might've been in the room at the time of the victim's death. Or he may have carried away evidence since then." Frank put away the brush in a plastic bag and marked the outside "cat". He picked up a sheet of paper and blotted it against each of the cat's paws. "This is so that if he stepped in anything we'll have it later, no matter how small."

"Is that why he has to go to the shelter?" Bobby asked, curiosity and concern in her eyes.

"He'll be fine, ma'am." Frank handed Gage a set of keys. "Why don't you get our friend caged in the back of the truck so I can get started in here."

Bobby, with the cat in her arms, followed Gage to the truck. In the back were several cages and some bottles of water. She slipped the cat inside and scratched his head. Gage pulled out a bowl and poured the cat some water.

"What will happen to him?" she asked as they watched the cat lap up the water.

"Once we're sure he won't be needed as a source of evidence, he'll be offered up for adoption. Why? You in need of a cat?"

"It's not his fault his world changed so suddenly because the person who loved him died. He shouldn't be punished by losing his home, too."

"You sure we're talking about the cat?"

The compassion in Gage's voice almost brought tears to her eyes, but she hadn't asked for pity nineteen years ago when she needed it. She wasn't about to accept it now. She'd come to this town to do a job and today's events had just made it harder.

"Of course I'm talking about the cat." She pulled away from his grasp and stalked back to the house.

Behind her she heard his phone ring. She paused to watch him. He looked at the caller ID, his eyes narrowed and his jaw muscle seemed to twitch with agitation. He pushed a button, immediately hanging up on the caller before joining her on the sidewalk.

From the look on his face, he had no intention of

ever talking to whoever had called. Why did she care? The man could drive anyone to drink.

Her nerves were just on edge from seeing her first dead body. Yeah, right. And nothing to do with the big man who keeps touching you every chance he gets.

On their way back to the house they were stopped by an audience of two elderly people, standing on the sidewalk.

"What's goin' on, Sheriff?" asked the little old man. "Somethin' wrong with Harley?"

"We haven't seen him outside last night or today," the white-haired lady said. "And you know he prunes his roses in the backyard every day."

Gage put his arms on both the elderly couple's shoulders, his face softening. "Mr. and Mrs. Clarke, I'm sorry to have to tell you this, but Harley is dead."

"Oh dear." Mrs. Clarke put her hand to her mouth.

Mr. Clarke's hand shook as he reached to hold his wife. "Do you know what happened?"

"We're not sure just yet. It appears to be an accident, but the department has to be sure." Gage squeezed both their arms. "Did you see anyone coming to visit him in the past few days?"

"Well, I'm not sure," Mr. Clarke shook his head, glancing at his wife. "We've been neighbors of Harley's for nigh onto fifty years. Ever since he was a little boy who came to our house for cookies after school. Edna always bakes her special chocolate cookies in the fall."

"Do you need to sit down, ma'am?" Bobby stepped forward, gently grasping the elderly woman by the elbow and casting a questioning look at Gage. "Maybe

I could come home with you and we could talk there while the Sheriff works here."

"I think that's a very good idea. This is Ms. Roberts," Gage introduced her, steering the couple toward their house. "I'd appreciate it if you'd tell her anything that you saw the past few days."

"We'd be happy to, Sheriff," Mr. Clarke said.

"Our grandson Jason is one of his deputies," Edna said as Bobby walked with them back to their house next door. "He talks to Joseph and me about the sheriff all the time."

"Says he wants to be just like him when he finishes his courses over at the community college." Joseph led them onto the porch and helped his wife sit on the quilt-covered metal porch glider. "You two ladies sit right here and I'll go get Edna some water."

"Are you the sheriff's girlfriend?" Edna asked once Bobby was seated next to her.

Bobby felt her cheeks heat. "Me? Oh, no. I'm just helping out over at the office."

"Gage's father was such a good man. We need another man like him to watch over things here. We're all hoping Gage will stay and run for sheriff again, but so far no one's been able to talk him into it. Jason says he wants to go back to Columbus."

"Jason says the sheriff misses the action of the big city." Joseph handed his wife a glass of water. "Seems like he'd want to take his father's place here, but I guess young people need lights and action more than the peacefulness of a small town."

"People really seem to care about each other here," Bobby said, trying to turn the conversation away from

Gage's personal life.

"Oh we do." Edna laughed a little twitter of a laugh. "Sometimes too much. Harley used to say that gossip is the biggest activity in town."

"So you've known Mr. Evans a long time?" Bobby pulled off her big black bag from her shoulder and took out a pen and the spiral notebook.

"Oh, dear, yes. Like Joseph said, he was such a dear boy. He'd come by after school and have cookies and milk. His mother was a schoolteacher and often had to stay late, so he'd just stop in and visit with us."

"We always knew he was a little different, if you know what I mean." Joseph said as he sat in the rocker opposite them.

"You mean he didn't have any girlfriends."

Joseph winked and nodded, as if that was all he had to say.

"But he was always such a sweet man." Edna patted Bobby's hand as if to reassure her. "He'd come and check on us once a week, make sure we didn't need anything. When it was winter, he'd drive us to the church services, so Joseph wouldn't have to drive on the ice or snow."

"Did he go to church this past Sunday?"

Edna looked at Joseph. "I believe he was at both services, wasn't he?"

"Yep. Took up the collection like always. Saw him Wednesday night, too." Joseph nodded again.

"And did you see him yesterday?"

"Can't say as I did."

"How about visitors? Did you see anyone coming to visit Mr. Evans in the past two days?"

The elderly couple exchanged looks then shook their heads.

"No, can't say as we saw anyone visiting in the past two days. But don't rightly know about the nighttime. We're usually asleep by eight," Joseph explained, tapping his hearing aid. "We both take ours out at night. If there'd been someone coming to see Harley we'd have slept right through it."

Bobby jotted the notes down. Some of this conversation might prove important if Harley's death wasn't an accident. She thanked the couple, promising to stop by again.

On the short walk back to Harley's house, she worked her way through the crowd that had assembled on the sidewalk outside. Whispered words of "who is she" and "wonder what happened to Harley" filtered past her.

"Ms. Roberts." Tobias Rawlins stepped directly in her path, stopping her progress. The newspaperman was at his side along with two men she'd never met before. "I didn't know you knew Harley."

"Mayor Rawlins." Jeez, news certainly brought out the big guns in this town. "Actually, I've never met the man."

"Really? Then may I ask why you're here?"

Not that it was any of his business, but she didn't want to make more waves, especially since Gage already gave her a cover story as his fill-in employee. "I was with the sheriff when he came to check in on Harley."

"So someone reported Mr. Evans' death to the sheriff?" Mr. Davis asked, taking out a notepad and pen to make notes.

No way was she giving an interview for the paper.

"No. I believe the sheriff had another reason for speaking with Mr. Evans, now if you'll excuse me I need to get back inside."

As she stepped onto the porch, an older man dressed in the same deputy's uniform she'd seen Cleetus and Jason wear stopped her.

"No one can enter, ma'am."

She gave him a smile. "You must be Daniel."

"Daniel Fischer, meet Bobby Roberts," Gage said as he stepped up behind the deputy. He searched the crowd on the sidewalk, his eyes narrowing. "Bobby's helping out at the station and is a new deputy, Daniel. You can let her in and no one else. Especially the local politicians and press." The last part he added loud enough to be heard all the way to the street.

"Yes, sir." Daniel opened the door and stepped back to let her inside. "Sorry, ma'am. I didn't know."

"That's okay, deputy. I'm sorry we have to meet under such circumstances."

Daniel's face grew somber. "Me too, ma'am. Harley was a harmless fella."

"You knew him?"

"He was a few years ahead of me in school."

Gage clapped him on the shoulder, his mouth drawn in a line of concern. "You going to be okay watching the crime scene for the night, Daniel? Or should I have Mike come over and you can man the station?"

"I'll be okay, Gage. Just seems a damn shame someone would do this to Harley."

"You're sure it wasn't an accident?" A chill ran over Bobby. Seeing someone dead was one thing, finding out his life had been cut short by someone else gave the situation a whole new sinister feel.

"I'll show you what we found if you think it won't upset you." Gage stepped back so she could get into the living room.

"It will probably upset me, but I'll try not to get sick."

Frank was taking pictures of Harley's body. They'd turned him over to get a look at the wound. The right front and top of his head were a bloody mass. Bobby swallowed hard several times to keep from gagging at the sight.

"You okay?" Gage put his hand on her back.

She nodded, not trusting her voice at the moment.

"Okay. Frank, show her what we found."

"At first glance, this looks like Harley tripped over the rug and hit his head on the corner of the table." Frank pointed to the table. "But see the bloodstain there?"

Again, Bobby nodded.

"It's a smear of blood. No tissue that I can find."

"And that means?" she asked, finally in control of her emotions again.

"It means the blood smear was planted. Probably by our killer, to make us think this was an accident." He pointed to the wound on Harley's head. "This wound isn't consistent with hitting the corner of the table. If that had been the cause of death, the injury would've been more of a gash, similar in shape to the table's corner."

Bobby leaned a little closer to look at the wound. "It looks like he was hit more than once."

"You're right, Gage. She is good."

Gage had complimented her to this expert? The knowledge warmed her a little and eased her nausea.

Frank pointed to the left of the body. "And the pattern of blood splatter to the side of the carpet over here suggests that the person was hit with blood and tried to clean it up."

Daniel stuck his head into the room. "The ambulance is here, Gage."

"Good. You ready to transport the body, Frank?"

"I'm pretty much done with him." He set his camera down. "Let me get the body bag from the truck."

While the men covered the body and loaded it onto the ambulance's gurney, Bobby looked around the room, careful not to disturb anything. The papers on the table seemed harmless. Just old bank statements and some correspondence. She wandered over to the bookcases. Many of the classics lined the shelves, along with mysteries and thrillers. She smiled. She and Harley had the same taste in books. He seemed to have every one of Robert Ludlum's novels. She did too.

She leaned against the shelves and stared at the fireplace across the room. Something wasn't quite right about it.

"What's wrong?" Gage asked, coming to stand in front of her.

She moved to the side, continuing to study the fireplace. "The mantle. Does it look odd to you?"

He turned to look at the other side of the room, too.

"No. Why? What do you see?"

"It's what I don't see. It's asymmetrical."

"Okay, I'll bite. Why is that a problem?"

"Look at the rest of the room," she waved her hand in the air. "Everything is neat, orderly, exact."

"Yes. We already discussed that. Harley was neat to the point of obsession."

"Not just neat—precise. Those maps are hung exactly equal distance from the ceiling and floor. The books are alphabetized and grouped by author. Now look at the mantle. There are two candlesticks, one on each side of the mirror. Two vases, one on each side of the mirror."

"And only one statue of a horse."

"Right."

"I believe Ms. Roberts has just discovered our murder weapon, Gage," Frank said from the doorway. "Good work."

Despite the seriousness of the situation, Bobby smiled.

"That she did. You might think she's a trained investigator," Gage said, winking at her. "Let's spread out and see if the killer dumped it anywhere in the house. I'll take the back trashcans. Bobby, you take the house cans."

Thanks to the victim's penchant for orderliness and neatness, the search was quick and futile. The only thing that Bobby found out of place was a bottle of bleach.

"That would explain why we couldn't find a real blood splatter on the floor around the body," Frank said when she carried the bottle out to him. "Our killer knows enough to try and eradicate blood with bleach. We'll bag this up and run it for fingerprints back at the lab."

"Can the bleach completely wipe out the blood evidence?"

"Not entirely. I'll have to bring out the county's Luminol and UV source. I didn't think I'd need them when I left the office."

"No weapon in the back trash," Gage said, entering through the kitchen door. He held up an envelope. "But I did find this."

"What is it?"

"The return address is White, Taylor, Davis & White, Attorneys at law, postmarked from Cincinnati."

Bobby inhaled and exhaled slowly. "That's Chloe's law firm."

Chapter Eight

By the time they finished processing the remainder of the crime scene, an act that yielded nothing new, the streetlights had come on. Most of the crowd had lost interest in finding out the gossip about the activity at Harley's house and gone home.

"I dread going to the café or the tavern for dinner tonight," Bobby said as she scooted into the truck's passenger seat. She glanced out the window at the crime scene house once more, her skin feeling as if a thousand ants crawled across it. She rubbed her arms. "Everyone in town will be asking questions."

Gage snorted a laugh. "You're learning what life in a small town is all about. It's one of the reasons I'm leaving when this term's finished. Sometimes I feel like a shark in a giant fishbowl."

The anger in his voice caught her attention. His

mouth had set in a hard line once more. She'd quickly learned that meant the subject was closed, at least for the time being.

The man fascinated her. He professed a desire to shake the town's dirt from his shoes, yet knew everyone in town by name. Over the past two days she'd seen his concern and compassion for the citizens, and watched their love of him as a friend and respect of him as their chief law enforcement officer. She wasn't sure who was confused, her or him.

He put the truck in gear and drove down another house-lined street. The homes on this street were a mix of style, some two-stories, a few Cape Cods that were popular after World War II and a few more modern ranch-style houses.

"Where are we going?" she asked, since they weren't headed back into the heart of town or toward her motel. A tremor went through her and she shivered. Her heart started pounding. What was wrong with her? Being alone with him was what she wanted, right? Why was she suddenly so nervous?

"You're right about dinner. No way can we have a quiet meal after this mess." He glanced at her a moment before focusing his attention on the road again. "Do you like steak?"

"Ribeye with a little pink in the middle. Why?"

"I know a place where you can get it cooked just like that, some steak fries on the side and no gossips bothering you while you eat."

"Sounds delicious. Where is it?"

He pulled into the long drive of a two-story house, parking in back next to the detached garage shielded by eight-foot ficus hedges. "Here. I cook the best Ohio grain-fed beef steaks you'll ever taste."

"I'll be the judge of that."

"Trust me. You'll be very impressed."

Even as he teased her, panic suddenly flowed over her. What was wrong with her? She'd never felt like this before. She needed to get out of the truck now. To walk, run, move, or something.

Just as she climbed out of the truck her cell phone went off again. She glanced at her watch. Six o'clock. Dammit, must be Chloe.

"Your sister again?" Gage stood next to the truck, leaning one hand on his door and staring at her with alert intensity.

"Yes. I'm surprised she waited until now to call. She's never been one long on patience." She pushed the talk button. "I told you I'd call you back."

"That was like four hours ago and you said you'd call me back at five. It's six. What have you learned?"

"There's been a complication…" Bobby walked the width of the backyard between the hedges.

"What sort of complication?"

Turning, she paced back toward Gage. "The bank loan officer won't be able to help us…"

"What do you mean, he won't be able to help us? He's the one who filed the lien on the property, wasn't he?"

"I don't know—" She pivoted and stalked back across the yard once more, faster.

"Just ask him."

Bobby pivoted again. Her pulse rapidly playing the drumbeat from Bolero in her head, faster and faster. "I can't. He's—"

"What do you mean you can't? For crying out loud, sis, you're making this more difficult than it should be. All you have to do is ask him if he got my letter and interview him on how the lien came to be."

"Dammit, Chloe, stop interrupting me." Her feet kept moving. She was almost jogging as she traveled back and forth across Gage's lawn. "He's dead, Chloe. Dead. As in his eyes are wide open, his heart isn't beating, he can't answer any damn questions, D-E-A-D, DEAD!"

God, her head hurt, her heart hurt. She closed her eyes as she paced. "Oh God, oh God, oh God."

Suddenly she slammed into something hard and warm.

Gage.

She gripped his shirt in her hand and tears rolled down her cheeks. A sob escaped her. Then another. The dam broke.

Removing the phone from her hand, he wrapped his arm around her and held her tight against his body. He held the phone to his ear, his eyes never leaving hers. "Chloe, this is Sheriff Justice. Your sister will have to call you back in the morning. Yes, she's fine, just a little upset." Then he hit the end call button.

"You…can't…" she hiccupped between stutters and sobs. "You…can't…hang…up."

"I just did, sweetheart," he wrapped both arms tight around her and rubbed her back. "You don't need to talk to a lawyer right now, even if she is your sister."

"Don't…know…what's…wrong…" she managed between sobs.

He led her up the steps, into the back door and through the house. "It's okay. You'll be fine soon. It's the adrenaline."

"Adrenaline?" She sobbed and sucked in air, realizing he'd pulled her down beside him on a couch.

"It happens to rookies at their first big murder scene. Men usually go out and punch something," he said as he rubbed his hands up and down her back, his body so warm against hers. Her body continued to tremble.

"And women?" She ran her hands up his chest, feeling each rib and the solid muscles beneath his shirt.

"Never had a female rookie. Saw a few cry like you just did, but never knew if it worked for them."

"I need to do something. I feel like I'm going to explode." She nuzzled his neck, nearly climbing astride him.

He lowered his lips, claiming hers. Her body seemed to be on fire, and he was the one stoking the furnace. She wanted the flames to lick her all over and consume this need inside her.

His hands kneaded her back muscles, making their way lower and lower, until he cupped her butt cheeks. He broke the kiss, panting as hard as she was. "You're sure?"

"Stop now and you're dead meat, Sheriff."

"Far be it from me to allow you to commit a felony."

"Bed," she whispered.

"Bed?" he croaked back at her, sounding like a teen trying to get to first base. The woman truly could read his mind.

"Yes. Now, please."

Gage grabbed her by the hand and hauled her off the couch and up the stairs before she changed her mind. Outside his bedroom door, he stopped her, crushing her to him in another heated kiss. She tasted of honey and raw need. Soft beneath his hands, yet strong in spirit. No woman should've seen what she did today, yet she hadn't given in to the urge to flee. She stood her ground. Her fire fed his own, until now he needed her as much as she needed him.

Press her against the wall. Strip her and take her. Now.

His body demanded it plunge into hers.

Stop.

She deserves more than a fuck against the wall like some streetwalker.

He broke the kiss with all the self-restraint he had left. "Wait here" he murmured, pushing her away from him and up against the hall wall.

She panted and nodded, as if she knew he wouldn't be able to resist her if she touched him again at this moment.

Inside his dark room, he stumbled to the window to be sure the blind was down. He pulled the heavy curtains closed. No use giving the widow Munroe more images to titillate her nights, not to mention gossip for her quilting bee friends. He searched his bureau drawer until he found the condoms he'd tossed in there nearly a year ago.

Damn. Had it been that long since he'd had sex? No. Longer. Since before he'd been shot.

He tossed one on the bedside table, thought about it, tossed a second. Picked up several pairs of boxers from the floor and threw them in his hamper so neither he nor Bobby would trip on them on the way to the bed.

"Gage?"

Her sultry voice coming from the hallway sent new heat through him. Best get her undressed and in the bed before her ardor cooled. He turned toward the lit hallway, stopping dead in his tracks.

She stood silhouetted in the doorway.

An earth goddess of sexual desire.

Femininity personified.

A temptation to sin.

Nude.

His.

"Oh, God," she murmured, stepping back. Timidity replacing the sex-siren call in her voice. "I knew I should've waited to do this in the dark."

"No. Stop."

The command froze her retreat.

He swallowed hard. Every inch of her was now highlighted in the lit hallway. Full breasts—not perky like a teen or porno queen, but not nearly middle-aged, with full dark nipples. The soft swell of her abdomen—not hard like a man's. The gentle curve of her hips, the kind a man could hold on to without fear of breaking her.

For the first time, in a long time, he realized there had to be a heaven…and it was missing an angel.

"Gage?" The tremor in her voice broke the spell.

In three strides he closed the distance between

them, his hands cupping her face, he stared into her eyes the color of milk chocolate on a hot day. "You are beautiful."

She inhaled, her breasts rubbing against his arms.

He slowly lowered his lips to hers. The kiss started slow. He wanted to show her just how desirable she was to him. She moaned beneath his lips and all gentleness fled.

Her fingers at his shirt, she opened it as he maneuvered them back toward the bed. She started to pull it off, and he stilled her hands. He broke the kiss, panting against her.

"What?"

"I have scars," he whispered, shoving the covers out of the way.

"I have fat hips and a big ass."

"I love your ass."

"You do?" she asked as he gently pushed her down in the bed.

"I've been dreaming about your ass since the first time I saw it." As quick as possible, he shed his clothes before stretching out beside her.

"I just bet you have." A sultry chuckle escaped her.

Good. She wasn't crying anymore. That had to be a good sign. And she was naked beside him. That was a very good sign. He slid his hand over her hip to cup a butt cheek firmly. "This was the first part of you I ever saw, and lady, you were made for squeezing." Which he proceeded to demonstrate and pulled her tight against him.

She gripped his biceps with one hand, arched her neck and moaned again. The sound thrilled him and stoked the need inside him.

So much for going slow.

With a growl, he lowered his lips to her neck, tracing the column from her collarbone to her jaw. She tasted of heat and smelled like lemons and some sweet flower, which poets probably knew the name, but he didn't give a damn. All he knew was he wanted more. With a need he hadn't known before, he slid his lips across to hers, not just kissing her, but memorizing the taste and feel of her. Claiming her, marking her as his.

A tremor raced through her body.

God. He had to slow down. This desire was consuming him. He needed to give her time. He broke the kiss off, panting heavily as his hands caressed his favorite part of her anatomy.

"Sorry." He dragged in another breath, opening his eyes to meet hers, which were half opened in arousal. "I'll try to go slower."

"Don't," she whispered, almost a plea.

"You want me to stop?" Not that. Anything but that.

"Don't...go slower." She stroked her hand down his side and across his hip until she held him in her hand. "I need you. Now."

Yes, there was a God!

He reached for the foil packet and ripped it open with his teeth. She took it from him and sheathed him. Her hands shook. The knowledge that they did from either nervousness or need touched something primal inside him. Something that made him want to both claim and protect her.

Gripping both her hands, he lifted them high over

her head and rolled her onto her back. She parted her legs beneath him and surged her hips up, pressing her mound tight against his hard-on. He took it for permission and entered her with one deep thrust.

A sound escaped Bobby. Half moan, half groan. He filled her so completely. She sucked in a breath, slid her feet up the back of his calves and pulled him in tighter.

It was his turn to groan.

All further thought escaped her. She rode the adrenaline rush and thrill of having him inside her. Each time he thrust, she parried with one of her own. The need inside her grew hungrier, the rhythm faster. The sounds of pleasure echoed in the dark.

Finally she clasped him to her with her legs and arms, her body arched beneath his as she crested the wave of passion. Above her he shouted out his own completion, clenching her to him.

Her eyes closed, she smiled and ran her hands over his back to soothe him as he collapsed upon her. As her finger crossed the two pucker marks on his back, she forced her hands not to linger, but gently caressed over all his sweat-covered skin.

Curious how he got the scars—she knew from crime photos she'd studied they'd come from bullets—she didn't want to think how much pain he'd been in or why. And asking him questions would spoil the moment.

Slowly, as if the effort used more energy than he had, he lifted up onto his elbows to stare down at her. The intensity in his gaze made her heart flutter a beat or two. A soft smile lifted the corners of his lips and he brushed her hair from her cheek with his fingers, caressing her cheek with his knuckles.

"Better?"

"Mm-hmm, much," was all she could manage. If she said any more, she'd either beg him to repeat the experience or cry tears of gratitude that he'd made her feel so good.

He leaned forward, his chest brushing the sensitive nipples, and placed a gentle kiss on her lips. He teased her lips with his tongue then slid it over her jawbone up to her ear.

"I'm still hungry," he whispered into her ear, sending tremors across her body once more.

He couldn't be serious? As spent as she was, she doubted she could do it again right now, even if the entire free world depended on it.

"I don't think that's possible right now," she whispered back, even though she clenched herself around him where he remained inside her.

He chuckled, and lifted his chest back off her. "Sweetheart, I meant I'm still really hungry...for dinner."

Even in the near-dark she felt the blush start at her toes and shoot up her entire body like a Roman candle. "Oh God. I thought... I mean... Oh." She slapped her hands over her eyes.

He chuckled again, nipping her lips with his own as he slid off her body. From between her fingers she watched him stride from the room in all his naked glory.

He was magnificent. All sinewy muscles and

arrogant male pride.

And she'd made love to him. Or at least had sex.

She couldn't believe she'd just done that. With a man she'd known less than a week.

What must he think of her?

That I'm an insatiable sex kitten?

Or desperate?

She groaned and pulled the sheets up over her body and curled on her side.

When he returned a few moments later, he stopped to pull on his jeans and a t-shirt. He brought her one of his own flannel shirts from the closet. "Bathroom's down the hall. I'll go start the grill."

He leaned forward for another kiss before leaving.

Nonchalant. That's how he wanted to play it. Okay. She could be nonchalant, too.

Grasping the shirt, she climbed out of bed and slipped it on. Taking a deep, steadying breath she rolled the sleeves up to her elbows and buttoned the front.

So what if her fingers shook a little bit? She was nearly forty after all. Sex should be no big deal. True, it had been the best sex she'd ever had. Not that she'd been *that* experienced. Losing one's virginity to the high school nose tackle, Adam "the moose" Bartholomew, and sleeping with the occasional boyfriend over the past twenty years didn't really qualify her as sexually active. More like a sexual bystander. This time with Gage was definitely…different.

At the end of the hall she found the restored Victorian bathroom and cleaned up as best she could.

She glanced at her face in the mirror. Her mascara had smeared during either the crying jag or her hot wrestling match with Gage.

Great. So much for looking like a sex goddess. What she needed now was something to scrub it off.

A bar of soap lay in the soap dish on the sink. Don't suppose he had anything gentler?

She flipped open the medicine cabinet and searched through its contents. Toothpaste, shaving cream, razors, deodorant. No cold cream. Something odd caught her attention. Shoved back in the corner was a glass jar.

What the heck? She pulled it out and studied the contents. The gold wedding band was obvious. The other thing inside was a mashed and mangled piece of metal.

Oh, my God. She nearly dropped the jar. The metal must be one of the bullets that had left the scars all over Gage's body. The ones she'd felt while holding him tight against her. Symbols of his shooting and a possible marriage.

She sat down on the toilet seat—hard.

Why hadn't he told her he'd been married before? Or was he still married? No, she would've heard something about his wife, if he still had one, in the two days she'd been in this small town. Of that she was certain. So he must've been married once before, but not now. But why hadn't he said something?

Well, it's not like she'd asked and he'd lied. And he was almost forty. At least she guessed he was her age. There were few never-married men or women their age, at least not straight ones. Besides, his past was his business. She hadn't asked for strings when she'd begged him to make love to her, and he hadn't given any either.

Turning the jar she studied the contents.

Why keep them stored together? Were they two separate events or connected in some way?

One thing she knew for sure. The man didn't want to talk about them. And he'd probably be pissed that she'd found this.

Carefully, she slid the jar back where she found it and replaced the toothpaste in front of it.

Somehow she'd go downstairs, have dinner with him and pretend she hadn't found his secrets. She'd also pretend she was as carefree as him about having sex. So she'd think of it simply like a physical release to the things she'd seen today.

She lathered the soap onto a washcloth and began cleaning the smeared makeup off her face.

Yep. That's what she'd do all right. Think of it as two people helping each other through a physical need.

No big deal.

Downstairs, she stopped in the doorway and watched him cleaning potatoes. His body, even clothed, would tempt any woman. She liked the way the jeans hugged his hips and thighs, the thickness of his arms in the t-shirt shouted all-male with every move.

Her heart jumped and her nipples tightened just at the sight of him.

No big deal, my ass.

"Hope you're as hungry as I am." He glanced up and smiled at her without breaking stride on the spuds.

Yes, I'm hungry, but meat and potatoes probably won't cure what ails me. Nonchalant, remember? Keep it light.

"Starving." Focused on looking around the kitchen, she didn't remember seeing any of it when he'd led her inside earlier.

Unlike the upstairs bathroom, this wasn't a Victorian remodel, but a vintage nineteen-fifties kitchen. Black and white linoleum tiles checkered the floor. The cupboards were painted white with chrome handles. On the wall hung a red Coca-Cola clock and signs advertising bottles for five cents. The table and stools looked like they'd come right out of a soda shop, complete with chrome edging.

She walked over and ran her fingers in the ridges of the chrome along the edge of the table. "This is fabulous."

"Thanks. My dad loved the fifties." He leaned onto the Formica counter as he explained. "He was a teenager then and collected stuff from stores and shops that closed over the years. When we moved here, he worked on making the kitchen what you see. The only modern conveniences are the stainless-steel appliances he added about five years ago. He always wanted a juke box, but none ever went on auction at a price he could afford on a sheriff's salary."

"You grew up with this?" She fingered the stainless two-sided napkin holder and tall glass sugar dispenser on the table. Framing the doorway that led into another room were framed vintage record covers of Elvis, Jerry Lee Lewis and several Motown R&B groups.

"Yeah. For a few years as a cocky teen I resented

his worship of old rock stars in favor of punk sounds. But with age comes wisdom. Dad really did impart some good taste into my life."

"You miss him, don't you?" It really wasn't a question. She saw how his eyes lingered on objects in the room and heard the pride in his voice as he spoke of his father.

"Dad was the finest man I've ever known." Gage turned and searched in the fridge, coming out with two steaks. "Now, you take a seat while I prepare you a feast."

"You want me to help?"

"Nope." From a drawer he pulled a pad of paper and pen and handed them to her. "I want you to write down everything you can remember about your sister's client and his case. Don't leave anything out, no matter how insignificant you might think it."

"You think it might have something to do with Harley's death?"

He nodded as he seasoned the steaks with salt and pepper. "Seems awful strange that you're here to investigate some lien against a property, and the man who would've been in charge of making the supposed loan winds up murdered less than forty-eight hours later."

"You don't think I have anything to do with it, do you?" She sat at the table, waiting for him to say just that.

He winked at her, picked up a knife and started slicing the potatoes into long strips. "Sweetheart, if Harley was killed last night, I know exactly where you were, remember? If you'd even tried leaving that motel room I'd have known. The walls are that thin."

Heat shot into Bobby's cheeks. Apparently she wasn't the only one aware that a thin wall separated them last night. Had he had as many problems sleeping as she did?

"Don't look at me like that or neither one of us is going to get any dinner."

She blinked and realized she was looking at him like a hungry tiger stared at a newborn calf. "Don't forget, I like my meat a little on the rare side," she said with more sass than she really felt.

"Why does that not surprise me?" He laughed.

She smiled and relaxed. If someone had told her a week ago she'd be sitting in the kitchen of a man as sexy as Gage, flirtatiously chatting and making comments with double entendres, much less having had incredible sex with him, she'd have sent them packing to the nearest insane asylum.

"So when did you first hear about the case?"

She picked up the pen, trying to focus on the task he'd given her. As she made her list, she talked aloud to save time so he'd hear things as she remembered them. "Everything started three weeks ago when Chloe called for one of her regular chat sessions."

Both her sisters called on a weekly, sometimes daily, basis to keep her informed of how they were doing since she was as close as they'd come to having a parent in twenty years. But she suspected they also called to check on her. They feared she spent all her time hibernating in the townhouse she'd raised them in like some hermit. When she'd told them she'd taken and passed her PI licensure test, they'd both laughed until they realized she was serious.

"Did she ask you to look in on the case?" Gage watched her from across the counter.

Bobby shook her head. "No, she really did just call to talk. But I always ask about her work, and she started telling me about this case. She was sure it was simply a clerical error. Just in case there was something to the bank's claim, she'd sent a letter to the bank a month earlier and had never received a reply."

"And her bosses were putting pressure on her to get the matter settled quickly."

"How did you know?"

He shrugged, tossed the pan with the steak fries into the oven and picked up the steaks. "I know a lot about lawyers, both junior and senior partners." His lip set in that I'm-done-talking-about-it line once more. Carrying the steaks to the back door, he paused a moment. "You write, I'll fire up the grill."

Whoa. The man really didn't like lawyers. Maybe he'd had a DA lose a drug case he worked hard on. That was a tried-and-true plot on all the crime shows she watched. She shook her head and focused her attention on writing down the events leading up to her trip to Westen.

***

An hour later, after a bottle of wine, melt-in-your-mouth steak and crispy fries Gage sat back and studied the woman across from him. "You were very good over at Harley's today."

"Yeah, right. I nearly keeled over when I saw him...like that." She took a deep drink of her wine as if the image of Harley's body still shook her nerves.

"But you didn't. And I have to tell you, you're one hell of a detective. You've got instincts people trained for years haven't acquired."

"Really? How?"

Her eyes sparkled from his compliment. Or maybe it was the wine. Either way, he meant what he'd said. He might've doubted her abilities the first day he met her, but today she'd proved her mettle.

"Figuring out the murder weapon, for one. Both Frank and I missed that."

"Thank you." She blushed.

He liked how she'd do that whenever he teased her or complimented her. He didn't know women her age could still blush.

"So how did your sister come to ask you to take on this case?"

Bobby sipped her wine. She slid her tongue out to catch the drop on her lip and shrugged. "I begged."

He chuckled. "You begged?"

"Yes, sir." She grinned at him over the rim of her wineglass. "I told her this would be a simple case for me to get my feet wet on. I'd had my license about six months, but hadn't gotten any field experience. This would be a relatively safe job and I could put on my resume that I'd worked for a prestigious law firm in Cincinnati. I can advertise it on a website and any publicity in the papers will help to get me more clients."

She wanted to solve the case to get her name in the papers. It was a logical business move, but it reminded him of Moira's craving for media attention. The acid in his gut churned a bit harder.

Was she the same kind of woman—a manipulator who didn't care who she hurt on the way up the ladder? He remembered how kind and patient she was to Cleetus and Jason's grandparents. Moira never would've treated them as Bobby had. He prayed he wasn't wrong about Bobby.

He finished his wine in one long drink. "And your sister bought this?"

"Well, I did have to turn on the guilt, just a little bit." She drained the last of the wine in her glass, too. "But I really can handle this case."

"It's no longer a simple bank error, Bobby." The suspicion that had nibbled at the back of his mind when they'd found Harley hadn't gone away. "You know what that envelope in the trash means, don't you?"

She nodded. "That Harley Evans had the letter my sister sent about the lien at his house."

"Which could mean?"

"That Harley, the friendly neighbor, staunch deacon, dependable employee had bank property at his house that he might've been hiding from someone—possible proof that something illegal is going on. And someone else killed him for it."

Damn, he loved the way the woman's mind worked. It was a sexy thing. Combined with the things her ass made him want to do, she was one tempting package. A temptation he intended to enjoy, again.

"So what do we do next?"

No way could she read his mind. She had to be talking about the case. Trouble was, at the moment both his heads had no interest in Harley, the bank or

Bobby's career as a PI.

"Frank said he'd have the autopsy report and fingerprint analysis for me tomorrow."

"What about DNA results?"

"You watch too many TV shows. That can take six weeks if the state puts a rush on it. I hope to figure out what's going on long before then."

She nodded. "So what else do we do?"

"Tomorrow, I have a little talk with Harley's boss and fellow employees down at the bank."

"Just you."

The hurt in her eyes kicked him right in the chest. For some reason this lady had gotten under his skin. Too bad he wasn't interested in something more than good hot sex. And he'd learned his lesson long ago not to let civilians get messed up in an investigation. Bad shit was bound to happen. Might as well let her learn up front how things were going to be, no matter how much those dark eyes pleaded with him.

"Just me. You've already gone in the bank today."

"But they think I was just there to open a bank account. A legitimate account, I might add."

He stood and started cleaning the dishes from the table. The idea of her walking around town alone with a killer loose twisted something deep inside him. "If you go in with me tomorrow, and if someone at the bank is responsible for the events that led to Harley's death, your official presence as a PI in town will put everyone's antennae on alert."

"But I'm not just a PI now. You made me a deputy today, remember?"

Damn. She had him.

"Right. And as your boss, I'm making an executive decision that you're not going to the bank with me in the morning."

"So you want me to continue to just be office help?" She'd followed him around the counter to the sink, her eyebrows knit in puzzlement.

"For now it might be best to keep your real reason for being in town between the few people who know— me, you and Cleetus." He squirted soap over the dishes and turned on the hot water.

"I'd sort of be undercover."

"Yes, you'd be undercover."

"When you worked narcotics, did you work undercover?" she asked, picking up a towel and taking the clean wet plate he handed her.

"Yes. For the last three years before I quit."

"Did you like it?"

The woman was far too smart and curious for her own good, and his. For a moment he considered her question. "I wanted to get the big dealers off the streets. Catching them in their own business. I liked that. Pretending to be someone I wasn't. That was hard."

"Why did you quit?"

"A case blew up in my face, literally. Someone close to me blew my cover. I was shot and left for dead." He scrubbed the last plate, not wanting to see the look of pity on her face. He'd sworn he wouldn't let another woman get close enough to hurt him.

"That's a pretty good reason to quit. I'm glad you're here to teach me how to be undercover."

The cupboard behind him opened. The ceramic

plates clanked as she put them back where they belonged. She'd given him space, accepted his shortened version without question. Just when he was sure he had her figured out, she did something else to impress him.

He turned and trapped her against the counter between his hands. Leaning in close, he sniffed her. Flowers. Lemons. Clean. Woman. He rubbed his face against the soft skin of her neck and trailed his lips lightly up to her ear.

"And would you like to get undercover with me?" he asked, letting his hands slide down and fill with the fullness of her round ass cheeks naked beneath the tails of his shirt. Damn, she'd left her panties in his bedroom.

Need slammed into him.

"Mmm, I think I'd like that," she murmured, her voice breathless.

He squeezed her close until her breasts were pressed tight against his chest and her body so molded to his she couldn't mistake his intent.

Her hands came up to clutch his hips, keeping her secure against him. "I'm looking for adventure, officer. What do you think?"

Just when he thought he couldn't get harder, her words sent desire racing to his groin. For a moment he considered throwing her over his shoulder and carrying her to the bedroom, but despite her whispered show of bravado, that would probably send her flying out the back door.

And he couldn't let that happen.

He turned his head and crushed her lips in a searing

kiss, one meant to tell her the urgency of his need. She met him with equal passion, her tongue parrying each thrust of his.

He needed her. Now.

In the kitchen? On the counter?

He grasped her by the butt with both hands and lifted her until she sat on the edge of the counter. Her legs parted and he pressed in between them, amazed how easily this woman aroused him.

When her hands cupped his face, he pulled her tight against him, arching her back to claim her lips in a deeper kiss. Her body quivered against him, her heart beat pounded against his chest in a chaotic beat that thrilled him to the core. In response, he ground tight against her.

"More," she whispered against his lips, breaking the kiss a moment and running her hands down his back to grip his shirt in her fists and pull it up and over his head.

"Yes," he murmured, his hands opening the buttons of his shirt she wore and slipping inside to cup her breasts. He lowered his lips to take one taut peak in his mouth. Another soft moan filled the room, and he sucked harder.

Her fingers fumbled at his pants.

Suddenly the sound of his phone filled the kitchen.

"Damn," he muttered against her breast, which quivered with her panting breaths.

"Do you *have* to answer it?" she whispered as it rang a second time.

Her need so apparent in her voice he couldn't help but smile. "Yes, sweetheart. I am the town sheriff, remember?"

She growled softly in frustration, her hands loosening their hold on his back. With a chuckle, he nipped at her lips before stepping away from her spread thighs to answer the old wall phone. His gaze stroked her from head to toe as he let his hand rest on the receiver for a third ring.

Sitting so exposed on his kitchen counter—his shirt open to her waist, the swell of both breasts visible, her shapely legs open with only the shirt tails tucked between, lips swollen from his kisses and dark hair tousled in wild abandon—she shouted sexy and whispered vulnerable at the same time.

Their gazes locked as he grabbed the phone. "This better be good," he growled into the receiver even as she began buttoning the shirt.

"Sheriff, this is Walt Sanders. Sorry to bother you so late."

Gage glanced at the clock. Nine fifteen. Not that late, but Walt was near seventy, so probably felt late to him. "No problem, Walt. What's up?"

"Well, you know that little lady I rented a room to yesterday?"

"Ms. Roberts?" The hairs on Gage's neck stood on end again and he turned to look at her, now primly sitting on his counter with her hands folded in her lap, her head tilted to the side as she listened to his end of the conversation. This vision of her tore at his gut as much as the sexy vixen had moments before. "What about her?"

"Seems someone broke into that room and tore it all to pieces."

Chapter Nine

They hadn't left one thing untouched. The closet doors hung by one hinge. Dresser drawers were strewn about the room. The knife-ripped mattresses of both beds lay helter-skelter with their tops gaping open and their internal stuffing scattered about like white nylon snowbanks.

Standing in the middle of the chaos, Bobby shuddered and rubbed her hands up and down her arms. "Why would someone do this?" She lifted her favorite sweater off the floor. Hopefully the dry cleaners could get the wrinkles and dirt out.

"Obviously they were looking for something." Gage said, standing just inside the doorway.

No kidding. "What were they looking for? Who could do this?"

"That's an answer I'd like to know." He turned to

Walt, who stood out in the dark night, peeking in from the side of the door. "Did you see anyone drive in or out today?"

Walt shook his head. "There were some truckers here last night, but they pulled out not long after you two left this morning. We had a couple stop by last night, but they've moved on, too. About two hours ago, the new set of truckers stopped for the night. You know we always get more business once the sun goes down."

"You've been watching the parking lot all day and night?"

"Well, now you know me and the missus watch the news and then our shows at seven. But I can't say as I've seen anyone snooping around this room. Least-wise no strangers actin' suspicious. Gonna set us back a few pennies for new mattresses." The old man's shoulders drooped a little more as he took in the room's devastation. "Good thing I didn't let my insurance lapse this month."

Bobby shook her head. It was so unfair that someone would cause this nice man such trouble. "I'm so sorry this happened."

"Well, it ain't your fault, miss. I'm thinkin' it was just some hooligans tryin' to cause trouble, is all." He gave her a gentle smile. "I think I can get another room ready if you be wantin' it."

The possibility of spending another night in a motel with such obvious lack of security sent another shudder over Bobby. "Um, that's very nice of you, Mr. Sanders, perhaps..."

"No need to go to the effort, Walt," Gage

interrupted her, his attention on the motel owner. "Ms. Roberts will be staying with me."

"Well, if you're sure, Sheriff. I best be calling Martin over at the insurance agency. Bad news always comes at night, don't it?" The older man just nodded his head and headed toward his office.

Bobby waited until Mr. Sanders was out of hearing range before she shoved her hands on her hips and narrowed her eyes at Gage. "I am *not* staying with you."

He crossed his arms over his chest and arched one brow. "You're not?"

"If I stay with you in twenty minutes the entire town will know about it. And you have a reputation to maintain." Her voice broke a little and she swallowed to keep from giving in to the tears that threatened to overtake her. The last thing she wanted to do was cry in front of Gage. Better to be angry than watery and wimpy.

"I do?" He asked, taking a step closer.

"Of course you do. You're an elected official..."

"Technically, my Dad was the one elected. I was more or less drafted to finish his term." He drew closer. "And where exactly were you planning to stay, if not with me?"

She took a step back only to have her legs slam into the upturned mattress behind her. In an effort to keep from toppling back over it like a scene from a well-scripted *I Love Lucy* show, she grasped hold of the mattress' edge with one hand, and Gage's George Strait T-shirt with the other. Her balance restored, she let go of Gage. "I'll stay at the Westen Inn."

"And put Adele Carlisle in danger? The woman is near eighty." He'd gone back to arching his brow at her, and he'd pressed his lips into that stubborn line again.

"What makes you think she'd be in danger?" Really. No one but him and Cleetus knew who she was and why she was here.

"Look around you, sweetheart." He spread his arms wide. "Someone believes you have something they want or need. Since you showed up in town, I've had one arson fire, one dead body, and now one breaking and entering with willful destruction of property."

"You think all this was *my* fault?" The nerve of the big lug! "I didn't do any of this."

The muscles of his neck worked as he swallowed, took another deep breath and heaved a huge sigh. "Bobby, I didn't say you were responsible for what's been going on. The timing suggests your appearance here is the trigger."

"You think whomever's behind Harley Evans' death is also responsible for the arson fire and now this mess? And that they may know why I'm here?" Another shiver ran through her.

"I don't know. But I do know it's a lot of coincidence they all occurred since you arrived in town." He reached out and took her hand in his. "I don't like this many coincidences. You'll be safer staying with me until I can figure out what the hell is going on and who's responsible."

The way he held her hand securely in his comforted her. When she looked into his dark-green eyes, she saw both concern and tenderness. Had a man ever looked at her like that? Something deep in her heart flipped.

She dropped her gaze first and shrugged. "I'd hate to put Mrs. Carlisle in any danger."

Gently, he slipped his other hand under her chin and lifted until her gaze met his once more. "Thank you."

Fighting the desire to throw herself into the safety and strength of his arms, she bit the inside of her lip. "Okay, so what do we do now? Wait for Frank and the crime scene division people to get here and process this stuff before I pack it up?"

A deep rumble started in his chest and filled the air with his laughter as he turned to take in the room. "This isn't like TV, sweetheart. I doubt anything we found in here would tell us who did this."

What did he find so funny? "What about fingerprints or DNA?"

He looped one arm around her shoulder and led her carefully through the maze of mattresses and drawers. "This is a motel. Despite Walt and his wife's best efforts at housekeeping, I doubt they've removed fingerprints from every surface after each person checked out. Then there's the DNA specimens probably left on a nightly basis on the mattresses."

God, men could be so gross. Bobby pulled away from him and smacked him in the chest. "Please. I don't even want to think that I slept on them." This time the shudder running down her skin was from the creeps instead of fear.

"Okay. You pack up your stuff and I'm going to have a look around the outside perimeter."

"What for?" She followed him to the doorway. "You just said nothing here would be of use."

"Just looking for tire tracks. I won't be far." He retrieved a flashlight from his truck cab, and began methodically searching the gravel parking lot from the hotel room back toward the highway.

For a moment Bobby continued to watch him, listening to the soft crunch of gravel beneath his boots. She shook her head as she started folding her clothes into her suitcase. The man was like a bulldog with a bone sometimes. If she looked in the dictionary for the word intense, she'd find a nice picture of him, grimly set lips and all.

As she made her way through the chaos of the room, collecting her belongings, she quietly catalogued each item in her head. Three pairs of jeans—the skinny-day ones, the fat-day ones and the pair on her body. Four sweaters or pullovers, all in various stages of wrinkles. Her good black pinstriped suit.

"Crap."

"What?"

Less startled than all the other times he'd snuck up on her, she turned and held out the evidence. "Just look! Whoever destroyed this room mauled my best silk suit just like a day-old newspaper."

"It's a suit." He stared at her like she'd climbed out of a flying saucer from the planet Odd-women-who-worry-about-clothes.

Now that really hacked her off. "This suit cost almost two weeks' salary!"

"Let me get this straight," he said with that patiently placating voice men sometimes used when explaining things to women. "You weren't pissed off because someone broke into your room, rummaged through your belongings and could have hurt you if you'd been here. That's okay with you. But because he wrinkled some suit you paid way too much for, *now* you're angry?"

"Yes, I'm angry. I'm angry that someone trashed my belongings. I'm also angry that they trashed this room which will cost Mr. Sanders time and money to fix. If your theory is right, I'm also angry at this person for stealing Harley's life and setting that fire." She mopped her eyes and returned to finding all her belongings. "Yes, I'm angry and a little scared. The suit was just the icing on the cake."

His arms came around her. "I know you weren't expecting all this when you came looking for adventure, but I promise to keep you safe."

"How? By keeping me under twenty-four-hour surveillance?"

"If I have to, yes." He hugged her tighter for a moment then released her. "You just about done now?"

The odd tightness in his voice took the edge off her anger. She focused on gathering up what she could see. "Just about. I suppose if I forgot anything, Mr. Sanders can let me know."

A knock sounded on the door. They turned to see a man in a deputy's uniform and holding a camouflage-colored baseball cap in his hand, standing halfway inside the room. He looked to be about thirty-five with dark hair and brown eyes. "Man, someone went a little crazy in here."

"Wes Strong, meet Bobby Roberts, our newest deputy."

"Ma'am." He nodded and lifted the corner of his mouth in a half smile, which didn't go to his eyes.

"We're going to gather up her things, and she'll be staying with me. But I'd like you to make a few rounds here tonight, just to be sure Walt doesn't have any more trouble."

"Yes, sir. By the way, I checked with Geraldine Taylor over at the bank to see if Harley called in sick."

"And?" Gage slipped his arm around Bobby's waist.

"Someone called Harley in sick, but Ms. Taylor can't be sure if it was him or not."

"Great. Let me know if you see anything unusual here, or hear anything more about Harley."

"Yes, sir." Wes nodded again, turned and left.

"He's a very sad man." Bobby said.

"Dad hired Wes before I came home. He's ex-military and very closemouthed about his past."

Once she'd finished packing, paid her bill and was seated in the passenger seat of his truck another idea hit her. "You need to take me back to town."

"You already agreed not to stay at the Inn," he said, glancing at her as he drove. The grip of his right hand on the steering wheel tightened the leather beneath his fingers, which creaked slightly in the cab's silent darkness.

The man certainly knew how to hold his temper. Wonder if he learned it from his years working undercover?

"I haven't changed my mind."

"Good."

The arrogance was back. Well, she hated to burst his man-bubble, but he wasn't going to like what she said next.

"We need to get my car. It's still parked outside the bank."

"It'll be there in the morning."

She waited until they reached the red light. They were the only ones at the intersection, but he stopped nonetheless. "Gage?"

He turned to stare at her, giving her his undivided attention. The right-turn signal clicked like a slow metronome.

"My laptop was in the backseat of my car."

"Oh, hell." Without saying anything else, he flipped the turn signal to the left, and headed back to town.

***

Now where was the sheriff taking the woman?

Good thing the tweaker did his damage and left before the old man saw them. Meth made them so damn paranoid and out of control who knew what might've happened.

Couldn't follow the woman now. The sheriff might not want the job the council thrust upon him, but no way was he stupid. He'd spot a tail for sure on nearly empty roads.

Think.

The woman hadn't had anything incriminating among her possessions. If she had anything to incriminate Harley in the land-grab scheme, she had to have it hidden somewhere other than the motel room.

The only evidence that anyone knew the property lien wasn't on the up-and-up had been the letter Harley had at his house. That was no longer a threat.

In fact, at the moment the only threat left to the plan was the nosy woman. If she kept poking her nose in where it didn't belong, she'd blow the whole operation. The associates wouldn't like it at all. Nope. Not at all. Something had to be done about her.

She was a piece of work all right. Drove into town this morning and walked into the bank like a regular customer. Smooth.

It would've been good to search her car, but with it parked in front of the bank and the deputies making rounds every hour, it wasn't wise to chance it. Once she moved it to a parking lot out of sight, it could be searched for incriminating evidence.

Of course if the woman and sheriff disappeared completely things could return to normal.

Nothing else to do tonight. Time to go check on production levels for the day.

***

Once they'd retrieved the laptop and discovered no harm had come to Bobby's car, Gage managed to convince her to leave the car parked two blocks from the sheriff's office. Despite the devastation they'd found at the motel Gage had to thank the perpetrator for one thing. After their hot, mind-blowing sex earlier, he'd wanted nothing more than to keep her with him until they'd quenched this crazy fire between them. He'd known she would've insisted she keep up appearances by staying at the motel. Now, thanks to the perpetrator, she'd be ensconced right in his home.

As he drove through Westen's deserted streets back to his house, Gage surreptitiously watched her in the truck's dark cab. She leaned against the door, her face pressed against her hand, her crushed suit and laptop both clutched against her chest with the other.

The sadness in her touched something primal deep inside him.

Someone had hurt her. Someone had dared to invade her privacy, trampled her belongings and scared the hell out of her. He wanted to find the person who did this and return the favor, preferably with both fists.

He gripped the steering wheel tighter. Concentrate on the road, not the woman. She's not your responsibility to protect.

He glanced at her once more.

It wasn't just sadness radiating from her, but fear.

Anger flared inside him. She'd come to his town looking for a little adventure, not real danger. Her simple estate investigation had turned into something darker, something evil. Something that had hovered just under his radar and he hadn't seen coming in this small, sleepy town. Somehow he'd been lulled into believing this town didn't have problems like the city did. Her arrival triggered events that put her life in danger and shone a light on a part of his town where darkness lay.

This was his town and his responsibility to protect everyone in it—another glance at her silent figure—especially her. Despite her calm head and cool thinking, Bobby was vulnerable and out of her element.

The primal need grew. He didn't like it.

"You should go home."

Her head jerked around. "What?"

"It isn't safe for you here, now. You should go home and let me handle this. I'll give you the credit with your sister once I figure out how all this ties together." He pulled into his drive and parked behind the house once more. They sat in silence for a moment.

"No." She climbed out of the car and stomped to the back door without waiting for him.

"What the hell do you mean, 'no'?" He grabbed her suitcase out of the back and strode right up behind her on the porch.

"No, the opposite of yes." She'd crossed her arms over her chest, still clutching her laptop and that damn suit. She stood looking at him like his eighth grade science teacher.

The upstairs light next door at widow Munroe's house clicked on and Princess started barking. Great. Just what he needed, an audience.

With a growl of frustration he unlocked the door and waited for her to get her fanny inside. Once inside, he set her suitcase on the table and locked the deadbolt. She moved away from him, her belongings still clutched to her like some magical shield. To protect her from this new fear or him, he wasn't sure. He wanted to grab her by the shoulders and shake some sense into her.

Instead, he stood across the chasm of the kitchen from her and sucked in a deep, calming breath. "This case is dangerous now."

"Believe me, after seeing Harley this afternoon and my motel room tonight, I have a clear picture of the situation."

"Then why are you refusing to leave and let me handle this?"

"Believe it or not, I'd like nothing better than to turn tail and run back to the suffocating confines of my classroom."

She raised a hand to stop him when he started to agree that's just what she should do. The honest look in her eyes stilled his words on the tip of his tongue. The least he could do was listen to her.

"When I made the decision to become a PI, it wasn't just some harebrained idea, despite what you and my sisters believe. I didn't just choose to do this for the glory. Average people need someone to speak for them, to ferret out the truth. Someone who isn't obligated only to looking until the letter of the law has been reached, but who's willing to go the extra mile beyond that."

"That's my job, too." He started toward her, but she shook her head.

"Hear me out. When I came to Westen I didn't expect to find a dead body. It was supposed to be a simple case. If I turn tail and run because of one dead body and one desecrated suit what does that say about me? I agree this has become a dangerous situation, not exactly what I expected. If I quit now, I'll always regret it." She glanced out into the dark night, then back at him, her eyes shimmering with unshed tears.

"Someone killed Harley. No matter what his involvement is in the Byrd case, he didn't deserve that. I want to help bring his killer to justice. I want to make sure Chloe's client isn't being swindled. I know you can make me go home, but please don't. I'm not a coward. No matter what this killer believes, I don't scare this easily.

"Besides, who's to say the killer won't follow me home? Wouldn't I be safer here where you're watching me and know the danger, rather than at home where the police have no vested interest in assuring my safety?"

Damn. The woman had a point. He rubbed his hands over his face—hard. At some point he was going to regret this. "Okay. You can stay."

"Thank you."

"Don't thank me, yet." He walked over to her, removed her laptop from her hands, laid it on the counter and her suit on top of it. Resting his hands on her shoulders, he stared down into her eyes. "You can stay, but we're going to have some ground rules."

"Okay."

"You go nowhere without telling me or in the company of me or one of my deputies."

"That's a little on the drastic side, don't you think?"

"Already you're arguing with me?" He winked and leaned down to stop her next protest with a soft kiss. "This is for practical purposes. I need to figure out who's doing this and why before anyone else gets hurt. I can't do that if I'm spending all my time worrying about you. If you say you'll be somewhere, I need you to be right there. I want you to keep your phone charged and with you at all times. Until I know who's trying to hurt you, I need to know you're safe with me or one of my deputies."

"Okay. I can live with those restrictions." She smiled. "Besides, I can't leave until I've unraveled the labyrinth Ruby calls a filing system."

He slid his hands down her arms to rest on her hips and pulled her up against him. "I knew there was a perfectly good reason to keep you around."

"Ah, you need me for my filing skills."

Slowly he pulled her hips tighter, grinding into her pelvis just slightly. "Yes, I need you for your skills."

With a soft smile, she slid her hands up his chest to his neck and pulled his head toward her. "I like you for your skills, too, Mr. Sheriff-Man."

"Oh sweetheart, you ain't even seen half of them yet." He slid his mouth over hers, giving her a soft kiss that promised untold pleasures. Deepening it when she moaned, his tongue slid in to tease hers with light strokes. He tried to pull her tighter, leaning her backward against the counter. When a soft whimper escaped her, he eased back, both of them panting.

"Mmm, why don't you take me upstairs and show me some of those skills," she managed to say while he caught his breath.

He took a step, but kept one hand on her hips. "It would be my pleasure, ma'am."

"Mine, too," she said with a wink as they mounted the stairs together.

Inside his room he stopped her at the bed, his hands stilling hers at her sweater's hem. "Let me, this time."

Grasping the edge of her sweater, he pulled it over her head. Next, he unfastened her pants, slipping them over her hips and down her thighs to pool at her feet. A shiver ran over her as she stood before him in only her bra and panties.

The hour was late and after all of today's events she had to be tired, but visions of how she'd looked just an hour earlier standing in the chaos of the motel room, her face pale and anxious, filled his mind. Anger had come over her as she realized someone had invaded her privacy and tried to destroy her belongings, making her face flushed and tense. Finally, she'd withdrawn into her fear on the ride home.

Tonight he wanted to take all those memories away from her and replace them with only hot images of them together.

Slipping his index fingers under the straps of her bra, he slid them down off her shoulders and over her arms to hook in her elbows with extreme leisure. The goose bumps that sprang up along the path of his fingers thrilled him. He followed her bra's lace over the mounds of her breasts with his thumbs, slipping the cups off, her nipples taut in the room's cool air. Leaning in, he kissed her shoulder, letting his lips suckle softly along the ridge of her collarbone to the pulse at the notch.

"Oh God," Bobby whispered in a hushed moan, her knees wobbling and her arms trapped at her sides by the bindings of her bra. For the first time in her life she was at the mercy of a man. One strong enough to press his advantage yet touched her with such tenderness instead.

Another shiver of excitement shot through her.

Encouraged by her passion, he licked up the column of her neck to her ear, his thumbs flicking softly across her nipples. His hard body, with all its planes of muscle and scars that spoke of his inner strength, pressed against hers. She wanted to pull his shirt off and feel every inch of him. She wanted all that strength to take her without any preamble. He teased her earlobe with his mouth, teeth grazing the sensitive skin as his hands slid down her sides to cup her cheeks and pull her in tight against the bulge straining at the zipper of his jeans.

Okay, preamble was good.

She moaned again.

"Mmm, that's it sweetheart, purr for me." That exotic flower scent filled his senses. *Plunge into her now. Take her.* He banished the thoughts to the far corner of his libido. He'd take it slow if it killed him.

Another sweet moan escaped her.

And it just might.

Banking his need as best he could, he gently pushed away from her. He let his body caress hers as he slid down to kneel at her feet. His face even with her breasts, the dark nipples pointed at him, begging for attention. Not to comply with their demands would be a sin against nature.

"I want to taste you. All over," he whispered over one taut bud, his breath caressing it. It tightened further against his lips.

"Yes... Please."

The breathless plea was all the permission he needed. He slipped his lips over the peak and suckled hard. The sound of her sucking in air filled his ears and sent more heat straight to his straining erection. He repeated the effort on the other nipple, watching her eyes drift closed and her head loll back, her dark hair hanging loose behind her.

Keeping her arms trapped at her side by the thin lace bindings of her bra, he skimmed his lips down her stomach to her navel, laving it with his tongue. In and out, darting like a feather into its depths.

"Oh, my God." She tipped her hips forward as he slid his mouth further down over the swell of her lower belly. *Why hadn't she done more sit-ups?*

"Mmm, sweetheart you're like satin honey. Smooth and tasty."

Finally, he slipped his hands in the band of her silk panties, sliding them over her hips and down her legs to join the jeans around her feet. When she looked down, he'd sat back on his heels, his hands softly kneading her buttocks and his face mere inches from the apex of her thighs. The very spot where her body's heat now swirled like the vortex of a sensual whirlpool. Lifting his head, their gazes locked.

He wet his lips. "All over."

All she could manage was a slight nod. Never in her life had she been this vulnerable, this needy, standing before him nearly naked and completely at his mercy. She could slide her arms out of the lacey binding and stop him if she wanted to, but at this moment his idea sounded like pure bliss.

"Open your legs for me."

Stepping one leg to the side, she obeyed his command. Determined to take all he had to hand out.

"Damn, you're beautiful."

His breath caressed her tender folds with the declaration, teasing them, increasing the heat flowing to them, the moisture gathering in anticipation. If he didn't hurry and touch her, she'd die.

As if he read her mind, his tongue slid along the center of her lips, parting them and sending fresh heat throughout her body.

"Yes. More, please."

"Your wish, my lady." He began an assault on her like none she'd ever had before.

The man truly had a magic tongue. His mouth latched onto the nub protruding at the top of her lips and suckled. It was all she needed to hurl her over the abyss. Her hands flew to his head, holding him pressed to her, every muscle in her body tensed, as she exploded in pleasure.

He held her to him as he lapped up her sweet essence, felt her body trembling like a willow caught in a tornado. With great tenderness, he eased his mouth from her, hands still cupped around her ass cheeks. Her weight supported on the strength of his arms.

"Easy sweet, take it slow." His face rested against the soft swell of her belly, licking her taste from his lips, his own breathing keeping pace with the speed of hers.

"Gage. I...oh, that was..." she cradled his head against her, the words coming out as soft whispers.

"Shh, we're not done yet."

A soft laugh escaped her. "Speak for yourself, big boy. I don't think I can do any more."

He leaned back on his heels, gently guiding her to sit on the bed in front of him. "You can handle it. You're a lot tougher than you look." He slipped his hands behind her, unhooked her bra to release her.

Wiggling back on the bed, she licked her lips and

watched him remove his clothing. As he reached for the condom on the bedside table the intensity in his gaze confirmed her fears. He wasn't finished with her. The idea thrilled her. The man certainly knew how to follow through.

With skilled movements, he slowly crawled over her body, a predator seeking his prey. His body all sinewy muscles, bulges in places most athletes would envy. The heat of his body warmed her chilled skin as it rubbed along hers. The sensation threw her back into need-mode. As he finally melded his body on top of hers, chest to chest, hip to hip, she slid her hands hard up the planes in his back.

"Oh, yes, baby," he whispered and lowered his mouth to hers, kissing her hard.

His gravely moaned words sent a thrill through her. Never before had she elicited such pleasure sounds from a man. Just to hear them again, she pulled her hands back up the hard muscles of his back a second time. She tasted her own passion on his lips as he moaned into her mouth.

That was all it took for her to surrender to him once more, opening her legs and rubbing her swollen sex against his erection.

He lifted up on his arms to stare down at her, the tip of him poised to slide into her wet folds. "I wanted to go slow, sweetheart, but I don't think I can."

"I need you inside me…now." To emphasize her words, she bent her knees and tilted her hips, making the head of him slip inside.

With a growl, he thrust all the way in, his shoulders gripping her tight to him. Nothing in her life had ever felt so good as this man thrusting in and out of her, his body straining against hers. She wrapped her legs around his thighs and met him thrust for thrust, staying with him as he drove them to the peak. The sound of their mixed climax filled her ears.

It seemed to take forever for her breathing to return to normal, the pleasant listlessness filling every fiber and muscle of her being. The man truly knew how to fulfill her fantasies. If she stayed around him too long, he'd probably kill her with pleasure.

Slowly, Gage lifted up on one elbow, moved one strand of damp hair from her cheek and stared down into her eyes. "You okay?"

"If the house caught fire right now, I couldn't lift a muscle to escape."

A low, satisfied male chuckle rumbled from him, as he eased off her to stretch out on his back. "Glad I could help you relax."

Rolling her head to the side, she gave him a weak smile. "I'm so relaxed now, I feel like Jell-o."

With another chuckle, he pulled her to his side, her head resting on his chest, and pulled the covers up over them. "Good. Maybe you can get some sleep now."

"I hope…" a yawn interrupted her words, "…so."

In the late hours of the night he held her close, feeling her breath softly caress his chest. He hadn't held a sleeping woman after sex in years. Not since Moira. Or had he? Come to think of it, his ex-wife had never really slept in his arms after sex. Instead, she'd hurry to her computer, using the excuse that sex invigorated her and she needed to use the energy to work on her cases.

A soft snore slipped out of Bobby. Looking down at her face completely at ease against his chest, he smiled briefly then grew serious. The desire to protect her filled him once more. He tightened his arm around her. Because of her, his life had become complicated again in the past forty-eight hours.

A year ago he'd come home to nurse his wounds physically and mentally in the peaceful rural town where he'd spent his happiest days as a kid. He'd wanted to take some time away from the crime and danger he'd found in the city. What he hadn't noticed was that beneath the veneer of this quiet small town, something sinister had roosted waiting to rear its ugliness.

With a soft murmur, Bobby turned onto her side, her back to him. Like hell he was letting go of her tonight. He rolled to his side, his chest pressed to her back, spooning into that delicious ass of hers, one arm draped over her, his mind still churning over the events of the past two days.

In the morning, he definitely needed to interview Harley's co-workers and look at the books regarding the Byrd property. There was no question in his mind that they were connected, along with the attack on Bobby's motel room. But what about the fire? If the murderer was also into setting fires, things were going to go from bad to worse in a hurry.

Chapter Ten

The strains of *Georgia on My Mind* erupted from Gage's cell early the next morning. Bobby curled around his pillow as he climbed out of bed and searched through his clothes for it.

"This had better be good," he grumbled into the phone. He began pacing the room as he listened to the caller, rolling his free arm as if to work out a kink in his shoulder. "A tweaker?"

Barely awake and half-listening to his end of the conversation, Bobby watched him move about the room. Dear Lord, the man's body. Even the three scars didn't detract from the vision. If anything, they gave him a dangerous edge, like a warrior from days past.

Technically, as the town sheriff he was the modern day version of a knight. A physically and mentally strong man sworn by his honor to protect the people around him. There he stood, in all his naked glory, hers to watch.

Hers?

When had she started thinking like that? She barely knew the man. A hot flush ran over her body. Oh God, she'd done the one thing she'd harped on her sisters never to do. Jump into bed with a man after the first date and think she was in love.

Had they even had a date? Not really.

When she'd traveled north to Westen, she hadn't been looking for romance, just adventure. Well, she'd found adventure, all right. Maybe being with Gage was another kind of adventure. She'd lived her whole life for others, taking the safe, conservative route. Why not take a chance and have a hot fling with a sexy man? No regrets, no commitments.

Suddenly, Gage stopped pacing, his whole being taut with concentration. He signaled her to get out of bed.

"Yeah, I can be there. How long can you keep her there? Half an hour?" he asked whoever was on the other end. His eyes on her, she realized he was also asking her if she could be ready that fast.

True to his words of last night, he was including her in whatever was going on. She nodded, quickly scrambling out of the bed and grabbing the sheet around her, she headed to the bathroom, tripping over her makeshift cover all the way down the hall.

Why was it men felt comfortable prancing around in their grand nakedness and women always felt the need to hide their imperfections?

No time to reflect on the differences between men

and women now.

She jumped in the shower and gave herself a once over, wishing she had the time to let the hot water pound her muscles. Some of the places she ached she never knew existed. Heat filled her cheeks. How was she supposed to spend the day with the man after the things they'd done last night? Well, at least the day wasn't starting with awkwardness. Whoever had called Gage wanted them somewhere pronto.

Who called and what had they said to set off Gage's intensity meter once more? It was scary that she could already read this man so easily and he seemed to be in tune with her as well. Most of her adult life she'd flown under men's radar.

Stepping out of the shower, she toweled off and finger-combed her hair. She paused and looked at herself in the mirror. Nope, same old Roberta Roberts, she hadn't morphed into Cindy Crawford overnight.

A firm rap sounded on the door. She grabbed the towel and held it in front of her. Yeah, like he didn't know what hid behind it. She cracked open the door.

"I put your suitcase in the bedroom. I'll be downstairs. We have fifteen minutes to meet Clint." He started to walk away, stopped and looked back, taking in her bare legs below the skimpy towel. "Leave the shades pulled in the bedroom until you're dressed."

"Why?"

"My neighbor is a bit of a voyeur." He winked, and sauntered down the hall. "By the way, nice legs."

She looked down and groaned. The man must be nuts. Her calves were trim from climbing the stairs in her townhome, but mid-thigh up, well, apparently he'd never looked at fashion and beauty magazines.

Once he was safely downstairs, she hurried to the bedroom to get dressed. Thinking about what lay ahead in their morning, she grabbed her other pair of jeans and a pink lightweight sweater from her suitcase that he'd tossed on the rumpled bed.

Who was Clint? Oh yeah, the town's doctor. The cousin's husband. What was so important they had to get out of bed so early? She glanced at the clock. Okay, seven in the morning might not be early, but she felt like she could've slept ten more hours.

As she dressed she tried to remember what little she'd heard of the conversation. All she could remember was something about a girl. So much for her skills at eavesdropping. Of course she'd been a little distracted by all that naked man.

Get a grip. You have a job to do.

Pushing Gage and last night's activities out of her mind, she grabbed her big black bag, which he'd brought upstairs along with her suitcase and laptop, then hurried out of the room.

"Ready?" He stood at the door, dressed in the all-too-familiar jeans and blue button-up shirt—which apparently made up his idea of a uniform. This morning he also wore a jean jacket and his Indians baseball cap sat perched on his head. Not quite tapping his foot in agitation, but she could see he wasn't used to waiting on anyone.

"All set." She grabbed her own jacket and started by him, but he caught her by the arm and stopped her. "What?"

"Just this." He cupped her cheek in his hand,

leaned in and kissed her slow and soft, thrilling her to her bones and heating her from the inside out. His lips lingered a moment longer before breaking it off. "In case I don't get a chance to do that the rest of the day."

Still stunned, but glowing from his kiss, she let him gently push her out the door into the morning light and crisp spring air.

"Good morning, Sheriff," a feathery voice called from the other side of the fence. A tiny bird of a woman, pink sponge rollers in her white hair, a pink chenille robe wrapped tight around her body, and a sly smile on her wrinkled face, stood on her back porch.

This was the voyeur?

"Aw, shit," Gage murmured under his breath, ushering Bobby to the truck's passenger side. "Good morning, Mrs. Munroe. How's Princess today?"

Bobby slipped into the cab, but held the door open to hear the conversation between him and the elderly little lady.

"Oh, Princess was restless last night, but I think she's doing better today. It makes me nervous when she's restless. You know she can hear things I can't."

"I'm sure Princess will take good care protecting you, ma'am." Gage hurried around the truck and climbed in.

Bobby would swear his cheeks were redder. The elderly neighbor's dog hearing them last night had embarrassed him? "You don't think little Princess heard us last night, do you?"

"Trust me, Princess isn't anything I want to mess with."

"You aren't afraid of Mrs. Munroe's dog, are

you?" she teased.

"Take a look at her porch," he said, slowly pulling back out the drive.

Bobby turned to see Mrs. Munroe smiling and waving at them. Beside her sat the biggest black-and-brown pit bull she'd ever seen. Its teeth snarled at them as if smiling. "That's Princess?"

"Yep. When Mr. Munroe died a few years ago, Mrs. Munroe said she wanted to get a dog for protection. Dad helped her find one he was sure would protect her."

"And she named a *pit bull* Princess?" She laughed at the absurdity.

"Could you imagine would-be burglars learning that Princess isn't a cute little yappy dog, but one capable of ripping out their throats?" He winked at her and returned to driving.

They wound their way through the streets of Westen for a few minutes. The place looked like all those commercials for small-town living floating on television now. Well-maintained homes with neat, trimmed lawns, and flowerbeds springing with daffodils and tulips. A nice little peaceful town— where two nights before there'd been a murder.

"Where are we going?" she asked, rubbing her arms against the sudden chill that ran over her.

"We're meeting Clint over at the clinic."

When no further explanation followed, she rolled her eyes. Okay, I guess I'll bite. "And *why* are we meeting him there at this early hour? Most doctors I know don't open their doors before nine."

"Because a tweaker beat the crap out of his

girlfriend, also a tweaker, and left her on the clinic's doorstep." He flexed his fingers one at a time on the gearshift. The other hand gripped the steering wheel as if his hand was the only thing keeping the vehicle from defying gravity. Was it the tweaker part that bothered him, or the beating and abandonment of the girlfriend?

Getting information out of him was worse than convincing Brent Adler to tell why he hadn't done his homework for six consecutive weeks. Of course, Brent hadn't wanted to tell her his father lost their job and they were all living in one room out of his grandmother's house.

Deep, patient breath. "And a tweaker is?"

He heaved a sigh and slumped his shoulders slightly. "A tweaker is a meth addict. Meth labs have been creeping into midwestern rural towns over the past decade. Most of the activity has been in the southeastern part of our county, but occasionally we have a tweaker or two travel through Westen."

"And this guy just beat up his girlfriend and dumped her?" Sometimes the stupid decisions people made amazed her.

"When a meth addict is in their tweaking stage, they don't sleep, sometimes as long as a couple of weeks. They're paranoid, irritable, prone to sudden violence." He pulled the truck into the drive of another three-story, mid-nineteenth-century home. He parked and came around the truck to help her climb out. "This is the Westen Clinic."

She followed him up the porch stairs. Before he could rap on the door, it was swung open by a gray-haired, middle-aged woman dressed in maroon scrubs.

"'Bout time you got here, Sheriff. Doc's in back with the woman."

"Good morning to you, too, Harriett," he said, ushering Bobby inside in front of him. "This is Bobby Roberts, she's..."

"...helping out at the Sheriff's office while Ruby's laid up. Heard all about it yesterday." Harriett didn't even look over her shoulder at them as she led them to the rear of the clinic.

Bobby looked at Gage, who simply shrugged as if to say, small-town news travels fast. What did she expect? An apology? At least the nurse hadn't said she also knew they were sleeping together.

"Gage and his lady friend are here, Doc," Harriett announced at the doorway before heading back down the hall.

Okay, so much for discretion.

The room she'd led them to looked like a bed and breakfast re-do circa 1940's. Soft pastel floral print wallpaper covered the walls and framed Norman Rockwell prints gave the room a calm, peaceful feel. Two wrought iron twin beds, each covered with matching pastel log cabin quilts, flanked the wall opposite the door. Beside each bed sat a wingback chair.

Currently, one of the beds held a body curled beneath the quilt and away from the door. A tall man unfolded himself from the wingback chair, a clipboard in his hand. Bobby blinked twice. The man looked like that actor in the Navy lawyer show.

"Gage," he said in a low voice, offering his other hand. "Sorry to wake you so early."

"Don't worry about it, Clint." Gage shook his hand, turning slightly. "This is Bobby Roberts, my newest deputy. Bobby, Dr. Clint Preston, Emma's husband."

"Ah, the lady helping out in Ruby's stead. Emma told me she'd met you yesterday. She didn't say anything about you being a deputy." His lips tipped in a gentle smile as he shook her hand.

At least he didn't comment on why they were together so early in the morning. Bobby liked him instantly. He made a perfect match to the redhead she'd met the day before.

"So how is she?" Gage asked, craning his head around to try and see the woman in the bed.

"Asleep." Clint turned and looked at his patient. "I gave her something to bring her down and she crashed hard."

"She going to be okay?"

"As far as I can tell, her boyfriend didn't hit any vital organs and nothing is broken. Which is a miracle, considering tweakers usually don't have any impulse control left when they start hitting."

"Damn, I would've liked to interview her. Find out the boyfriend's name and where he's staying." Gage shoved one hand down in his jacket pocket, the other rubbing the back of his neck.

"Don't know that it would've done much good. Most of what she said didn't make sense." Clint went to the bedside table, lifted a small recorder and handed it to Gage. "Uncle Ray used this to make tapes of things so he or Harriett could transcribe them later. I recorded everything she said while I was stitching her up. Thought you might use it."

"Doubt it's admissible in court, but it might help me find the son-of-a-bitch who did this." Gage stuck the recorder in his jacket pocket.

"I took some pictures, too. I'll have Harriett..."

"...print them up." As if conjured by magic, the nurse appeared in the doorway with a manila file in hand. She handed them to Gage and moved to sit in the chair by the woman's bed. "Emma has breakfast ready, Doc. She said bring Gage and his lady friend with you. I'll keep an eye on our patient."

"We don't have time for breakfast," Gage started to refuse the invitation out in the hallway.

"Sure you do," Clint gave him a gentle shove on his shoulder in the direction of the front entrance. "You and I both know our victim isn't going to wake for hours, maybe days. Might as well have some of Emma's cooking to start the day. Besides, she'll give me hell if you don't come see her and the boys. Yesterday she pointed out you hadn't been over for a month."

Frustration and resignation crossed Gage's features in a flash, replaced with a smile just as quick. "Last thing I want to do is upset a pregnant woman."

"Smart man." Clint laughed.

When they stepped off the porch, Bobby headed for the truck, only to have Gage grip her arm and turn her toward the street. "This way, sweetheart. Emma and the doc live close enough to walk."

Clint lifted an eyebrow when Gage called her sweetheart, and Bobby flushed with embarrassment. What he must think that meant. *Get a grip. It's not like you'll be seeing these people after this case is done.*

The two men led her across the street to a three-story Victorian apparently in the midst of a remodel. Lumber and tools lay in neat piles on the wide veranda. Next to them sat large pails of paint and putty.

"How's the upstairs coming?" Gage asked as Clint opened the front door.

"The boys' room looks like a cowboy bunkhouse now. Which has them yee-hawing and galloping all over the place," Clint grumbled, but the smile on his face told how little he minded it. "I'm just hoping they outgrow it before they earn their knot-tying badges in Scouts."

A moment later two redheaded boys, Bobby would guess about seven years old, barreled down the stairs, shouting, "Gage!"

Emma came around the corner. "I'm so glad you could join us," she said to Bobby as she waved them all into the kitchen connected to the great room—a newly remodeled portion of the house.

Moments later, seated at the oak country table that was the center of the kitchen, Bobby listened to the boys try to tell Gage about everything that had happened in the past month, each finishing the other's sentence between bites of pancakes in their haste.

"Brian, Ben, slow down," Clint ordered, but with a smile. "You're going to end up choking on your food. Gage isn't leaving before his breakfast is finished."

"But the bus..." Brian said, shoving half a piece of bacon into his mouth.

"...will be here soon, Dad," Ben finished.

As if on cue, the sound of a school bus horn blasted from the street. Chaos ensued. The doctor went to hold the bus, while the boys grabbed their backpacks and their mother did a quick once-over to be sure their faces and clothes were clean for school. As the boys ran out the front door, their mother following behind them, Gage chuckled beside Bobby. "They're like two spring tornadoes."

"I'll bet they're a handful."

"They used to be worse. Before Emma married Clint. She never knew what they'd get into. But now they mind both Em and the doc without question." He sipped his coffee, nodding his head as if he approved of his cousin's family.

"How long have they been married?"

"A little over a year."

Before she could ask any further questions, a movement from the hallway caught her attention. A white-haired, frail-looking lady stood in the doorway, a confused look on her face as she rubbed her hands one over the other in nervous agitation.

"Aunt Isabelle?" Gage carefully set his coffee mug on the table and eased his chair back. He approached the elderly woman with slow, gentle movements. "Is something wrong?"

She looked up at him, no recognition on her face. "Do you know where my little girl is, sir?"

"Emma is out on the porch with your grandsons." Gage smiled and took her by the shoulders, leading her into the kitchen. "Why don't you sit with Bobby while I get you some breakfast?"

His gentleness with his aunt amazed Bobby. It was

a new side to him. She'd seen his anger, most of which was directed at her, his patience with Cleetus, and his disdain—that's the emotion he used with the mayor and his entourage. But gentle kindness? Out of the big tough sheriff?

Who'da thought it?

Isabelle blinked and her eyes seem to focus on her nephew. "Gage, it's so nice to see you. I'd love a cup of coffee, please." She glanced at Bobby, smiled and leaned closer. "It's about time he brought you to visit us, my dear. I thought your name was Mary, or Maureen, or…what is your wife's name, Gage?"

"Her name *was* Moira, Aunt Isabelle," he said as he set a plate of pancakes in front of her and a cup of coffee. "Remember, we've been divorced more than a year."

"Oh, dear. I'm sure your father is very disappointed." Isabelle sipped her coffee.

A brief flash of pain crossed his features, from the mention of his father or the divorce, Bobby wasn't sure, but Gage quickly replaced it with a smile and a pat to his aunt's hand. "Don't worry about Dad. By the end, he was as glad the marriage ended as I was."

For a moment, an uncomfortable silence filled the kitchen then the front door closed.

"Well, they're off," Emma said as she and Clint joined them once more. She leaned over and kissed her mother on the forehead. "Good morning, Mama."

"Good morning, Emma. We need to plant the spring vegetables today, dear."

Emma heaved a heavy sigh as she retrieved a bottle of medicine from the cabinet. "Not today, Mama. I have nursing classes. You'll be going to the day center. Remember?"

"Oh yes, with that lovely girl, Libby."

"Yes, Mama, Libby Wilson." Emma glanced at Bobby. "Libby is a social worker and a friend."

"She always has the most interesting things for me to help those poor elderly people do," Isabelle said, almost to herself.

Emma doled her mother's medicine into her wrinkled and frail hand. The unshed tears in the other woman's eyes made an ache around Bobby's heart and she wanted to hug Gage's cousin.

Since her parents died so young she'd never been around an elderly person in such an intimate fashion, especially not one so obviously suffering from Alzheimer's. Emma certainly had her hands full with her mother, sons and a new baby on the way.

Clint cupped his wife's face and kissed her. The worry around her eyes softened immediately.

Bobby swallowed hard. If she could look as happy as these two, she'd gladly trade places with Emma, despite all her responsibilities.

"So did you get a chance to look at those pictures?" Clint asked, sitting across from Bobby and Gage once more.

"Not yet." Gage glanced at his aunt, seated next to him and staring off into space. He opened the file in front of him.

Emma gasped, Gage muttered a curse and Bobby swallowed hard at the gruesome sight in front of them. The young woman—at least she appeared to be young, she was so thin—had stringy blonde hair. Her left eye, black and blue, was swollen nearly shut and the skin just below it over her cheekbone had a long gash that Clint had stitched closed. When Gage turned to the second picture of the woman's torso, Emma left the room looking rather green and Bobby turned from studying the images.

"You have no idea who the bastard is that did this?" Gage asked through nearly clenched teeth.

"No. I never saw him before this morning. Harriett was at the clinic early to type up files for all the summer baseball physicals we've been doing, when the guy knocked on the door. She called me, and as soon as I got there, the guy bolted." Clint drank his coffee. "Figured I best take care of the girl, then call you."

"You know," Gage spread the pictures out on the table, lightly tapping the full-frontal one. "She looks a little familiar."

Clint and Emma, who'd returned looking pale but not so green, leaned in to study the picture.

"Yeah, I think so, too. But not anyone I can put a name to." He looked at his wife.

Emma cocked her head to one side. "It's the color of her eyes, er…eye," she said, since only one was open enough to see the iris. "Such an unusual shade."

Bobby leaned it to see more. Yep, almost a translucent green.

"Well, hopefully someone will know who she is." Gage scooted his chair back, gathered his and Bobby's breakfast dishes and took them to the sink to rinse.

Emma looked at her watch. "I need to get Mama over to the center. Libby wanted to do some special memory exercises with her today."

"Do they help much?" Bobby couldn't help but ask, rising from her seat.

"Actually, for a day or two they do seem to help. Clint is also considering increasing her medication dosage." She smiled at her husband as he wrapped his arms around her. "We'd like to keep her home with us as long as possible. Once she's in a care facility, I'm afraid her memory will completely disappear."

"We're hoping she'll get to see her newest grandchild before that happens." Clint kissed his wife on her cheek.

Afraid her envy for their obviously happy relationship was written all over her face, Bobby looked at the pictures on the table once more. "It's a shame no one knows this girl. She didn't have any identification on her?"

Clint shook his head. "No. It's as if he was through using her and threw her away."

"Hold onto this for me," Gage said, handing Bobby the tape recorder. She slipped it into her black bag as he started to gather up the pictures. His hand was on the last one, when Isabelle placed her hand on top of his, stopping his movements.

"She looks just like her mother."

The foursome grew very quiet, exchanging startled looks with each other.

"Who looks like her mother, Aunt Isabelle?" Gage asked in a quiet voice, laced with his own anxiousness.

"Teeny."

"Teeny?"

Isabelle tapped her hand on the photo. "Teeny

Miller. Her real name is Tina, but she was always such a little shy thing—not really bigger than a minute, barely came up to the middle of her mama's chest—that everyone called her Teeny. Her mother used to come to church on Sundays looking like this." Isabelle tapped the picture of the battered woman and leaned closer as if whispering a secret to them. "Twyla always said she'd hit her face on the door, but we all suspected it was her husband's fist instead."

"So you know Teeny, Mama?" Emma asked.

"Oh of course, you'd already gone off to college by the time she came to my middle school girls' classes at church on Sundays. I tried so hard to get her to stay out of trouble, but she just couldn't seem to stay away from him."

"Who?" Gage asked, sitting next to his aunt once more, apparently thrilled to hear some gossip.

"Oh dear, what was that boy's name?" Isabelle stared off into space a minute. "Something like dirt. Or dust. No that wasn't it. Rust! Rusty Davis. That was his name." She leaned closer to her nephew. "He was a no-good troublemaker, always sneaking out during services to smoke. Teeny couldn't stay away from him."

Gage and Clint exchanged looks. Gage patted Isabelle on the arm. "Do you think Teeny is dating this Rusty fellow still?"

"Oh yes. Like two peas in a very bad pod they were."

"Do you know what he looked like?"

"Who, dear?" Isabelle's eyes clouded over once more. Her period of lucidity apparently finished.

***

"Do you think he might be the one who did this?" Bobby asked as she and Gage sat in his truck behind the sheriff's office. It had taken only a few minutes to travel the four blocks from

the clinic.

"I don't know, but at least I have two names to start searching for information with." He pulled off the baseball cap, which seemed to be his version of the sheriff's hat and ran his hands through his blond hair.

Trying not to remember how her hands had felt doing the same thing in the early morning hours, she closed them into tight fists. *Get a grip, girl. Yes, it was the best night of sex you've ever had and will probably ever have again, but there are more important things going on here.*

She looked down at the closed file in her lap and the contents it held. How could someone be so cruel to another person? "Do you think this Rusty-the-tweaker has anything to do with Harley's murder?"

"I doubt it. I'd think he'd be more likely to be involved in the fire two days ago, *if* there'd been some evidence of a meth lab. Damn." He turned to her, complete frustration in his eyes. "Last week I lived in my own version of Mayberry. No big-city crime, no worries. Hell, I even had my own Barney Fife. Now, I wonder what the hell is going on. A fire, a murder, breaking and entering, assault and battery. It's like I woke up in an episode of *The Twilight Zone*."

She shook her head. "Or *The Wizard of Oz*."

"At least I have my own Dorothy to keep me company." He reached out a hand to flip her dark hair off her shoulder.

Their gazes locked and tension sizzled in the air between them. Bobby inhaled air like a deep-sea diver. This whole affair was too intense for her, even after last night. She blinked first. "So what are your plans for today?"

He studied her for a moment longer, as if he tried to decide whether to let her hide behind all the chaos around them or force her to acknowledge this thing growing between them. He swallowed, his decision made.

"I think it's time I found out just what's going on in this town."

"How are you going to start? With the murder, the fire, or finding Rusty?"

"Good question. I think this morning, I'll see if I can find Rusty. We'll have to postpone our trip to the bank a little while."

"We?" She perked up at his reference. "Does that mean you've changed your mind about me helping?"

"You and I will go to the bank this afternoon for some answers. While we're doing that, maybe one or two of my deputies can canvas the foreclosed farms in the area." He climbed out his side of the truck and she followed suit from hers.

"And this morning?" God, she hated sounding like a hopeful puppy.

He winked at her and headed for the back door of his office. "You get to unravel some more of Ruby's secret filing system."

"Oh, great. Leave me with the work while you go have fun."

Holding the door closed, he drew her up against his hard body and grew serious once more. "You saw what this tweaker did to Teeny. I'm not letting you get within a hundred feet of him, *if* I find him and *until* I know he's out of the violent stage."

The intense protectiveness rolling off him shook her to the core and Bobby had to fight to take in another breath. She should be pissed he was taking the big, bad alpha male role with her. For all of her adult life she'd been in charge of what she did and where she went. No one had protected her or tried to take care of her. Now here she was with a man who wouldn't take no for an answer. Of course he had way more experience than she did with crazy drug addicts.

"Okay. I'll stay here."

Her acquiescence relaxed him once more. He lowered his head and kissed her. Long, slow and with just enough intensity to make her melt up against him. Slowly he eased his lips from hers, smiling. "Besides, yesterday you found the fire pattern buried in the mess. Who knows what other secrets you'll find in there."

She laughed. "Maybe Ruby has the answers to who shot Kennedy hidden in those files."

With a shake of his head, he opened the door and held it for her. "You never know what surprises we'll find waiting to pounce."

***

"The shipment's ready." Rusty Davis paced behind the cookhouse. He shook his other hand wildly. It felt like he'd been stung by a dozen fire ants. The kind that drove him crazy while living one summer in Florida with Grandma Pen.

"Did you take care of our little problem?" the man asked. The cold in his voice sounded like death.

Rusty leaned his head to hold the phone against his shoulder while he scratched at his arm. God, he hated the feeling. He'd just bet bugs were crawling on him. "Yeah, the bitch won't be talkin' to no one. Not for a long while."

"I told you to get rid of her."

"No, man. She's cool. By the time she comes down and wakes up, she'll know..." he whirled and paced again. "She won't say nothin'."

"I told you. After this batch, I'm shutting down shop for a while. No loose ends."

"Yeah, yeah, I got it." He glanced around to see if anyone was watching. Someone was always watching. He'd just bet the cops wanted to know where he was cooking the meth. But he was smart. Smarter than the law. Smarter than Teeny. Hell, he was smarter than the Man. Of course he'd never say that out loud.

"Meet me at the usual place in one hour. Bring half the latest shipment."

"Sure thing. I'll be there."

"And Rusty, make sure no one follows you."

The warning had him looking over his shoulders again. The man knew he wouldn't let anyone follow him. He was so good at hiding, he was invisible. But he'd made sure this time. No one was gonna find his cookhouse.

He laughed, the shrill sound hurting his own ears. Yeah, anyone looking here was in for a big surprise.

Chapter Eleven

By eleven that morning, Bobby wanted to take all
the files and set them on fire, toss in the phone and
quite possibly Cleetus, since she felt guilty wanting to
throw the injured Ruby onto the pyre.

With a sigh she glanced down at the shiny deputy's
badge Gage had pinned on her chest before leaving on
his "tweaker" hunt. She guessed starting a deadly fire
wasn't in her official duties now.

So far she and Cleetus had worked their way
through traffic offenses, stolen vehicles and DUI.
Drunk driving had several thick files going back to the
mid-fifties. Seemed it was a popular past time with the
local teens then and now.

They'd also managed to get the assault and battery
cases into the computer. Most of these were found
under marital problems. Sadly, Ruby had filed them

correctly. Why was it men felt the need to take out their frustration on the women they were supposed to protect?

Bobby glanced at the folder on Gage's desk. She had to admit, in a few of the cases the woman had been the instigator. Stretching her arms over her head, she arched her back to loosen the muscles.

She didn't understand people. Why did they try to destroy the ones they loved? Didn't they realize how fragile life was? How unsure the future? One man's senseless drunk driving and her parents' lives had ended, the marriage they'd worked so hard to keep together gone, and three daughters left to pick up the pieces.

"You done with that file, Miz Bobby?"

Cleetus looked up from the computer screen he'd slowly begun to master today. The man's gentle nature, so at odds with his choice of profession, amazed her. It was an oddity that seemed to fit in this small town. She handed him the manila folder. "One more to cross off our list."

The office phone rang on the dispatcher's desk. Cleetus started to rise from his spot, but she stopped him with a hand on his shoulder. "I'll get it, Cleetus. You're in a groove on that computer."

"Westen Township's Sheriff's office, how may I help you?"

"I need to speak with Gage, right now," the clipped feminine voice demanded.

"I'm sorry, Sheriff Justice isn't in right now," Bobby couldn't help saying with just a little extra sweetness.

"Look, I've been trying to get the bastard on the phone for two weeks. You put him on right now." The woman's anger slashed across the phone lines.

Like hell I will.

"The sheriff is currently out of the office, but if you'd like to leave a message, I'll be sure he gets it." *When snow falls in July.*

The woman growled into the phone and Bobby considered slamming down the receiver. Instead, she patiently counted to ten and waited for the rude woman to make her decision.

"Okay. I'll leave a message," the condescending words almost dripped through the phone. "You tell my husband to call me as soon as he gets back. You tell him it's urgent. You tell him his wife needs him."

Before she could reply the woman disconnected. Bobby held the receiver a moment, staring at it.

Wife?

Slowly, she replaced the phone into the cradle. She turned to the only source of information she had available. "Cleetus? How many times has Gage been married?"

"That'd be once, ma'am," he said, not looking up from typing on the keyboard.

She dragged a chair over and sat across the desk from the deputy. "Aren't they divorced?"

"Yes, ma'am, but the sheriff, he don't talk about it too much."

Bobby rested one elbow on the desk and braced her hand in her chin. "Do you know what happened?"

"I don't think he'd mind you knowin'." Cleetus stopped his typing and leaned back in the chair. "The sheriff, Gage's daddy, he was so excited when Gage got married. Said he was finally gonna have some grandbabies. But Gage and his wife only came to visit once. When he left the sheriff was sad as a hound dog on a short leash. Said Gage had married one cold fish. That she wanted to keep her job with DA's office in Columbus. He doubted there'd ever be babies and Gage was headed for a lot of heartache. The sheriff was right, all right."

"So? What happened?" she gently prodded.

"One night the sheriff gets a call that Gage was shot and in surgery over in Columbus. When he and I got there Gage was barely hanging on in that ICU. I only went in once to see him. All them tubes and monitors beeping." Cleetus shuddered. "Made me real nervous. But the sheriff, he never left his son's side. Not 'till the docs said he was gonna live.

"Funny thing, that wife, Moira," Cleetus turned hard, angry eyes toward her and Bobby was very glad she wasn't Moira. "That woman never once came to see Gage or his daddy."

Oh my, God! What kind of bitch had Gage married? "Never once?"

Cleetus nodded. "Worse. Seems Gage was undercover on a drug case when he was shot. He'd been home a few days earlier and told his wife a big bust was comin' down. Guess she wanted to be the one to get credit to impress her boss, so she had this PI followin' Gage. That's how the drug dealers knew he was a cop and tried to kill him."

Oh God. No wonder he'd treated her so badly when he found out she was a PI. Poor Gage. Betrayed by the one person in the world who should've put his safety above everything else.

Pain struck Bobby as sure as if she'd been the one shot.

***

Gage cursed and slammed his hand against the rusted slats of the nearly dilapidated mobile home in the back corner of the third trailer park in the county's northeast corner. All morning he'd been chasing the elusive Rusty Davis from one sketchy lead to another, until finally someone remembered he liked to hole up here.

And once he got here. Nothing. No Rusty. No meth lab. Nada. Just a trashed-out trailer a hazmat unit should destroy. With his luck somewhere in this mess was a clue to where Rusty might be, or who his meth dealer was. Which meant he, or one of his men needed, to sift through the trailer's contents.

He glanced at his watch. Nearly noon. Great. By the time he got back to town the bank's officers would be at lunch. Time to call in the reinforcements. He flipped open his cell and dialed the station.

"Westen Township's Sheriff's office. How may I help you?"

Bobby's voice, sounding just a little too sweet, sent desire sizzling through him. A rush of relief mixed with it. If she was on the phone, she was safe.

Damn. What was wrong with him? He'd assumed that once he'd had sex with her, her nearness wouldn't affect him so much. But it just seemed to get worse, like a growing addiction.

"What are you doing answering the phones?" he

asked, a little too harsh.

"Good morning to you, too," she replied and he just bet she had that sarcastic little grin on her lips. The one that made him want to grab her and kiss it gone.

Oh yeah. He had it bad. He gritted his teeth as he sat in his truck. "Find anything in those files?"

"You'll be happy to know there have been no kidnappings reported for the past fifty years, however dog custody cases seem to have a special place in the citizens of Westen's hearts."

Gage sighed. She was making small talk to give him time to get his temper under control. Smart woman. "Mr. Waddle and Mrs. Turnbridge."

"Seems those two have an ongoing battle over a Tennessee Blue Tick, whatever that is."

"It's a coon hound."

"A coon hound?"

He smiled at her confusion. "A dog used for hunting raccoons."

"Ah, I can see the need for this feud for the past thirty years. Wait, can a dog live that long?"

The left side of his mouth twitched into a half grin. "No, the feud isn't over one particular dog, but breeding rights from the original litter they both owned when they were married."

"Oh. Sort of like child custody suits. I get it." There was a pause on the other end. The gears in her quick mind were grinding as she switched tracks. "So want to tell me what had you ready to bite my head off?"

"Sorry. That was just frustration talking." He pulled off his sunglasses and rubbed the bridge of his nose. "I'm out at the Summit Trailer Park, the last known residence of one Rusty Davis."

"Bad tip, huh?"

"No, there's plenty of evidence this was his place. In fact, too much. It's going to take hours to sift through this mess to see if there's any lead as to where he is or who his supplier might be. That's why I called."

"You're going to be stuck there and want me to go to the bank on my own?"

Even though her voice suggested she was teasing the idea gripped him tight in his mid-section. After last night's mess at the hotel and Harley's murder, he didn't want her going anywhere by herself. No way was he going to let her go in the bank on her own and with no authority. He wanted this investigation official. He wanted some answers. No more secrets.

"What I need is for Cleetus to call in Daniel, Mike and Wes. Tell them I know it's their day off or not their shift, but we're going to need everyone's help to find this guy. They'll have to meet me here for instructions." He repeated the address.

"Okay. Got that."

There was a pause. He could almost see her writing down his every word. "As soon as they're started here, you and I'll head for the bank. In the meantime, give Clint a call and see if Teeny has woken yet. I need to find out if she has any idea where Rusty might be hiding."

"I talked to Emma just a few minutes ago. She said Teeny is still out cold."

"Damn. I'd hoped for a break somewhere. Maybe

she'll be awake by the time I get back to town."

"I found something interesting in the files."

"Really? What?"

"Seems your Dad was curious about Rusty or Rusty made it onto his radar somehow. He had a file on him. Of course Ruby had it hidden in a file marked persons of interest."

"Dad never mentioned any of this to me."

"Your dad probably didn't want to burden you when you first came home. And I imagine it slipped his mind there at the end."

Her understanding and sympathy brought a lump to his throat. "What did it say?"

"It just has his arrest record. Minor stuff—pot possession—and his military record. Seems Rusty was on the bomb disposal unit while over in the Gulf War. He had an honorable discharge."

"Damn. I'll bet he's the meth cook. With that background he probably knows the chemicals to make it. He could also be our firebug. Okay, tell my deputies to get out here ASAP."

"Yes, sir. By the way, ham or turkey?"

"Both. Why?" His stomach growled just to emphasize to his brain its barren state.

"Because while you've been out gallivanting all over the county, Cleetus and I have been very busy and need some sustenance. I'm going over to the Peaches 'N Cream to get sandwiches, but didn't know what you liked."

Panic gripped his gut. Breathe. Relax. As much as he didn't want her wandering about town on her own with a killer, an arsonist, and a woman-beater all on the loose, she was probably safe walking across the street to the café in broad daylight. Besides, no one messed with Lorna in her own restaurant.

"Tell you what. You order for both of us and I'll meet you there as soon as you get those other deputies out here."

"Your wish is my command, oh Sheriff, sir." The laughter in her voice wiped out some of his worry. Maybe things weren't so bad.

***

Things were spiraling out of control.

It all started when Harley saw the sheriff haul the woman out of the bank's trash. The little worm had balked at the first sign of trouble and had to be dealt with. He'd worked very hard to stage it as an accident and it should've taken the sheriff weeks to find Harley's body, not days.

The barn fire should've spread and consumed most of the Turnbill farm like a brushfire, so it could be swallowed up in another foreclosure, only it hadn't. Deke Reynolds had called in the arson investigator, so now he couldn't approach Turnbill with a buyout without raising suspicions. He needed all the farmland attached to the original property. The property his ancestors had been forced to sell.

To top it off the meth shipments were due in Columbus and Cincinnati at the end of the week. His partners paid half up front. He'd used the money to finance the land scheme and to buy the supplies his cook needed to make the product. With the last two pieces of property almost within his reach maybe it was time to tie up all the loose ends. The cook, Rusty, wouldn't be a problem any longer. Soon, neither would the tweaker girlfriend. Hell, it was time to close production after this shipment and retire from the drug business.

Problem was, you didn't mess with his partners. If he couldn't deliver he was dead. Literally. Maybe, if he planned it right, he could convince his partners to look for a source elsewhere, and still finish acquiring the land this town stole from his family.

To top things off, that damn woman from out of town was snooping though files over at the sheriff's.

He took out a handkerchief and wiped at the sweat dripping down his neck. He sat tapping his fingers one at a time on the top of his desk and stared out across Westen's main street at the sheriff's office.

It was his fault. He'd gotten greedy in the past year. The old sheriff took sick and his son stepped into the sheriff's role. Distracted by his father's illness, everyone knew Gage was just killing time in Westen until he could move on. The lax authority made the town ripe for the picking. And he'd picked property like apples off the ground. He'd made promises. And now he had to find ways to keep them.

The door opened over at the sheriff's and out stepped the woman.

He sat straighter in his chair.

Where was she going? She looked around then started across the street for Lorna's.

He glanced at his watch. Past noon.

He shut down his files and stepped out of his office.

Time to grab some lunch and catch up on the local

gossip at the Peaches 'N Cream. Maybe he'd get lucky and find out if the woman and the sheriff were getting close enough to be a danger.

***

Nearly every seat in the café was occupied when Bobby entered. Men wearing jeans, different-colored flannel shirts, and baseball caps filled the counter seats. Probably farmers or truckers stopping in for lunch, since several big rigs and pickups filled the lot next to the café.

Several groups of men in suits and ties sat at tables along the front windows. She didn't recognize anyone from the bank among them. And two families sat in the booths along one wall, looking very Norman Rockwell-ish. All that was missing was the family dog.

In one corner, a group of women sat laughing and eating dessert. Bet they knew every secret in town. She grinned and headed to the counter.

"Well, someone seems pretty happy today," Lorna said as she entered from the kitchen with a tray of sliced pies in hand. "Come here and hold these for me, Bobby, so I can get them in the dessert cabinet. We went through the first batch in record time. Always happens on Baptist Women's meetin' day."

Bobby balanced the tray low enough so Lorna wouldn't have to bend too much when putting the plates inside the refrigerated glass pantry. "How often do they meet?"

"Every other week. Can't make up enough desserts for them." Lorna gave her a conspiratorial wink and leaning in close, she whispered, "They eat nothing but soup and salad, then get the biggest slices of pie I have. Sort of cancels out all those calories they save."

Bobby couldn't help but laugh.

"Let me hold that for you, Ms. Roberts," a smooth voice slid over her neck as two hands took the tray from her. Of course half the load was already gone.

Bobby glanced over her shoulder. Yep, should've known a politician would show up just as most of the work was completed. "Hello, Mayor Rawlins."

"You remembered. But please, call me Tobias."

He flashed a smile meant to dazzle her, and in the normal scheme of things it might, except these days she'd acquired a taste for things, tall, blond and often on the moody side. But that was no excuse to be mean, so she smiled back, glancing around the restaurant. "Seems half the town must be here today."

"That's because Lorna has the best food in town."

Lorna harrumphed beside them, her lips pinched like she'd been sucking on lemons. "That's because other than the tea room over at the Westen Inn, I have the *only* food in town." She grabbed the now empty tray from the mayor's hands. "Bobby, you go on and get that last booth before someone else does."

Bobby slipped around the mayor and slid into the open booth in the opposite corner from the Baptist ladies, with her back to the wall to watch for Gage. Unfortunately the mayor followed her.

"How are things coming over at the sheriff's office? Still getting those files on line?" he asked as he sat on the opposite seat without invitation.

"Things are coming along slowly. Ruby had a rather unique filing system, but Cleetus and I are making some progress."

"I'm sure Cleetus isn't exactly the best help." The corners of his lips curved slightly giving his smile a bit of a sneer.

Thankfully, Rachel arrived with glasses of water and menus, saving her from defending Cleetus and wiping the scornful look off Tobias' face.

"The sheriff meeting you here?" Rachel asked, nodding at the empty booth seat by Bobby.

Heat filled her cheeks. Did half the town just assume she and Gage were an item? Or had the voyeuristic neighbor spread the news of where she'd spent the night? Oh well, not like she'd be living here.

"Yes, he's on his way, but he told me to order for him." She ignored the mayor and studied the menu for a minute. Lorna had several salads and soups on the list.

Rachel pointed to the daily specials. "Today's special is chicken-fried steak with gravy, hash browns and green beans. That's one of his usual favorites."

Heart attack on a plate. Figures. All those calories and the man remained whipcord lean. "Well, let's make the sheriff a nice turkey and Swiss sandwich with fruit salad on the side today. And I'll have the chicken-salad plate and fruit."

"If you're sure. Gage really likes the chicken-fried steak."

"Yes, but his heart will appreciate the turkey."

Rachel shrugged and wrote down the order.

The mayor ordered a salad and diet soda. Funny, he appeared the same age as Gage, but even eating salads hadn't kept the extra weight from sagging his face slightly. In ten years he'd probably have deep jowls.

"So how long will you be staying in town?" he asked, leaning back and resting one arm on the back of the booth.

"Probably until the job is finished." Let him assume she meant converting the files to the computer. He didn't have to know she had a different job.

Rachel returned with their drinks, salads and a basket of fresh, homemade rolls. "I'll bring the sheriff's out once he gets here," she said as she served their food.

The meal looked delicious and Bobby wished she could just dive right in, but she really would've preferred not sharing her meal with Tobias. In fact she had a much different companion in mind. And what was keeping Gage?

"So, have you found anything interesting in the files?" Tobias asked casually between two bites.

Something in the way he asked the question—just a little too casually—sent warning bells like a toy monkey's brass cymbals clashing up and down her spine. Too many years watching the nuances of her more manipulative students told her the man was fishing for information.

Was there some tidbit in the files he wanted? Or maybe something he didn't want to see the light of day?

Forcing the sudden anxiety down, she took a forkful of the chicken salad and smeared it on a cracker, smiling innocently at him. "Nothing more than a feud over a hunting dog and a large number of DUIs over the past few decades." She ate her cracker slowly and drank some water before asking, "Why, did you think I'd find something mysterious?"

He shook his head a little too quickly. "Oh no, just curious. This is just a sleepy little town. Not much going on for excitement."

Yep, nothing much except for land fraud and murder, possibly arson. And despite what little evidence she and Gage had collected, they both knew it deep down that the three were somehow connected.

"The records do go back nearly ninety years. Maybe we'll find something interesting from way back then."

"Well, you'll have to keep me informed if you do. My Grandfather was mayor about sixty years ago. I doubt he had any more trouble than I have." Tobias focused on his meal as he told her bits and pieces of the town's history. "We've always had an odd character or two living here. The town used to be a stop on the coach route between the state capitol in Columbus and the port city of Cleveland. Not too far from here are some old canals built as part of the Erie Canal system from the early eighteen hundreds."

"Really?" The noise level in the café had dropped a bit. Bobby glanced around as she ate her lunch and half listened to his tale. The hairs on her arm stood up and she had the eeriest feeling she was being watched.

"All the land around the town once belonged to a wealthy merchant family who raised and sold grain to the ferryman for their animals they used to pull the barges along the canals."

"One family?" She factored his words into the back of her mind as she watched the people in the café.

The Baptist ladies were leaving, but a few took a

moment to stare at her on their way out the door. She doubted it was more than idle curiosity. Not something to set her nerves on edge. The two families still busily chatted in their booths, while several of the seats at the counter had emptied. Her gaze fell on a table of businessmen. All three seemed to be studying her and Tobias.

"The estate also served as a stop on the Underground Railroad."

With a tilt to her head she focused her attention back on the mayor. As a teacher she'd studied the state's history of active abolitionism before the Civil War and always found the subject fascinating. "Many old homes claim the same thing."

"Yes, but it's been recorded in the county record since after the war. They say the old estate has hidden rooms and tunnels beneath the house." Tobias winked at her between bites of his salad. "Of course no one knows for sure, since Gilbert Byrd bought the place nearly half a century ago."

"Really?" Now he'd said something to catch her attention. "This Mr. Byrd doesn't allow visitors?"

"Old Gil never liked people in his home when he was alive. He was a bit of an odd duck." He grinned at his own pun.

Finally, some information about Gilbert Byrd. "He recently died?" Trying not to let him know she already knew this, she spoke as casually as her rising pulse would allow.

"Maybe a year back. The bank holds the lien on the abandoned property and no one can get in to look around it."

She drew her brows in and gave him half a grin in encouragement. "Just how do you know all this?"

"I'm not just the town mayor, I sit on the bank's board of directors."

"Aha, a man with his finger on the town's financial pulse?" Setting her fork aside, she leaned in a little closer. "So, tell me, has there been anyone out to the Byrd place to check those rumored tunnels?"

Before he could answer, the three businessmen, including the newspaper reporter with the limp handshake, approached their table. Bobby quickly picked up her fork so she wouldn't have to shake hands with anyone.

"You ready for that fiscal planning meeting, Tobias?" one of them asked.

"Sure am, Thomas." Tobias finished his soda. "Ms. Roberts, allow me to introduce you to two members of the town's council. Thomas Yoder, the town's legal advisor and this is Harold Russet, civil engineer and head of road maintenance and planning. And I believe you've met Richard Davis, the newspaper's owner and chief reporter."

Bobby smiled and nodded to all three men.

"Thank you for an enjoyable meal," the mayor said as he scooted out of the booth. "Perhaps we can do it again sometime?"

"Well, that will depend on how long it takes me to finish my job." She gave him a smile to soften the sting of her words, watching the group saunter out the café's door.

Despite Tobias joining her uninvited for her meal, she'd learned some useful information. Something in those files had the mayor nervous. He'd tried to hide it, but she wondered how far she'd have to dig to find whatever it was he wanted to keep buried in Ruby's filing system. What really had her excited was the news that the old Byrd place might have underground tunnels and hidden rooms.

Wonder what might be hidden there. Something worth committing murder to cover?

Bobby glanced at her watch, then out onto the street. No sign of Gage or his truck. He'd been getting in her way for days and now when she needed him, he was nowhere to be found. Typical.

She'd just have to find the Byrd place on her own.

But he'd made her promise to stay with one of the deputies or him. Well, maybe if he knew where to find her, that was just as good, wasn't it?

She took her bill over to the cash register.

"Not waiting for the sheriff?" Rachel asked as she rang up her bill.

Bobby handed her the money. "I'm sure he'll be along anytime now. But I was hoping you could give me some directions."

Chapter Twelve

"**D**amn the woman," Gage cursed as he sped along the highway leading east of Westen. "I left her specific instructions not to go anywhere without me or one of my deputies."

When he'd been halfway back to town from the trailer park, he'd gotten a phone call from

Cleetus telling him to head out to the Byrd property to meet Bobby. A cold chill had washed over him, followed quickly by red-hot anger.

At the turnoff, he slowed down just enough to keep from rolling his truck as he made the hairpin turn and hit the gas again. His sweaty palms slipped on the steering wheel and

he adjusted his grip.

"Doesn't she ever watch slasher horror movies? The woman who goes off by herself is the

one too stupid to live and is always killed!"

Leaving one hand on the wheel he punched in her cell phone number again. No answer. Or she was on the damn thing. It switched over to voice mail. Since leaving town he'd already left her three messages. The phone closed with a snap.

For a second he glanced at his speedometer. The red arrow sat on ninety. If he didn't slow down he'd be the other horror movie cliché—the lawman who gets killed before he can get there to rescue the stupid heroine.

He eased off the gas, but his temper stayed in hyperdrive. When he got hold of her he was going to shake some sense into her. He ground his teeth. And she better be in one piece so he could tear her apart.

What the hell had Tobias said to her to send her out here without a thought to her own safety? The mayor better pray nothing had happened to her, or he was going to beat the shit out of him.

Gage drove past Aaron Turnbill's farm, past the charred remains of the barn on the abandoned MacPherson land next to it. As he neared the old Byrd property on the other side, he slowed and scanned the area. No other vehicles were on the road.

A lot of the vegetation had grown up around the drive's entrance in the year since Gil had died. The truck bounced over several deep potholes in the gravel as he drove to the front of the two-story colonial. The trees and bushes around the property all needed pruning and several panes of glass in the upper windows had been broken.

Parked in front of the porch that covered the front of the house from one side to another was one very familiar brown Toyota.

"At least her car's okay," he muttered, pulling in behind it.

He climbed out of the truck and stood perfectly still. Slowly he counted to ten. Then counted again.

Even though they'd spent the night together, Bobby wasn't his responsibility. She was a grown woman, with the right to put herself in danger if she wanted.

He was full of shit.

Anything happened to her, he'd never forgive himself. And knowing that scared him as much as anything.

Taking a deep breath, he started up to the porch. As he neared the other car, a feminine arm reached out dangling a brown paper bag.

"Don't worry, Cleetus. He just pulled up." She peeked out the car window at him and grinned, disconnecting her call. "I brought your lunch with me."

"You want to explain to me *why* I shouldn't haul you back to town, lock you in a cell and throw away the key?"

The pallor that crept over her face at the mention of the cell took some of the starch out of his anger. But he wasn't ready to let her off the hook yet. He leaned his hip against the hood of the car, took the sandwich from the bag and sank his teeth into the sourdough, turkey and swiss combo.

The car door opened and Bobby stepped out.

He let his gaze start at her feet and the red lacquer-tipped toes peeking out of her open-toed sandals. He slid it up over her jean-clad legs that had wrapped around him the night before. As his gaze continued upward, he stared hungrily at her rounded hips and the sweater clinging to the breasts that had filled his hands. Finally, he focused on her lips that he'd feasted on the night before. All he could think about was stripping her naked and repeating every moment.

"I know I didn't stay physically in Cleetus' presence, but I did stay in touch with him." She wiggled her phone in front of his face. "Besides, you don't want to lock me up."

"I don't?"

She held a paper cup just out of his reach. "Nope. I remembered to bring you a cup of Lorna's sweet tea, too," she said with a grin.

Her sass was back. Good. He'd only been half teasing about locking her up, but after her reaction he doubted he really could do that to her again. Hell, he never should've done it in the first place.

Lifting one eyebrow to warn her not to press her luck, he held out his hand for the drink. She'd remembered how much he liked his drink sweet. Three years of marriage to Moira and he doubted she'd even known he liked tea, much less go to the effort of bringing him some of his favorite kind.

"So what was so important you had to risk your life coming out here now instead of waiting for me?"

"I knew you'd be mad that I left town without someone to act as bodyguard. It's why I kept Cleetus on the phone the whole time," she said as she rested her butt against the car's hood right next to his.

He slashed her a skeptical look. She had the sense to blush at his censure, lifting her shoulders in a little shrug.

"I had the choice of waiting for you or dragging Cleetus out here. Frankly, I'd rather have you help me search this house."

She trusted him to protect her. That felt right. He *wanted* to protect her. "I won't tell Cleetus you said that."

Her lips lifted in a half smile. "I'd appreciate that." Their gazes locked for a minute and another blush filled her cheeks.

"The reason we're here?" he prompted and took another bite of the sandwich.

"Tunnels."

Cleetus had told him she'd eaten lunch with the mayor. Another fact that had sent his anger up another notch.

"Tobias told you the old rumors that there are tunnels beneath the old Byrd place and you believed him? Instead of the two of us sitting in the bank getting some real answers about the property lien and possibly Harley's death, you drag us out here to see if some town myth might be true?"

"The bank and their employees will be there tomorrow." Bobby rolled her eyes at him and pursed out her lips a moment. She waved a hand at the house. "But just think about it. What if the rumors are true? Tobias said Gilbert Byrd was a near recluse, something his nephew said too, and wouldn't let anyone on his property. What if there are secret rooms and tunnels beneath this place? What better place for your missing tweaker to hide?"

Okay, she had a point.

He finished his sandwich and drank the last of the

tea. Pushing himself away from the car, he stretched a moment. "I always wanted to see what Gil kept hidden inside this place."

"Let's go, then." She took one step toward the house, and he grabbed her arm to stop her. "What?"

"If Rusty is in here, he may be very dangerous." Removing his sunglasses, he slipped them into his shirt pocket and fixed his most serious expression on her. He wanted her to know he meant business. "We do this my way. You follow me. I tell you to stay put or to get out of the house, you do exactly that. No questions. No arguments."

She nodded.

"Good. Wait here a second."

He went to his truck and retrieved both the heavy-duty flashlights he kept in the backseat for emergencies and his gun from the lock box under his front seat. He wasn't taking any chances. Checking the lights, he walked back to her and handed her a flashlight. "You take one and bring your cell phone, just in case."

"Do you think the gun is necessary?" She lifted her brows, her head cocked to one side as she stared at his weapon.

"Normally, in Westen, I'd say no. But after these past few days I figured I'd best be prepared for anything." He slipped the gun into the back of his jeans and led the way up the porch.

"At least you didn't say it was all my fault this time," she muttered from behind him.

He bit back a grin, forcing himself to concentrate on the search and not the woman behind him. The doorknob didn't twist under his hand. Taking out his wallet, he pulled out a credit card, slipped it into the door and jimmied it lose. With a little shove the door opened.

The musty stale air hung around them like dragon's breath as they entered the house.

"If someone's hiding in here, they certainly haven't aired the place out," Bobby said mere inches behind his left shoulder.

He glanced over at her. If she was this nervous walking into this huge house, wonder how she was going to handle the cramp dark confines of a basement or even a tunnel if they should find one? He didn't want to get caught with her having some sort of panic attack. One word from her and they'd leave now.

"You going to be okay?"

"This doesn't smell nearly as bad as Harley's place the other night." She wrinkled her nose at the memory then nodded. "Lead on, Sherlock."

To let her know he admired her spunk, he winked at her and eased further into the paneled foyer. She followed him so close, the beam of her flashlight shining on the floor in front of them, he could feel her body's heat against his back.

"Doesn't look much like Harley's either," she whispered behind him. Her warm breath sent heat straight down his body and his mind to things other than their surroundings.

Somehow he needed to get control of his reactions to her. Before either of them got hurt.

Flashing his light into the front room, he saw stacks of old newspapers and magazines lining the back wall, books lay piled about the floor and in tiers on every surface.

"Seems Gil was a bit of a collector."

"More like a hoarder. You know I read an article not long ago that said hoarding was a sign of depression. Maybe Gilbert's reclusion was less about wanting to be alone and more about mental illness. That would explain why he had no contact with his family. Maybe he was paranoid as well as depressed."

Maybe her babbling was a way to keep from thinking how scared she was. He reached behind him and took her cold, clammy hand in his.

"Gil's been dead a year. Don't think he needs psychoanalyzing, do you?" With a squeeze to her hand he led her through the house. "Keep your eyes open for any sign someone a little less dead might've been in here recently."

Her light beamed up the walls to the ceiling of the hall way and down into the dining room. She let go of his hand to step into the room. "Wow, look at all the ornate scroll work in the crown moldings." She scanned her light across the table piled with complete sets of china then down to the floor. "Inlaid parquet floors. People pay a fortune for this kind of stuff nowadays."

"They did back when this place was built, too." He watched her stroke her hand over the wood wainscoting and stop to check out the china pieces, her fear completely forgotten.

"My God. He has three different sets of Blue Ridge pottery. My mother used to collect pieces when I was a teenager." She fingered one serving platter before moving around the table. "There's a dozen Staffordshire teapots." She held up one, shining the flashlight on the blue and white design. "An antique dealer could have a heyday in here."

"Wonder why your sister's client hasn't been up here to cart this stuff off? Gil's been dead quite some time."

"His nephew only found out a few months ago that his uncle had died." Carefully, she set the teapot back in place and walked back out of the room. "Remember, I told you they weren't close. When he tried to find out about his inheritance he learned about the lien the bank supposedly held. Suspicious because of his uncle's mistrust in banks, he had Chloe immediately file an injunction to prevent anyone from taking anything off the property until his claim can be heard in court."

With her head tilted to one side, something he'd learned meant a sure sign she was going to ask a very interesting question, she furrowed her brows together.

"What I can't figure out, is why no one in town looted this place. Or at least came in out of idle curiosity to see what Mr. Byrd had hidden in here."

"Simple. Cowardice."

Her brows shot up in surprise. "The whole town was afraid of Mr. Byrd?"

"Yep. Gil owned this house as long as most of Westen's residents have been alive."

"Even you were afraid of him?"

"Yes. Even me, at least when I first moved here."

"Really? Do tell."

"First let's check out the rest of the house." Taking her arm in his, he drew her against his side as they moved deeper into the house. "Be prepared, I'm about to tell you a tale of my misspent youth."

Once they'd made sure the library, second parlor, a bedroom, downstairs bathroom and coat closet, all of which were packed with collections of items, were empty of any living creature they arrived in the kitchen. Typical of kitchens from the early part of the nineteenth century this room felt cavernous. It still had the original stone fireplace flanked by newer appliances. If you could call appliances from the 1940s new.

Although dust covered every surface, this room lacked the signs of hoarding found in the others.

"Looks like Gil kept this room very neat," Gage commented as they looked through the cupboards. "Tight as a ship's galley."

"And you've seen the inside of a ship's galley?" Bobby opened a cupboard or two. Finding nothing unusual, she set her flashlight on the counter and leaned her back against it. Her hands shook a bit, and she clasped them in front of her.

If he hadn't been watching he'd have missed the nervous tremors. Once again her determination and courage impressed him.

"Served two years in the Navy, right out of high school. Dad wasn't happy, but it gave me an appreciation for personal freedom and responsibility." He leaned one hip against the kitchen counter. Odd he should tell her that, but again he'd already told her things he hadn't told anyone else.

"So what is this childhood confession you promised to tell me?"

"I was twelve when my dad and I moved to Westen. Since I was the new kid at a school where everyone had grown up together, I wanted desperately to fit in." He leaned against the counter beside her so he could watch the back door and the hallway as he talked. "So one summer day I was riding my bike with my friends and we came up past this place."

"Let me guess, your new friends were the school troublemakers."

He blinked. "How did you know?"

With a nonchalant shrug of her shoulders she leaned back and crossed her legs in front of her. "I taught middle school for the last ten years. The new kid always falls in with the troublemakers first."

"Really?" Here he thought it was just him.

"Yep. So what did the guys dare you to do to Mr. Byrd?"

Wow, she was almost psychic. "I had to throw a rock through one of the upstairs windows. Since I'd been the shortstop on the baseball team at my old school, I had no problem hitting the target."

"How'd you get caught?"

"I was the sheriff's son. Gil recognized me and called my dad." He still remembered the tanning his backside had gotten for that. Worse was the guilt he'd felt for letting his dad down. "Dad brought me back here after dinner and made me apologize to Gil. Afterwards he made me cut lawns all summer, including Gil's, and every cent I earned went to repaying to have the window fixed."

"I wish more parents had your father's ethics. The world would be a better place. And it would make a teacher's job much easier."

"At first I was pissed off at him. But as the summer went on and I saw how much work it took to earn the money I learned to respect other people's property. I also learned that Gil might be eccentric, but he wasn't anyone to be feared just because he was different."

"Sounds like you learned a lot from the whole experience."

"Yeah, my dad earned my respect for the whole process, too. And there were some other benefits I hadn't counted on."

She tilted her head to the side and drew her brows together. "What extra benefits?"

"By the end of the summer I took pride in the fact that I'd paid for the whole thing myself. I also put on some muscle weight doing all the physical labor. Which paid off during football tryouts and meeting girls." He grinned at her and went to test the back door. "Locked."

She ran her hand over the counter. "By the layer of dust covering everything in here, we'd know if anyone had so much as stepped foot in this place."

He nodded at the door on the opposite side of the kitchen. "Does that mean you don't want to check out the basement to see if there are any tunnels down there?"

Shaking her head, she pushed away from the counter. "The word tunnel implies that it would lead somewhere away from here. I think we should check it out to be sure there's nothing or no one hidden down there. Don't you agree?"

Frankly, he hoped it was a total waste of time, but

she had her demons under control again. At least her hands didn't shake while she held the flashlight anymore, so he might as well check the basement out while he was here.

The basement door didn't creak when they opened it. Surprising. Ever since he'd gotten the message to meet Bobby here, he'd felt like he'd stepped into a B horror movie. Old Gil must've kept the hinges well oiled.

Gage flashed his light down the stairs. "Stay close, but be careful. These steps are steep."

"Don't worry, I'm right behind you," she whispered over his left shoulder.

They crept down the stairs without saying anything more. With each step, he felt her breathing pick up pace. At the base of the steps, he stopped. She stood one rung above him, but it only made her face equal to his.

The stairs opened onto a storage room. For a basement in the Midwest, it felt small—too small. Could it be because the house was built so long ago? Or were the rumors right? Were there secret rooms and a tunnel hidden somewhere down here?

Slowly, he swung his flashlight from one side of the basement to the other, covering every nook and cranny. He slid it over the tower of boxes, the line of crates and chests, and the table with its household tools. His actions intent on allowing her a moment to collect her defenses against her fear.

"You could wait upstairs if this is too much for you."

"Like I said before, I'd rather be with you. Staying

in an empty old house by myself will feel…"

"…claustrophobic?"

She gave a nervous laugh. "I was going to say creepy, but yes, a little claustrophobic, too."

"When did you first start feeling this way?" Please don't let her say when he locked her in the cell. "Or have you always been afraid of small spaces?"

"About nine months ago. I'd gone to a teaching conference with some of my fellow teachers. We had four people staying in one room. All they talked about was teaching or their families." A soft sigh escaped her. "Which usually didn't bother me, but after five days of enforced camaraderie and boring workshops packed with people, I felt suffocated."

"Did it get better after you left the conference?" he asked as he moved his beam back through the dark room, slowly searching each section of wall for an opening.

"I felt better once I got home. But the next week, when school started, I realized my classroom felt the same. Cramped, crowded, suffocating."

"What did you do?"

"First I opened the windows. That worked well, until the weather turned too cool. I tried to have the door open, which my boss insisted remain closed. Finally, I decided I needed some psychiatric help."

"You went to a shrink?"

She peeked over his shoulder. "A psychologist. You make it sound like I went to see a voodoo priestess. It wasn't that bad. She helped me talk about things—my life, raising my sisters, putting my dreams on hold—and that's when I realized teaching was the root of the whole problem."

The flashlight beam stopped on one panel of the wall as he turned to look at her. "Teaching was making you claustrophobic?"

She stepped down beside him on the concrete floor. "Apparently, now that my sisters are all grown and I no longer need to support them, my subconscious is rebelling over being stuck in a classroom. She also suspected the claustrophobia stemmed from my resentment over all the years I've worked as a teacher, putting my life on hold."

Grudgingly, he nodded. "Makes perfect sense. Is that when you decided to become a PI?"

"Yep. I thought being out of the classroom, dealing with different cases and people each day, and having some adventure would cure me. When I got my PI license and quit my job, I felt much better. When I left Cinci, I'd pretty much convinced myself I had it licked. That was before you threw me into a jail cell."

Her words, a soft censure of his actions, cut his pride to the quick. Guilt washed over him. Lowering his light a little, he stared down at her. "I'm sorry about that. It was a knee-jerk reaction."

There was no gloating in her eyes over his apology. She gently laid her hand on his arm. "I quite understand. Cleetus told me about the shooting and how the PI played a part in it. I'm terribly sorry, and I'm surprised you didn't throw away the key, too."

The air around them thickened. He swallowed several times. Memories, the betrayal and her easy acceptance of the whole sordid mess swirled around in his head. "Cleetus told you everything?"

"Yes." For a moment she looked at him and opened her mouth to say something, only to have her gaze shift beyond him. "Oh, my God. Look!"

Shoving the turmoil in his mind away, he stared at where she pointed. The flashlight beam illuminated a line three-quarters of the way up the opposite wall. If you looked hard enough you could just make out the entire outline of a doorway in the panel.

"I think we found the entrance to the tunnels."

Bobby scooted past him. Her fear barely under control, she began pulling crates laden with old, musty clothing out of the way in an almost maniacal effort. Any other time the antique material and clothing styles would've stopped her from madly thrashing through them to admire every piece of history.

Today, she needed to do something. The confines of the room and Gage's physical closeness clawed at her senses. One good thing about being in the creepy basement, at least the darkness had hidden her blush of embarrassment at admitting to such a cowardly character flaw.

The bottom crate had to have bricks in it. She gave it a shove. The only thing that moved was the dust in a loud cloudy oomph.

"Here, let me get that before you hurt yourself." Gage reached between her and the crate.

Grinding her teeth, she stepped out of his way. For two decades she'd managed to handle every problem or situation by herself. Now, in three short days she seemed willing to share the load with this man. Of course he never gave her much chance to argue.

As soon as he had the crate moved far enough to give her access, she squeezed behind it. "I'll bet there's some secret button to open this somewhere along here." Dust flew around them as she pressed her fingers over the panel. Suddenly, the edge popped inward and back out like a spring. Dank, musty air whooshed from behind it. "I found it!"

"I can see," he said, right behind her.

This time she didn't jump. Maybe she was getting used to him.

"If you'll move back out of the way, we need a little more room to get the whole thing open."

She shifted back past him, her body brushing softly against his hard planes. Trapped between him and the other crate, she fought desperately to take in a breath, to control the sudden panic that filled her.

"It's okay, sweetheart. You're safe."

Whispering the words, he ran one hand down her arm. Shivers of delight followed, quickly replacing the fear. As she glanced up at him, the corner of his mouth lifted in that smile that melted her heart the first time she saw him. Then he winked.

Air filled her lungs once more and her pulse slowed to its steady lub-dub rhythm once more. He was right. She'd been even closer than this to him last night, trapped between him and the bed. Safe. Secure. Well pleasured.

"Okay now?"

Not trusting her voice, she nodded and stepped back out of the way. Leaning his shoulder into the crate, Gage gave it a hard shove. The wood scraped across the floor as it moved another foot. "That should do it."

He picked up his flashlight from where he'd laid it on the top of the crate and handed it to her. "Hold this while I open the entrance more."

As he gripped the panel's edge and pulled it open, she flashed both lights into the widening crevice beyond. God, she hoped nothing popped out like rats or bats. She shuddered, making both beams wiggle into the dark tunnel beyond.

His warm hand settled on one of hers, slowly taking one of the flashlights from her. The edges of his brows knitted in concern. "We don't have to do this. We could go upstairs, call one of my deputies and you could wait outside in your car."

For a moment she took inventory of herself. Normal breathing. Normal heart rate. Heck, even her palms didn't feel sweaty. "No. I'm good. I want to see where this leads."

Whether she meant the tunnel or this thing between them, she wasn't sure, but she knew one thing for sure—she meant to explore both as far as they would take her.

He gently laid his hand against her cheek as if he knew she meant more than the tunnel in front of them. He winked again. "Okay. Hang on one second." Leaning over, he pulled an old bamboo cane from inside another tall crate.

"What's that for?"

"Spiderwebs." He rolled his eyes upward a moment and gave a little shrug. "I've never much liked having them hang over my head or clinging to my body."

The big, bad sheriff was afraid of spiderwebs? Just

like Indiana Jones' fear of snakes, his vulnerability only made him sexier. Suddenly her claustrophobia didn't seem such a bad thing. Everyone had something or other they feared. Some men feared commitment, some women being alone. She and Gage just manifested their fears more outwardly.

With a sweep of the cane, he pulled several cobwebs off the tunnel's entrance and shook them free. Only then did he step inside. Taking a fortifying breath, Bobby followed him into the tunnel.

An immediate chill ran over her, but not of fear. The cool earth lay behind the wood-planked walls, reminding her they were underground. Slowly they moved down the corridor. Gage bent slightly to fit into the short space and stopped every so often to sweep ahead of him for cobwebs.

Despite the narrow confines of the hundred-year old tunneling, Bobby realized she felt at ease following Gage. His mere presence assured her of safety and gave her confidence. Right now she could almost forgive him the cell incident.

***

He knelt down in the copse of trees watching the tunnel's exit. He'd driven up the old drive and seen both their vehicles parked out front. He'd quickly hurried over here to watch for them to emerge.

When he'd left town, he'd prayed they hadn't headed this way.

Had they found the hidden entrance in the old mansion? No one knew it was really there except for him, the cook and Gil Byrd. And they certainly weren't telling anyone from the grave. A quick glance at the watch.

Fifteen minutes. Fifteen minutes he'd been sitting in the damp grass and thicket beneath the trees. Fifteen minutes waiting to see if they'd found their way out.

He'd give them ten more. Hopefully, they wouldn't show. That would mean the tunnels and secret room were safe. He'd have time to finish tying up loose ends and close down the business before anyone knew what he'd been up to.

What if they did find the tunnels?

He'd have to find some way to make sure they didn't get any closer.

Chapter Thirteen

The odor hit Bobby's nose before they actually found the room.

"Oh, God. Not again." No matter what they told you on TV crime shows—or didn't tell you for that matter—she'd learned one thing this week, death had a unique smell. "I don't suppose that's some hundred-year-old corpse, is it?"

"No, I'm pretty sure this corpse is of the twenty-first-century type." Gage muttered a few curse words as they trudged closer to the offending smell.

"Who do you think it is?" Why she was whispering was beyond her. Not like the body was going to complain she was making too much noise.

"At this point I have no clue. But with the luck we've been having, it's going to be Rusty."

"After what he did to Teeny, wouldn't that be a

good thing?" She wasn't usually this bloodthirsty, but frankly, drawing and quartering was too good for the guy.

"Not really. He deserves to be punished for what he did to her, but I need someone to give me some answers. She's out of it and I'd hoped he could lead me to his supplier. If he's dead, so is the trail to the dealer." Gage paused to swipe more cobwebs out of the way, flashing his light farther into the tunnel. A large room appeared in front of them.

As he scanned the light down to the room's floor, a large mass came into view. It took Bobby's eyes a moment to adjust to the image, but slowly she could make out the shape of a body curled on its side—the back to them and a large pool of something dark beneath the head. "Do you think that's Rusty?"

"Won't know until we get a look at him."

As they moved closer, more of the room behind the body came into view. Where Gil Byrd's home hadn't seen visitors in quite some time, this place appeared well used. Scales and boxes were piled all over the table and floor.

"How did he die?" she asked without looking too closely.

"Looks to be the same as Harley. Someone bashed his head in."

"Wonder if they used the same statue?"

"That would be a little too convenient."

Gage stopped just inside the doorway and turned his head to look at her over his shoulder. Even in the eerie light she saw the concern in his eyes.

"I can't get you out of here very fast. So I need you

to keep your cool for a little longer. Do what we did at Harley's. Focus on the room and surroundings, not the body. Put those skills of observation you showed me at Harley's yesterday to good use and just tell me everything you see. Okay?"

Not trusting her voice to remain cool and collected in the light of his concern, she simply nodded. Had they just been at Harley's the evening before? That meant they'd discovered two murders in as many days. Say what you wanted about Westen—sleepy little boring town it wasn't.

Gage stepped over the body, taking her hand to steady her as she followed. Without a downward glance, she kept her back to the corpse and focused all her attention on the room's contents. Slowly she scanned the room's entire width and breadth. Two wooden cots lay upended against one wall. Another wall had two trunks piled against it, and the third wall had another exit carved out of it.

"That looks to be how they got in and out of here."

"Would explain why no one ever knew this was here and the lack of finger or footprints up at the Byrd house," Gage said from just beside her knee, where he'd squatted down to study the body.

"The table's full of boxes of plastic bags," she said as she moved closer. She reached into her purse and pulled out a pair of tweezers. Using them, she lifted one bag to study the contents in the flashlight's beam. "Crystal meth."

"And you know this how?"

"Sadly, we had a kid trying to sell the stuff on campus last fall. The principal and the police did an in-service with us to make sure we knew what it looked like if or when we saw it in our kids' desks. Seems the drug users and drug pushers are getting younger and younger."

"What grade did you teach?"

"Seventh grade history and computer technology."

"Ah, that explains how patient you are with Cleetus and the computers."

"Believe me, he's a much better student than some of my former ones." She laid the bag of drugs back on the table, took the tweezers and poked through the box, counting the number of bags inside. "There are a hundred bags just in this one box. What's the cost of one of these?"

"Street value?"

"Yes."

"Probably between ten and twenty dollars a bag."

"If there's a hundred bags in each box, that means there's about two thousand a box, times..." quickly, she counted the number of boxes, "sixty-five boxes, that's over a hundred thousand dollars here. Dear God."

"And more bad news," Gage said, standing up, holding a wallet and state ID. "It's definitely our man Rusty. Whoever is behind this is running very scared."

"He's killing off anyone who can connect him to both the bank fraud and the drugs."

"The way you think is downright sexy."

For a moment they stood and stared at each other, the intensity between them almost palpable in the room's small confines. She wanted him to kiss her, but she didn't want what they shared tainted by the grisly scene around them.

Almost as if he read her mind and agreed with her, he stepped to the side. "Tell me what else you see."

Slowly, she studied the room. "Some wooden dishes and old eating utensils probably left over from the Underground Railroad days. A modern scale, for measuring out the drugs, I'm sure. Couple of chairs."

"Good. Now what don't you see?"

Puzzled at what he was getting at, she considered the room and what she knew about meth. News reports talked about how easy it was for people to cook it in their own kitchens. "There's no stove to cook it on. No pots, nothing to manufacture it in."

"Right. Which means this is simply a storage space for the end product." He took her elbow and led her to the other exit. "That's a good thing for us."

"Why?"

"Meth labs are highly explosive and they leave the chemical residue on everything, even the air. Just inhaling the air in a meth lab can get you high on the stuff."

"So where are we going now?" she asked as she followed him up the new tunnel.

"We know where the other exit leads. Let's see where this one ends."

"What if it leads to the meth lab? Wouldn't that be dangerous?"

"Don't worry. I have a feeling I know exactly where this goes." He reached back to take her hand and steadily moved farther into the tunnel, which seemed to gradually lead upwards.

***

At the end of the tunnel, they encountered an old wooden door covering the exit's top. Gage reached over his head and gave one good shove. It creaked open halfway and stopped. He peeked his head out the opening. In the dim evening light he couldn't make out much.

Grass. Bushes. Trees. Nothing moving.

He lowered himself back into the tunnel and took Bobby's cold hand in his once more. For a woman with such a bad phobia, she was keeping a tight leash on it. "I know you don't like being in there, but I want you to stay here for a minute."

"Why?"

The slight tremble in her voice tore at his gut. "I want to be sure no one is waiting out here to jump us."

"Don't take any chances. I haven't finished all my fantasies when it comes to you." Before he knew her intent, she leaned in close and kissed him hard. She stopped just as abruptly, her eyes widened with worry. "One minute. That's all you get, then I'm coming out. I don't want you getting hurt to protect me."

"Make it two." Her concern touched that spot deep inside he thought he'd closed off for good. For the first time since his father's death he felt like his life mattered to someone besides himself. He slipped his gun out of the back of his jeans.

"All right, but that's all the time my nerves can take."

He had no doubt if he didn't return with in one hundred and twenty seconds she was coming out after him, not from her fear of the tunnel, but her fear for him. And that idea both pleased and scared him.

She rotated her wrist and flashed the light on her watch. "Go."

With a couple of quick lunges, he scrambled out of the tunnel's hole onto the ground beside it. He dropped into a crouch, paused and listened for any unusual sound. Undercover in the city, he'd known by the cadence of the cars and the movement of feet on pavement when danger was close at hand. Today, he had to draw on memories of days spent hiking and camping in the woods as a kid.

Birds chirped in the trees. Far off, he could hear bullfrogs calling and water running in the creeks that fed into the Mohican River. No cars grinding over the gravel road. No limbs cracking beneath errant boot steps. Nothing to say someone watched in the woods.

"One minute," Bobby whispered from just inside the tunnel.

Still squatting, he duck-walked forward a few feet. The light was fading fast, especially in the copse of trees, but he was able to make out the shape of something on the edge of the trees. He didn't have to guess what it was. Just like he suspected—the charred remains of the MacPherson barn.

He glanced around at the ground. The grass had been trampled here recently. No real footprints could be seen, but from the different depths of the dents in the grass, he'd say someone stood here for some time.

Watching the fire the other night?

A frisson of fear skittered across his neck, lifting the hairs. Watching the tunnel exit?

"Gage?" Right on time, Bobby peeked her head out of the tunnel.

He straightened, walked back over and slipped his gun back in the waistband of his jeans. Leaning over, he grabbed one of her hands. "Let me help you. It's a little slippery."

"Did you see anything? Anyone? Where are we?" she whispered as she scrambled out to stand beside him.

"We're alone now, but someone was definitely here not too long ago."

"How do you know?"

"Over here." He took her elbow, led her over to where the grass had been flattened and pointed out the area with his flashlight. "Someone stood here for a while."

"Could it have been a hunter?"

"Maybe, but I doubt it."

"Why?"

"This is a spot where someone could view anyone coming out of the tunnel over there." He swung his light to where they'd just exited the tunnel then back behind her. "And that's the barn that burned down just two days ago."

"So the fire, the land fraud, Harley's murder, Rusty's murder and the drugs are all connected." It wasn't a question. She'd come to the same conclusion he had. "So what do we do now?"

"First we get some help to lock these drugs up and out of commission then we figure out who's behind this mess." He took her hand and led her out of the woods to the open area behind the barn. Pulling out his cell phone, he called the office.

"Cleetus, this is Gage."

"Hey, Sheriff. No one's found any sign of that Rusty fellow, and the men pretty much finished cleaning out that trailer like you asked."

"I found Rusty."

"You did? Did he say why he beat up that poor little lady? How about who his supplier is?"

"He's dead, Cleetus."

"Dead? Well, damn."

Trust his deputy to feel bad about a tweaker dying.

"I need you to call the county coroner's office. I'm also going to need you to get hold of someone over at the state DEA office. We have a whole lot of meth down here."

"Meth?"

"Apparently our boy Rusty wasn't just a tweaker. He was a supplier and quite possibly the cook."

"I'll get Daniel to take over the station and make those calls, Sheriff."

"Good. Let's try to keep this information just between us for now."

After he hung up, he called Deke to drive out to the site. He wanted his input as to what exactly was going on and just how likely they were to find the meth kitchen before the whole situation exploded.

***

Bobby sat on the hood of her car, watching Gage talk to Frank Watson and the county coroner's team as they walked the blanket-draped stretcher with Rusty's body on it to the ambulance. He'd moved both their vehicles from the Byrd place closer to the burned-out barn and the tunnel entrance while they'd waited for everyone else to arrive.

"Lorna sent you some tea and sandwiches," Cleetus said setting several paper cups and a bag on the hood next to her.

"That was nice of her. How did she find out about this?" Bobby took the lid off one cup and swallowed some of Lorna's special sweet tea. She'd suffer for the calories later, but right now she was starving and thirsty.

"Lorna's one smart woman. She saw the coroner's ambulance go by, then Deke Reynolds stopped in to get his dinner to go, something he doesn't ever do, and she just figured something was up."

Bobby took a bite of a chicken salad sandwich. Manna from heaven couldn't taste this good. She chewed and swallowed quickly. "I keep forgetting how small this town is. News really does travel fast."

"Yeah, Lorna knowing something's up is only one of the things the sheriff isn't gonna be too pleased about," Cleetus said as Gage and Deke neared the Toyota.

Gage had introduced her to the fireman about an hour earlier as they waited for Frank to process the body and photograph the crime scene. It took all her willpower not to stare at the ridges of scars covering the left side of Deke's neck and lower jaw like an angry poisonous vine. His deep, raspy voice suggested the fire he'd obviously been caught in had damaged his vocal cords, too.

"I didn't expect this murder to stay quiet for long. Town's too small for that. I'm just glad the mayor, town council and the newspaper reporters aren't here mucking things up," Gage said, reaching for a drink.

His arm brushed Bobby's in the process. He stopped and stared at her a moment. "You want to get inside the car where it's warm?"

She shook her head a moment, still trying to come to terms with how a simple touch from him had her body tingling from the inside out. "I like it out here."

"Okay." He went to his truck. Returning, he held a worn denim jacket in his hands, which he placed over her shoulders without further comments.

Thank goodness it was dark now, her cheeks were so red from the intimate act she probably looked like a lobster with a sunburn. He couldn't have announced their relationship any louder had he shouted it from the top of the barn's ruins.

She glanced around and caught Deke staring at her. After a moment he gave a brief nod. Hopefully, that meant he approved.

Why? Did she need Gage's friend's approval? It wasn't like they'd committed to a life-ever-after or anything. They'd simply had some good hot sex.

That's when it hit her. She'd liked having sex with him. She also liked teasing him, the way he made her jump by sneaking up on her, hearing how protective he was about all the quirky people in town. She loved how patient he was with his deputies, how he tolerated the small-town politics, and that he liked Lorna's cooking, but hated spiderwebs.

Damn, she didn't just like those things. She loved every single one of them. And she'd done the stupidest thing. In less than one week, she'd fallen head-over-heels in love like some young girl on her first date.

"What else is going to piss me off tonight,

Cleetus?" Gage finished off the last bite of the sandwich he'd almost devoured while she mused.

"I made that call over to the state DEA department. Seems they have a couple of raids goin' on in Cincinnati and Columbus tonight and can't spare a man to come get all this meth."

"Aw, shit." Gage turned and stalked off toward the barn.

Bobby started to scoot off the car and go after him.

Deke held up a hand, stilling her movement. "Give him a moment." The words rasped out over the cool night air. "He walks while he thinks."

"You've known each other long?" she asked, tearing her gaze away from watching Gage, who'd pulled out his phone, the dial pad glowing against his face as he talked to someone and stalked through the grass in the twilight.

The fireman took a long drink of tea before answering. Did using his voice still hurt from his past trauma? Guilt washed over her for asking him to speak again.

"Met him his first day at school when he and his dad moved to town. The gunslinger was a couple of years behind me in school, but I recognized something in him from the get-go." Deke stopped to take another swallow of liquid.

Even though she wanted to know everything about Gage, Bobby waited for Deke to tell the story at his own pace.

"I recognized the anger. He hated his dad for moving him to a small, rinky-dink town. He hated being the new kid in a school where most people had known each other almost from the time they were born. He hated his mom leaving them and hated himself for being angry with her. That anger made him edgy."

"That's a good thing?"

"If channeled right. It makes him aware of danger coming his way. It's what kept him alive all those years undercover."

Except for when his own wife nearly cost him his life. Silence hung between the trio. She wondered who or what had subdued Deke's edge and caused his scars.

"So how did Gage learn to channel that anger? I've seen teens just give into it, turn to drugs or gangs."

That made Cleetus laugh and the right side of Deke's mouth turned up in a half smile. "Until tonight, I'd say the worst drug problem we've had in Westen was the Saturday night pot parties. And as for gangs, there are only two that count."

"Two gangs? In this small town?" In the few days she'd been here, she hadn't noticed one group of kids hanging out at any of the places in town. No fights, nothing to suggest a gang.

"Yep, the baseball gang and the football gang."

Cleetus nodded. "Gage and Deke belonged to both. Best duo on the football field on a Friday night. Gage passing, Deke catching. Was a thing of pure beauty."

"That's how he got the nickname Gunslinger," Deke said.

Before she could question them more about Gage's past, he returned, pocketing his phone as he reached them. "The smart thing to do is lock the meth up in the jail, except I don't know who Rusty was working for.

My best guess is that's the person who killed him. No way could someone from Westen sell this much Meth on their own. The raids in Cincinnati and Columbus are not helping the situation." He shoved his hand through his hair, staring at Deke a moment, almost as if they read each other's thoughts.

"Moving the meth to town puts everyone at risk if the distributors need to replace what's seized tonight," Deke said, his facial muscles tightly matching the intensity in Gage's.

Bobby understood their concern. No way could Westen's citizens hold up under a drug war. "So what do we do?"

"We leave it here, under guard until the DEA can get here tonight or in the morning to claim it."

"Won't the killer try to take it?"

"My gut tells me this guy's trying to eliminate anyone who can lead us to him. Cleetus," Gage switched his attention to his deputy, who'd snapped to attention at his name, "I'm going to send Daniel out here with camping gear for the two of you. You don't let anyone near that tunnel, okay? Daniel can take the one inside the old Byrd place for the night."

"Yes sir, Sheriff."

Deke looked at Cleetus. "You two be careful out here. Tweakers are notoriously paranoid. They like to set booby-traps."

***

"Do you really think the killer covered his tracks by killing Rusty?" Bobby asked as soon as they headed back into town after dropping her car off at his place. Gage was surprised she waited that long.

"Yes, but that's not the important question of the moment." He watched the headlights on the highway and waited for her to come up with the right question.

"You mean, does Teeny know this guy's identity and does the killer know she's still alive?"

He loved the way her mind worked. Maybe she did have a knack for being a private eye. Which sucked, since he still didn't like them. Problem was, he found little *not* to like in Bobby. Before he could answer her, the sound of "Wild Thing" rang from her purse.

"Damn it," she murmured as she searched through the big black bag, finally pulling out her phone and flipping it open. "What do you need now, Chloe?"

Her face illuminated by the fluorescent dial numbers on the phone, he watched her roll her eyes and pause to listen. Her sister's voice, a slightly higher-pitched version of hers, came over the phone, but he couldn't quite make out what she said.

"No, I'm fine. Yes, we found a dead body. Actually, two. No, I don't need to come home yet. Yes, the whole thing involves the Byrd property. No, the sheriff wasn't rude. His name is Gage. Well, yes, I'd say he's handsome. Chloe Roberts, I don't believe that is any of your business."

She glanced at him and lifted her shoulders in a small shrug in the dim light of the truck's cab. Her sister had to have just asked if something happened between them.

Despite the evening's turn of events and what still lay ahead, he found himself relaxing a bit. No doubt because the conversation between the sisters sounded so normal.

"Yes, I'm focused on finding out the information your client needs and as soon as this is all handled to the sheriff's satisfaction I'll give you a complete report."

She'd put his needs before her case. *Interesting.*

He listened while she talked with her sister, her voice slipping from mildly irritated to placating, and back to irritated. Obviously the younger sister was giving her a taste of being worried and fussed over. Something he suspected happened little in Bobby's life. The idea ate at him. Bobby Roberts deserved to have someone worry about her.

"No, you and Dylan do not have to come here. You'll just be in the way. Besides, you're both too busy with your careers and school. Yes, I know you'd set it aside for me, but it's not necessary."

Growing up he'd wished for a brother or sister, someone to hang with or tease. Deke was about the closest he'd come. He'd been lucky, though— even though Dad had been the town sheriff, he'd always had time for him. Now with him gone, he'd missed someone fussing over him the way his dad had for years—the way Chloe was doing over the phone to Bobby.

In fact, there'd been a hollow place inside him since before Dad's funeral. One he'd grown accustomed to and accepted as part of his life from now on—that was, until Bobby fell into his arms.

Almost as if she knew what he'd been thinking, she reached out and took his hand lying on the truck's gearshift. Warmth settled in his chest at her touch. Different from the hot need he'd been fighting from the minute he'd met her. That hunger still hummed through his body, but this new need both pleased and scared him.

"Yes, I promise to be careful. Gage is quite capable of handling this. Yes, I'll tell him. I love you guys, too."

A moment later, she slipped the phone back in her purse.

"What did she want you to tell me?"

She gave a snort of a laugh. "She said to take care of me or she'll come here and kick your...um, butt."

"I'll bet she would, too."

"Chloe can be a bit obsessive at times."

"Probably makes her a good lawyer."

"And a pain in the backside," she said but the humor in her voice took the edge off the comment. "So back to the Teeny problem. Do you think the killer will go after her?"

He released Bobby's hand to grip the steering wheel with both hands, immediately focusing back on the problems the night's revelations had caused. "So far he's done his work without being noticed or tipping his hand. He doesn't like or want a big scene. But by now I bet he knows Teeny is hole up over at Clint's clinic."

"Oh my God," she said on a whispered gasp. "Your cousin's family."

Chapter Fourteen

"**I** called Clint as soon as I learned the meth was staying here tonight. He said Teeny was still semi-conscious and no one had been by to inquire about her," Gage said in an almost casual tone. "But just in case, I had Clint send Emma, Aunt Isabelle and the boys over to stay with Lorna at the café."

His words didn't fool her. Despite his implied lack of concern, the landscape had flown past them from the moment they'd gotten in the truck. Bobby glanced at the speedometer. Eighty-five.

Sure he wasn't worried one little bit.

Minutes later, they turned onto the main street of Westen right near the clinic. All the windows facing the street were dark.

Harriett greeted them at the darkened doorway. "Kept the lights out near the street. The doc said you wanted it to look like no one was here. You two look like you could use a bath," she said, leading them back to the room where they'd seen Teeny sleeping the day before.

At the door Harriett stopped them on the threshold like some warden of a special prison. She soaped up two washcloths and handed one to Bobby and the other to Gage. "Wash first, then talk."

Bobby didn't think she'd ever get used to the nurse's matter-of-fact bluntness. In the hallway's dim light she glanced down and saw the dirt and mud caking her jeans and sweater. Funny, a bath and changing clothes didn't seem like much of a priority right now.

The look on Harriett's face suggested that they not buck her orders or even try to enter the room without washing. With a glance at Gage, who appeared no happier than she about a bath at this moment, but obeyed nonetheless, Bobby quickly made work of removing any grime on her face and hands.

"Where's Clint?" Gage handed his grimy towel back to Harriett.

"Doc's in his office trying to find a bed at the county hospital for Teeny. He wants to get her in some place that can do drug rehab." The edges around Harriett's eyes and mouth softened as she walked over to the bed where Teeny slept in the dimly lit room. The nurse wiped a loose strand of hair from the girl's face. "Poor thing needs some food and care, too. Scrawny doesn't half describe her."

"That's the meth."

"Oh, it might be the immediate problem, but her

mother never had much meat on her bones, either. And I doubt either of them knew how to stand up to a man. What a shame."

Gage took Bobby's washcloth and set it on the edge of the sink. Taking her hand in his big warm one, he stood patiently beside her just inside the door. He rubbed his thumb across her knuckles, the caress reassuring her, despite his attention on the sleeping woman across the room. He seemed to wait for the nurse's permission to approach her patient.

"The few times she's drifted awake long enough to talk to me or the doc, she hasn't made a bit of sense. He's worried the beating or the drugs or both might've given her brain damage." Harriett tucked the covers around her patient before moving aside. "Might as well see if she'll wake up for you."

Instead of taking the seat by the bed, Gage leaned in close to Bobby. "Why don't you try talking to her?"

"Me? She doesn't know me at all." Was he nuts? She wouldn't know the first thing to ask the girl. She had nothing in common with a meth junkie. "You're someone she knows and you're also the town sheriff. Someone with authority."

"Exactly. I'm the law. She won't trust me. But you have skills for this I don't." He put his finger under her chin and lifted until her eyes met his. "Talk to her like a concerned teacher."

Great. He wanted her to do the one thing she'd always loathed about teaching—delving into her student's lives outside of class. She'd always preferred to leave that to the counselors.

"I don't think I'm what you're looking for."

"Yes, you are exactly what I need. I need you to do this," he said in an almost soft murmur. He held her gaze, his thumb caressing her knuckles once more. "Teeny needs our protection and I can't do that if I don't know who is behind all this."

Taking a deep breath, Bobby walked over to the bed and sat in the rocker. Out of the corner of her eye, she watched Gage move into the room's shadows.

"Teeny?" She reached forward and took the other woman's hand in hers. It felt cool. Small, scabbed-over sores dotted the nearly translucent skin stretched tightly over the bones. It was like holding the hand of an elderly person. There couldn't be an ounce of fat on her body. "Teeny, can you hear me?"

No response.

Bobby glanced to Gage's dark form. A movement of his head suggested he wanted her to continue.

How to reach this girl?

As a teenager Dylan had always been difficult to get out of bed in the mornings. Maybe she needed to be firmer with Teeny like she had with Dylan?

She switched to her "mom" voice. "Teeny. It's time to wake up."

The girl's pale lids fluttered.

"Open your eyes. We need to talk."

"Mom?" Teeny's voice cracked. Her lids drifted open, then closed. "Dry. Need a drink, Mom."

Should she give her something to drink? Bobby looked at Harriett for reassurance.

The nurse poured her a glass of water and brought it over. "Not too much. Just sips," she whispered.

Nodding her understanding, Bobby took the glass

and held the straw to Teeny's bruised, cut and chapped lips. "Take a little sip, sweetheart."

"Mom? I miss you. Lonely...without you." Teeny took a sip of the water, her eyes opening, but not really focused on Bobby.

"I know, sweetheart. I've missed you, too." Bobby hated lying to the girl, but when she'd been young there were many a night she would've loved to talk to her mom, even if it had been a blurred vision of her in a dark room.

Teeny took another sip of the water. "Rusty likes the fishman. Said the fishman was our friend."

Fishman? "Teeny, who is the fishman?"

"Rusty said he had to shut me up. The fishman wanted me to shut up."

"Teeny, can you tell me where the fishman is?"

"I hurt so bad. Don't let him find me, Mom." She sat straight up in bed and grabbed Bobby's hand in a death grip. "Saw what he did to the banker. I didn't tell no one, I swear it, Mom. I wouldn't do that to Rusty, Mom. You know that."

Had she witnessed Harley's murder? Is that why Rusty beat her? Even after he beat her nearly to death, Teeny wanted to protect her man.

Heart breaking for the girl and her wasted life, Bobby eased the battered girl back into the bed, gently smoothing her damp hair off her face. "Shh, sweetheart. It's okay. I know you didn't tell anyone. Go back to sleep."

"Mom? I love you, Mom." Her eyes drifted closed, her fingers slowly relaxing in Bobby's. "Don't go, Mommy."

"Sleep, sweetheart."

"Don't...go...Mommy."

Bobby, turned and stalked out of the room, not looking at either Gage or Harriett. Blindly wiping at the tears streaming unchecked down her face, she headed for the front of the house. Two strong arms wrapped around her, stopping her retreat.

"This way, Bobby. Out back," Gage whispered in her ear, turning her and leading her to the back door.

Outside, she gulped in air as he held her.

"It's okay," he said.

White-hot anger shot through her. She shoved hard against him until he had sense enough to let go.

"Don't," she said, stepping away from him. She dashed at the tears again. "Don't hold me. Don't try to make it right. That girl is half alive and I'm making her think she was talking to her dead mother!"

"I know."

"No! You don't know." She stomped down the steps into the dark yard. "Too many times I wanted my parents after they died and there was no mother to comfort me, no father to hold me. And now I just deceived her into thinking I was her mother just to get some information out of her."

He followed her down the stairs. "Bobby, stop it. You didn't do anything to her. She believed what she wanted."

She whirled and planted one finger right in the middle of his chest. "Don't you ever...ever make me do that again."

He held up his hands and backed toward the porch steps. "Yes, ma'am."

She followed him. "You want me to talk to someone, I'll talk to them. But I won't lie to them. Understand?"

His back against the porch, he nodded, hands still in the air. "I got it. No lying to anyone. No matter what."

"Okay." She stood less than a foot away from him, breathing deep to calm her anger.

"Done chewing me out?"

"I don't know."

He reached for her and pulled her in tight against his chest. This time she let the solid warmth of his body work it's magic on her. The tears flowed freely once more and soft sobs shook her.

"It's okay, sweetheart," he murmured against her hair. "You've had a very trying day."

No longer capable of words, she simply nodded and sucked in some air. It sounded like a hiccup to her. *Great.* Not only had she blown up at him like a Roman candle, now she'd turned into a watering can all over him.

"And I should've known she'd want her mom and that would hurt you. You're the toughest woman I've ever met."

She pulled back, wiped at her tears and stared up at him in the moonlight. "No, I'm a wuss."

"Nope. I'm the sheriff here and no one tells me off like you just did." He lowered his head and brushed her lips in a soft kiss, his hands rubbing the muscles of her back.

She pressed in closer, wanting more.

"Don't you have a murderer to catch?" Clint asked

from the porch shadows above them. "Looks to me like you have something else on your mind."

Gage ended the kiss and pulled her tight against his chest. "You okay now?" he whispered against her hair.

"I'm fine."

He turned and looked where his cousin-in-law was lighting a cigar. "Emma know you still smoke those things?"

"Yes. But only on rare occasions and only out on the porch. So what did you find out from Teeny? Anything useful? She kept asking Harriett if she was an angel."

"Harriett, an angel?" Gage eased Bobby aside. Taking her hand, he led her up the porch steps.

"Yeah. That's when I knew she was still hallucinating."

"What she said to us didn't make any more sense, either. She was scared of someone called 'the fishman'. Apparently Rusty was ordered to shut her up, that's why he beat her."

"I think she saw Harley's murder."

Clint took a drag on the cigar. "So Harley's death wasn't an accident?"

Great. She'd forgotten they'd let everyone believe he'd died from a blow to the head when he fell.

Gage wrapped his arm around her and pulled her into his side. "The official cause of death hasn't been determined, but his death wasn't an accident, and we have reason to believe his death is mixed up in all this."

"So the sooner you find this guy or I find a place to send Teeny, the safer we'll all be."

"That's about right."

"What's your next move?"

"Frankly, I don't know. I'm wondering if Dad might've kept some files on who Rusty might've been connected with over at the office. But with Ruby's filing system who knows where it's buried?"

"A word of warning. Emma just called and said the mayor and some people are looking for you. Might want to avoid the café for now."

"Thanks. You find a place for Teeny yet?"

Bobby's heart swelled again. There it was, Gage worrying about Teeny. He didn't see it, but every time she turned around, he had the welfare of another citizen of Westen on his mind. Even someone as helpless and hopeless as Teeny.

"Libby Wilson has an ambulance coming from a private clinic in Columbus."

"Libby Wilson, the county social worker?"

"Yes, she's become a great friend to Emma and me, since your aunt's Alzheimer's has grown worse." Clint paused to take another drag on the cigar. "Libby has a friend who's a psychiatrist at the clinic and willing to see Teeny, so we can have her evaluated and held for a few days. But after seventy-two hours, unless the doctor finds a psychiatric reason for keeping her, I'll need to find a drug rehab program to get her in."

Gage let go of Bobby and opened the door. Waiting for her to go past, he looked back at Clint. "Send the bill for the private clinic to me. I'll find a way for the sheriff's budget to cover it."

"That's gonna piss off Tobias and the town

council."

"Too bad."

***

For a town that usually rolled up its sidewalks by ten, Main Street was lit up like a birthday cake. Gage drove past the café, which was still doing a brisk business an hour after closing time. He turned into the alley behind the jail and parked.

"So, now what do we do?" Bobby asked, as she hopped out of the other side.

"Just what I told Clint." He opened the door and held it for her to pass through. "We need information on Rusty."

"Which means with Cleetus out at the tunnel, I get to search through Ruby's files all by myself."

"Once I get Daniel on his way out there, I'll help you search."

"Hope you're as good as Cleetus." She winked at him in that sassy way that always sent need coursing through him and made him want to grab onto her hips. This time he let her keep walking in front of him, even as he watched her hips swing softly with each step. Now wasn't the time to talk about what he'd really like to do to her sexy ass. The whole town of Westen depended on the two of them solving this mystery. Hopefully, he'd be able to talk her into staying once this mess was cleaned up.

Suddenly, she stopped in front of him. He put his hands on her shoulders as he slammed into her to keep her from falling into the main office.

Good thing, since it was crammed full of people. The mayor was seated in his chair. Richard Davis, the newspaper's owner, and two other members of the town council, Thomas Yoder, the town's legal advisor and Harold Russet, all stood in the room. Deke, who'd beat them back to the office, leaned against one file cabinet, his quiet stare taking in the group.

"Good of you to join us, Sheriff," Tobias said in his best, I'm-the-mayor-and-I'm-in-charge voice.

"Sorry, Sheriff, they wouldn't leave until they talked to you." Daniel came around the deputies' desk, his shoulders slung back in military precision. Daniel had spent ten years in the army and standing at attention was a sure sign he'd been trying for some time to hold his temper.

Gage gave Bobby a little shove into the room and followed her in.

"Hello, Gage," a deep, sultry voice he'd planned to never hear again said from his left.

The voice stopped him in his tracks. He turned his head just in time to see the woman unwind her long, lean body from her chair and saunter over. She wrapped her arms around his neck and pressed in close. "I've missed you."

A movement to his right caught his eye. Bobby dropped her bag on his desk and kept walking to the file cabinets, her back rigid. Finally, she turned to look at him, her face a mask of contentment, except for one arched brow. "Oh, I forgot to tell you. Your *wife* called earlier."

Oh, shit.

"*Ex-wife.*" He set the viper away and took a step back. Everyone else in the room watched them with rapt attention, except Bobby, who'd turned her back and was pulling out files. Icicles were forming in that corner.

For a moment he studied his ex. Tall and thin as a supermodel. Dressed in designer clothes her inheritance had paid for and fashion magazines dictated. Not a hair out of place, makeup applied like an artist. A beautiful cover for an empty, hollow person.

"What do you want, Moira?"

"We haven't seen each other in two years. Can't I just stop by to say hello?"

It'd been three years and he thanked God every day he wasn't married to her anymore. "You never do anything without a reason."

"Gage," Tobias picked that moment to move out of his chair. "I'm sure that is no way to speak to a district attorney with a reputation such as Ms. Dudson's."

"It's assistant district attorney and Tobias, don't get in the middle of this. You're way out of your league here. And by the way, why are you here?" he asked as he slipped behind his desk, keeping one eye on Bobby, who still hadn't turned around.

"The town council and I want to know what you intend to do about this meth-head lying over in the clinic?" Tobias glanced at his minions who all three bobbed their heads on cue. "Why isn't she in jail?"

"The *victim* is in Clint's clinic because she's unconscious and requires medical aid. You wouldn't want me to lock her up in the jail, then have something happen to her so she or her family could sue the town for refusing her medical care, would you?"

"Well, no. We certainly wouldn't want that." The

mayor backpedaled faster than a Tour de France racer going in reverse. "Why aren't you out trying to find the other one? You don't think he's holed up somewhere here in town, do you?"

"No. I know exactly where he is." Taking out his keys, he removed one and tossed it to his deputy. "Daniel, go over to my garage, get a couple of sleeping bags and some camping gear, then meet Cleetus out at the old MacPherson place. Take some walkie-talkies so we can stay in touch."

"What's up over there?" Daniel grabbed two hand-held radios off the docking station on Gage's desk and headed toward the back of the office.

"Cleetus will fill you in."

"Yes, sir." Without further question, Daniel marched out the door.

Gage wished he could go with him. He glanced at Deke. His friend just lifted the unscarred side of his mouth in return. Big help he was. Bobby, busily opening and closing files by the wall of filing cabinets, pretended to ignore everything in the room.

With a deep sigh, Gage turned to stare at his ex-wife. "Now, what are you doing in town and what trouble have you brought with you?"

"Ms. Dudson has brought you some information about the drugs infiltrating our town, which you didn't seem to know anything about," Tobias interrupted before Moira could respond. She just smiled in that calculating way she had when she had a suspect under her thumb.

A bolt of déjà vu shot down Gage's spine. To his left Bobby had stilled her movements.

Ignoring the mayor once more, he inhaled. The old wound caught, reminding him that with Moira there was nothing coincidental about her actions. He narrowed his eyes at his ex-wife. "What information is that?"

"That there may be a meth lab somewhere in your jurisdiction," Tobias announced.

Ignoring the mayor, Gage studied his ex-wife. "For months we've been getting fliers about rural areas all over the state being hotbeds of meth activity. What makes you think there's one specifically near here?"

"I have it on good authority the State task force believes a lab has existed in this area for some time. Whoever is behind it has stayed under their radar until recently," she replied.

"And you know this how?"

Moira flipped her long, dark-blonde hair with a toss of her head and gave him a sultry look. "Don't you think we should talk about this privately?"

"What I think," he said, slowly pushing himself out of his chair and reaching for her arm, "is that you need to sit right here." He gently pushed her into his vacated seat. "And tell me how you got this information."

He leaned against the corner of the desk and extended his legs, trapping her between him and the wall. He folded his arms over his chest and waited. Since what he really wanted to do was reach down and choke the hell out of her, his patience surprised him.

Moira glanced around the room, her calculating eyes seeking any source of assistance.

Gage slammed his hand against the desk. "Now, Moira."

She jumped, narrowing her eyes at him. "I have a friend on the task force."

"You're sleeping with one of the DEA agents." It wasn't a question. With Moira there was never friendship in her plans. When she wanted info, she slept with someone to get it. Something else he'd learned after his shooting. "So what did your source have to say?"

"Raids are going down tonight, Gage. All over the state. They plan to shut down the urban supply." She twisted her lips which meant she was holding something back.

He'd seen that look more than once, the last time before he'd gone off to get shot. "And?"

"They're hoping the dealers will panic and come for any drugs the rural suppliers have in store." She leaned forward, just enough to be sure her deeply cut top gave him and anyone looking a full view of her breasts. "It's our chance to beat them to the punch. You and I can bring in the drugs before the DEA gets here. We can call in the press to give us state-wide coverage. Think of how great that will be to both of our careers."

She laid one hand on his thigh and lowered her voice. "You could get out of this rinky-dink town and get back to real police work."

Slowly, he pried her hand from his leg, leaning close. "You're out of luck, Moira. I've already found the cook, the drugs and contacted the DEA. You'll have to go screw someone else to get your name in the paper."

"You bastard." She stood and drew back her hand

to slap him, but he caught it inches from his face.

"Careful. You wouldn't want to spend a night in this rinky-dink town's jail for assaulting an officer of the law, would you?"

Her eyes narrowed again like a cat considering her options. Finally she shook her head.

"Good decision." He released her hand and moved away from the desk. "Now I suggest you take your career and your ego back to Columbus."

With a feral growl, she snatched up her purse and slung it over her shoulder. She pushed past his leg and stalked from the room, her heels clacking hard against the ancient wood floors.

No one said a word until the office's front door slammed behind her.

"What do you mean you've found the drugs? How much drugs are we talking?" Tobias was the first to jump from his spot into Gage's face.

"Who was the cook?" One of the councilmen asked.

"What are you going to do about the drug gangs coming here?"

"That was your ex-wife? Did you get a rabies shot instead of a blood test before the ceremony?" Deke's comment cut through the yelling by the other men.

Gage ignored them all to stare at Bobby's back. She hadn't moved in minutes. "Did you find anything?"

"Not yet." Her voice a bit shaky, she closed the top file drawer and moved to the next one.

There wasn't anything he could do about her anger until he got the politicians out of his office. He turned his attention to the group of men. "Tobias, we discovered where the drugs are being stored and my men are guarding them until the DEA agents can get here. We're talking probably several hundred thousands of dollars' worth of crystal meth."

"And when did you learn about this illegal drug operation?"

"Today."

"Today. Really? Someone made that many drugs just today?"

The mayor's condescending attitude grated on his nerves. "No, I'd say this operation has been cranking out product for some time."

"Months?"

"Probably."

"Years?"

"Perhaps."

"So your father and now you had no idea this was going on. Isn't that your job to protect this town?"

The file drawer slammed behind them. Bobby whirled, hands fisted on her hips. "He *is* protecting the town. Considering everything Gage has been through in the past three years you should be thankful he even cares enough about this town to want to protect you and every other citizen from one of your own!"

Startled, all the men stared at her.

"You do realize this, don't you?" She took a step forward, her cheeks red with anger. Anger for him.

Other than his father, Gage couldn't remember the last time someone defended him, or even felt the need to do so.

"What are you saying, young lady?" Thomas

Yoder asked.

"It's very simple to understand," she lifted one eye at the lawyer as if she were explaining something to one of her students. "This problem isn't coming from some big, bad gang from another part of the state. It's homegrown. Someone in this town is responsible for making drugs, selling them and trying to hide the evidence with a fire."

"Fire? What are you talking about?"

"The MacPherson place," Deke replied, pulling a chair up and sitting near Gage. "It was Arson. We've pretty much decided the two things are connected."

Bobby stood next to the corner of the desk, her hands fisted on her hips and looking daggers at the mayor and his group of talking heads. "He isn't above murdering two people to cover his tracks, either."

"Murder!"

"Two murders?" Tobias looked like a Ping-Pong ball as he swiveled his gaze back and forth from Bobby to Gage. He moved in front of the desk. "What is she talking about?"

Now that Bobby let the news out, he didn't see any reason to keep the council members in the dark. "We found the body of the man we believe to be the meth cook with the drugs today."

"That's one, but she said two murders," Yoder stepped up beside Tobias.

"Harley Evans is the other."

"Harley? Didn't he die from falling and hitting his head on his coffee table? Now you're saying it was a murder?" Harold Russet joined the others crowding Gage's desk.

"*I'm* not saying it, Harold. The county coroner is. Someone staged Harley's death to look like an accident."

"Do you have any idea who?" Tobias asked.

Gage took a deep breath to keep from reaching over his desk and knocking some of the hot air out of the mayor. "No, Tobias, I don't. The only witness I have is currently unconscious over at the clinic and unable to talk to me. And given how badly she's been beaten, I doubt I'll ever get any information out of her."

"She hasn't said anything?"

He shook his head. "Not since Clint gave her medicine to knock her out. Before that he said all she did was mumble incoherently about a fishman. That's still all she says the few times she's drifted into consciousness since before going out again."

"A fishman?" Tobias drew his brows together. "Someone who likes to fish? We've got lots of trout fishermen in the area."

Gage shrugged. "Haven't a clue what it means."

Bobby reached down and pulled her big black bag off the desk and began digging through it. "Clint did record what she said. Maybe one of you know what she means." Finally, after dumping half the contents on his desk, she pulled out the small tape recorder Clint had given them earlier.

"Don't like...the fishman. Rusty said...fishman coming. Makes...my skin...crawl. Don't want...fishman...touch me. Got to hide. Rusty...hit...over and over...hurts to talk. Gotta keep…quiet. Fishman…said…shut…me…up."

Bobby pushed the stop button at the end of the tirade. They'd listened to Teeny's squeaky, high-pitched voice ramble in a manic whirlwind for nearly ten minutes.

"Doesn't tell us too much," Tobias said.

For the first time since they'd entered the office he didn't look like a politician trying for a photo-op. Maybe he had as much a concern for the townspeople as Gage, after all. She could almost forgive him his earlier insensitive attack on Gage. She hadn't been sure who she was angrier with, Tobias for not realizing pain and grief had kept Gage unaware of the drug lab's presence, or Gage for having an ex-wife who looked like a supermodel. She hadn't seen that one coming.

"Seems Teeny was either trying to keep quiet, or this 'fishman' wanted her kept quiet," Deke said.

"That's what Clint thinks," Gage answered. "Teeny can identify him, if she ever regains full consciousness and hasn't got brain damage from the drugs and the beating."

Something occurred to Bobby. "You know, something about this seems familiar."

Gage turned to look at her. "That's because you heard it over at the clinic."

"No, that's not it." She tried to ignore the way her heart jumped a beat as he stared intently at her. She wasn't forgiving him for the supermodel wife thing that easily. Hitting the rewind button, she went back to what Teeny said.

"Rusty said…fishman coming. Makes…my skin…crawl…"

"There. That's different than anything else she says. Reminds me of someone. Someone I met here." She looked at the group of men crowded around the desk. "Where's the newspaperman? Where did he go?"

"Richard?"

They all looked around. Richard Davis was nowhere in the office.

"Oh my God, it's him." She just knew it.

"Richard? You think Richard is behind this mess?" Thomas Yoder asked. "Be very careful whom you accuse, young lady. You have to be mistaken. He's been living here his whole life."

"Thomas is right," Tobias chimed in. "He's served on the town council and is a deacon over at the Baptist church."

"Why do you think it's Davis, Bobby?" Gage asked her, watching her with such intensity and completely ignoring the other men's protests.

"Because when I shook his hand it felt like I was holding a limp, wet fish." She shuddered at the memory. "And it made my skin crawl."

He shoved his chair, back, squeezed her shoulder and grabbed his hat. He headed for the door. Deke close on his heels. "Did you see where the son-of-a-bitch went?"

Deke shook his head. "He slipped out sometime after your ex stormed out the door."

The two of them stood on the sidewalk, scanning up and down the street. The others joined them.

"Tobias, do you know where Davis might've gone?" Gage asked, punching numbers on his cell phone.

281

"I thought I knew the man. But now, I don't know. The lights are out over at the newspaper office," the mayor pointed down the street.

"Clint?" Gage spoke into his cell phone. "Any sign of Richard Davis over there?"

He listened a moment. Bobby's heart seemed stuck in her throat.

Please God, don't let the murderer be there with Gage's cousin-in-law or Teeny.

"No?"

Thank God.

Bobby let out the breath she'd been holding.

Gage nodded at her, his face still serious. "Keep the doors locked and don't let him in if he shows up there, got it? Yeah, he might be our man." He hit the off button, studying the group around him. "Tobias, you and Deke go check out the newspaper office just to be sure he's not there."

The two men jogged off to their left.

He glanced at the café. Bobby followed his gaze. People seemed to be calm and enjoying a late night in town. "Thomas, you and Harold go over to the café and let Lorna know what's going on. Try to keep anyone there from leaving for a while."

The other two men nodded and headed to the right where the brightly-lit café sat. Gage walked past her, shoving the door to the office so hard it slammed against the wall.

"What are we going to do?" she asked, following Gage back inside.

"I'm heading out to the MacPherson place. See if you can reach Cleetus or Daniel and give them a head's up."

"I'm coming with you." She grabbed her purse and one of the sheriff's walkie-talkies off the desk.

"Bobby, this isn't a chance for you to make a name for yourself. These are my men out there. You'll have to get your publicity for your client and your PI career someplace else."

The words hit her like a sledgehammer to the chest. He still thought she was there just for the case? Just to get attention? After all they'd been through? All they'd shared?

"Don't be an ass. I care about what happens to those deputies, too. And besides, you might need help."

"I don't have time to keep arguing with you." He strode out the back door, Bobby right on his heels.

"Good. It'll save us both some oxygen." She scrambled into the passenger's side of the truck, barely closing the door before he threw it into reverse.

She handed him the walkie-talkie and strapped herself into the passenger seat.

"Daniel?" Gage barked into the walkie-talkie.

Only static came across the line.

"Daniel, Cleetus, are you there?" His voice tightened.

Still no answer.

"Dammit." He tossed the black box at her, as he turned onto the highway and pressed hard on the gas pedal. "Keep trying to get them." He fished his cell phone out of his pocket and punched a few buttons.

"Who are you calling?" She tried to keep the panic out of her voice.

"The rest of my deputies."

She pressed the talk button again. "Daniel or Cleetus, come in?" Each time she tried nothing came back but static. Was there something wrong with the walkie-talkies? Or had Davis gone to retrieve his drugs? Were both men dead?

The dark countryside passed by as they flew over the pavement. Gage made one phone call. Wes would meet them out at the MacPherson land after he got the other two deputies to cover the town.

"Do you think Daniel and Cleetus are okay?" she asked once he was off the phone.

"I'm praying they are…" Gage said, hesitant to say more.

"But?"

"Richard has lived in this town a long time. On the surface, and up until two days ago, I'd say he was a very benign person—completely harmless."

She stared at Gage's profile in the dark truck. "And Cleetus and Daniel won't know they're in danger until it's too late."

Chapter Fifteen

As they made the turn onto the MacPherson land, Gage turned off the headlights. The darkness gave way to eerie shapes in the moonlight shining on the path to the barn's burned-out shell. The sheriff's cruiser sat next to the old truck Cleetus drove when off duty, so Daniel must've arrived to stand guard with him.

"I don't see either of them," Bobby whispered, climbing out of the truck once they'd parked. She flicked on her flashlight to scan the area near the cars. She slowly pointed the beam back at a large dark form lying near the barn. "Is that a body over there?"

"Cut the light." Gage sprinted past her to kneel beside the body. "Daniel?" he said as he gently turned the man onto his side. "Daniel can you hear me?"

Obeying his order, Bobby shut off her light and stumbled close. She caught the metallic smell of blood

285

and saw the gooey thickness coating the side of the deputy's face. Was he dead? Please don't let him be dead.

As Gage eased him onto his back and carefully checked him for other wounds, Daniel gave a guttural moan.

Thank God.

Bobby knelt beside them.

"Daniel, where's Cleetus?" Gage asked even as he took the walkie-talkie from Daniel's pocket.

The other man did little more than moan again.

"Bobby, I have to find Cleetus." Gage grabbed her by the shoulder, thrusting his cell phone into her hand. "Call Clint and tell him to get over here. His number is the second one on the list. Deke's is the third. Tell him to come, too."

"Gage," she grabbed his hand, stopping him for a moment. "Are you sure you don't want me to come with you? In case Cleetus..." She couldn't bring herself to say the unthinkable.

Gage shook his head. "I want you to stay with Daniel. Listen for me on the walkie-talkie. If I find Cleetus, and he's still alive, I'll need you to tell Clint and Deke where he is. Okay?"

She grabbed him by the shirtfront. "Promise me you'll be careful."

"I'll be as careful as I can." He planted a hard quick kiss to her lips. "You watch carefully until Clint, Deke or the deputies arrive. Try not to make too much noise. Davis could be anywhere or circle back this way."

"I will." Her body trembling from his warning, she

scooted close to Daniel.

Gage crouched low and moved through the charred debris and overgrown brush toward the tunnel's entrance. After a moment she lost sight of him in the darkness.

Her chest hurt from thinking he might find Cleetus dead. Worse, Davis could attack him before he knew it in the dark.

She'd just found in Gage what she'd been looking for in a man and now he could be taken away from her by a crazed killer. To keep from calling after him, she bit her lip hard and forced herself to focus on her surroundings and Gage's instructions.

Keeping one hand on Daniel's chest to let his breathing reassure her, she punched in Clint's quick dial number. Once he answered, she filled him in on the situation, and then called Deke.

Suddenly she felt very alone and vulnerable. Every sound in the night seemed magnified. The bullfrogs' bellows matched the thumping of her heart. The chirping crickets seemed to scream in her ear as she strained to hear something in the direction Gage had gone. Why was it she could hear everything but the man she loved?

Panic threatened.

Breathe. Don't lose it now. Gage and Daniel are counting on you.

"Bobby." Gage's voice crackled over the walkie-talkie lying beside her.

"Yes, Gage?" She picked it up and whispered into the walkie-talkie.

"I found Cleetus. He's been shot."

"Oh, God, no!" She took a breath to calm her shaking hand. "Is he...is he..."

"He's alive. I've tried to stop the bleeding with my jacket."

"Where exactly are you?"

"Straight ahead and just to the left of your position. About ten yards from the tunnel entrance. Tell Clint and Deke to get here fast."

"They're already on their way. Do you want me to come stay with Cleetus?"

"No. Stay with Daniel until the others get here. Bring them to find Cleetus. I have to go after Davis before he gets away. He's down in the tunnel."

"Be careful, Gage...Gage?" Static buzzed in her ear.

Dammit. Why wouldn't he wait for help?

Because he's the big, bad cop, that's why!

No. He feels responsible. His men have been injured, his town threatened. He wants someone to pay for this mess. Him or Davis.

Please let it be Davis.

***

"It's mine. They won't take it from me. Not when I'm this close."

Davis' mutterings rambled up out of the tunnel's entrance Gage crouched beside. It took all his control not to rush down and confront the bastard—he'd been seeing red since finding Daniel unconscious, then Cleetus shot in the leg and bleeding from a hit to the head—but he needed to move with caution.

Despite Davis' small size—Gage still couldn't believe the quiet, unassuming man he'd known as the town's only reporter since the day he and Dad had moved to town was behind the drug operation and two murders—he'd laid out both Daniel and Cleetus, men nearly twice his size. Davis was armed and wouldn't hesitate to use the gun if cornered, just like he'd used it to shoot Cleetus. If he couldn't stop Davis, there was no one to keep him from going after Bobby out in the dark by herself.

The idea tore at his gut and bile rose in his throat.

In just a few days she'd worked her way past the barrier around his heart and become as important to him as air. And because he'd been blind to the actions of a madman in his town she could lose her life.

He damn well wasn't letting that happen, even if it took every last drop of his blood to prevent it.

"Can't carry it all. Not much time." Davis' voice became shrill with his own panic.

Carefully, Gage eased down into the tunnel's opening, loose dirt raining down around him. The noise sounded like fire alarms in his ears.

Once his feet settled on the inclined floor, he drew his gun from his jeans' waistband and paused, holding his breath to listen.

Davis had gone back to muttering. From the way he still slammed around in the secret room it sounded as if he hadn't heard any noise from the tunnel.

Gage exhaled and inhaled again, willing his pulse and breathing to slow. *Think. Calm. Breathe.* Too much depended on him getting the surprise jump on Davis.

With deliberate steps and holding the gun in front of him with both hands, he made his way down the dark incline toward the light and the racket his prey made.

"Got to get this out first. Come back for the rest," the shrill voice said with laughter.

"No. One trip. They'll be here soon. Take as much as you can get," Davis seemed to be muttering again.

If he didn't know better, Gage would think there were two people in the room up ahead of him.

Did Davis have an accomplice he didn't know about?

Shit.

One man he could take down effectively. Two meant more trouble. More danger. More chances for one of them to get away and find Daniel and Bobby where she hid.

He swallowed the bile once more. One step in front of the other he neared the room.

At the door he pressed his body up against the tunnel's wall, staying in the shadows and letting his eyes adjust to the yellowish light cast around the room by the ancient lantern sitting on the table. Shadows danced as Davis, his gun in one hand and his back to him, shoved baggies of the meth into the duffel bag he held. A second one bulging with more of the dangerous drug sat at his feet.

Deep breath. Exhale. Deep breath.

Extending his arms out, leading with the pistol, Gage crouched low and moved forward, checking for anyone else who might be in the room. Davis appeared to be alone and talking to himself.

"Richard, stop what you're doing."

Davis whirled. The wiry man's eyes wide as his

gaze darted around until he fixed it on him. "You're early, Sheriff. I hoped you take a little longer to get back out here."

"Put your hands up, Richard. I don't want to have to shoot you."

With a tight grip on the bag, Davis backed up from the table toward the crate against the room's far wall. "I'm not going to let you take it from me, Sheriff. I worked too hard for it."

"The drugs?"

He laughed—the same shrill sound Gage had heard coming up through the tunnel. The sound sent the hairs on his neck standing on edge.

"The drugs are just a means to an end."

"What did they buy?"

"All this." He waved one hand in the air around him. "It all belongs to me."

Gage moved into the room between the tunnel exit up to the manor house and the one he'd just entered. His focus never left his target, the center of Davis' chest. "All what, Richard? What is so important you'd kill two people and turn to the drug trade?"

"Land, Sheriff. Didn't you know? This is my ancestral home. My ancestors were the first settlers in the area. The ones who built the town with their wealth. It never should've left my family's hands. And I have it all back. All except the most important part."

He moved another step back toward the crate, which seemed to be pulled out from the wall. A dark shadow behind it.

Another entrance?

Damn. He thought he'd had all the escape routes

covered. Davis had a third escape route from the room.

Gage edged closer. "What important part?"

"The manor house. Gil Byrd wouldn't sell it to me, no matter what price I quoted. He just wouldn't listen."

Understanding settled on Gage. "You killed Gil."

"He was the first. So easy. He was a crazy old coot. Living out here by himself. No one came to look for him until it was too late." Another shrill laugh escaped him.

"Greed? You'd kill your friends and neighbors for simple greed?"

"Not greed. Restoration. It's my duty to restore the power in this town that once belonged to my family. To give my family name the respect that this town stole from it."

Okay, sanity wasn't Davis' strong suit.

"You can't expect to get away with this. Why don't you let me take you in, nice and easy. Maybe we can make a deal."

"I don't think I'll let you take me in, Sheriff. I've still got deals of my own to make."

With one quick movement he lifted his gun and fired in Gage's direction.

***

Muffled gunfire broke the tense, dark silence surrounding Bobby.

Oh, God! Gage.

With shaking hands she grabbed the walkie-talkie and pressed the talk button. "Gage! Gage!" She whispered hard into the mic, the words sounding like screaming to her own ears. "Are you okay?"

Lifting her finger from the button she strained to

hear a reply.

Please let him answer.

Only static met her ears.

Please God, don't let him be dead.

Maybe the walkie-talkie just didn't work underground.

Did she try again? What if the newsman had Gage's walkie-talkie? Would he come after her and Daniel? What if it Gage still had it but was injured? Would the noise lead Davis to him?

Again she pressed the button, released it and listening for any sound from Gage's end.

Nothing.

Off in the distance sirens sounded, growing louder as they approached. Thank God help was almost there. But were they too late?

She closed her eyes, seeing Gage's face once more. The intensity in his eyes when he made love to her, the patient way he spoke to the town's elderly members, the authority with which he led his deputies. She *would not* believe he'd been hurt. No way.

As the two cars pulled onto the dirt path to the barn, she crouched beside Daniel, leaving one hand on his steadily rising and falling chest. She turned on her flashlight to signal them where she was.

Car doors opened and shut. Deke, Doc Clint and Wes all ran toward her. A bit of relief slipped into her and she stood to wave them her direction.

Help had arrived.

Chapter Sixteen

As Davis lifted his arm to shoot, Gage rolled to the side. The bullet slammed into the ancient wooden boards behind him, at the level where his head would've been. Dust and wooden splinters rained down on him. He came up returning fire as Davis dived into the tunnel behind him.

Gage scrambled over the room's debris and plunged into the third tunnel's darkness in pursuit.

Suddenly a blast thundered ahead and above him, knocking him back into the hidden room. The earth shifted around him. Boards and dirt fell from the room's rickety walls.

His ears still ringing, Gage shook his head to stop the room from spinning. What the hell was that?

A booby trap! The dead tweaker must've safeguarded the exit to the meth lab and Davis tripped it.

Fuck!

He half crawled, half ran back toward the tunnel he'd entered.

Before he reached it a second explosion shook the exit leading to the manor house, slamming him to the floor once more. With a whoosh, the tunnel and exit collapsed beneath ancient timbers and tons of earth.

Geez, the fool must've rigged the other tunnels to go if the lab exit blew. He had to get out of here *now.*

Turning, he scrambled on his hands and knees to the remaining exit. Thick clouds of dust and earthen debris filled the room just as he reached the tunnel.

Above him, lightning flashed, thunder sounded farther up his escape route, not quite as loud as the other two. Or maybe it sounded less powerful to his already shell-shocked ears. It still had enough force to throw him hard against the tunnel's wall.

Frantically, he struggled to regain his footing.

Rocks and thick soil rained down, filling the tunnel in front of him.

He glanced back. Aftershocks from all three explosions sent more beams crashing into the room behind him, collapsing the century-old haven completely.

Trapped.

Alone.

Buried alive.

***

Just as the three men neared Bobby's position next to the still-semi-conscious Daniel, the dark night's silence shattered beneath a thundering boom. The earth beneath them shook, sending Bobby crashing back to her knees beside the wounded deputy. The flashlight and walkie-talkie flew out of her hands.

Gage!

She had to reach him. In the dark she searched the ground around her for the walkie-talkie. Only slight relief filled her when her hands wrapped around the radio. She gripped it tight, praying he'd answer her this time. "Gage? Gage!"

Static.

"Gage, can you hear me?" Please God, answer!

"What the hell was that?" Clint asked as he, Wes and Deke finally reached her side. He knelt beside her and immediately focused his attention on Daniel, who moaned when touched.

That was one good sign.

"Sounded like C4 to me," Wes said. "Where's Gage and Cleetus?" he asked Bobby, who still clutched the radio in both her hands.

She struggled to stand on wobbly legs. "Gage said Cleetus was ahead and to the left of this spot. About ten yards from the tunnel entrance. He's been shot and is unconscious, too."

"And Gage?" Deke asked, his stern and scarred features a mask of concern.

She cleared her throat, fighting the tears that threatened to spill. "He's in the tunnel."

Deke and Wes took off at a dead run.

A second explosion blasted into the night. Once again Bobby fell to the ground. Her chest hurt so bad, she couldn't drag in any air.

"Oh, God! Oh, God! Gage..." she sobbed, unable

to stop it this time.

Strong hands grabbed her by the shoulders.

"Bobby." Clint shook her gently. "I need your help here."

She lifted her blurry gaze to his, trying to focus on his face in the darkness. "Gage is still down there. He could be trapped...or...hurt...or..." she just couldn't bring herself to say the last.

"We don't know that. We aren't going to go there, either. Daniel needs our help. Focus on that. I need you to shine that flashlight on his head so I can assess how badly he's injured. Can you do that for me?"

Numb with fear, she could do little more than nod. She gripped the flashlight Clint pressed into her shaking hands.

"Good. Shine it right here." His hands on hers, he directed the light to the bloody gash on the downed deputy's head.

"Doc," Wes' voice came across the radio. "Cleetus is awake, and the pressure dressing Gage put on his wound seems to have stopped the bleeding from the gunshot. I'm bringing him to..."

A third explosion ripped through the night.

***

Just as Deke neared the tunnel's entrance, another explosion sent him face down into the wet grass. A cloud of dust flew out of the portal. "Shit!"

On hands and knees he scrambled over the edge and flashed a light into the debris-filled tunnel. A narrow passage let the light filter down through the dust on one side.

"Gage?" He strained to listen for any reply. He and

Gage had been friends since high school. The memory of another friend in the crumpled wreckage of a car in the dark of night begging him for help flashed through his mind.

No. He wasn't losing another friend. Not this time. "Gage, can you hear me?"

"Is the sheriff down there?" Wes asked.

Deke turned to see the deputy holding Cleetus beside him.

"I don't know." He leaned into the opening once more. "Gage? Answer me, man!"

He listened again.

Tap-tap-tap—taptaptap—tap-tap-tap, sounded from behind the rubble. Morse code for S.O.S.

"He's alive!" Wes shouted next to him.

"Gage! I hear you, man. Just hang tight!"

He wiggled back from the tunnel's edge on his stomach then stood.

"We just gonna leave him down there?" Wes asked.

"I need to get him some air down there." The problem was the only passage looked too small for him to get down through without sending the rest of the debris down and sealing Gage inside.

"What do we do?" Cleetus asked, leaning heavily on Wes.

"Let's get you over to the doc. I've got a couple of air tanks and rope in my truck." He started to heft the big man's other arm over his neck, when Cleetus pulled back.

"Wes can get me to the doc. You get the air to Gage."

Deke didn't hesitate another moment. He ran as fast as he could over the rough terrain in the dark. Past the brief light surrounding Clint, Bobby and Daniel. At his truck he pulled out two air tanks, masks, radio mics and one hundred feet of rope.

What else? He grabbed two bottles of water from the backseat cooler he always kept on hand and the giant flashlight. Now if he could get this stuff to Gage without collapsing what little access there was. There had to be some way.

He would *not* lose another friend.

The alarms of sirens sounded from up the road. More help for the wounded. He glanced in that direction and saw several headlights following the flashing lights in the distance. Too far away to help Gage.

He stopped briefly next to the doc where Wes had just deposited Cleetus.

"Gage?" Bobby's pale face and dark, worried eyes were full of questions.

"He's alive," Deke said. It was all the reassurance he could afford for any of them at that moment.

He handed Wes one of the air tanks and they jogged back over the dark terrain.

"You think we can get him out of there?" Wes asked.

"First we have to keep him alive, then we need to dig him out. Any chance there's an engineer with a backhoe in the vicinity?"

"Harold Russet's a civil engineer and head of road maintenance. He'd be the person most likely to get us what we need. And they started the new highway build between here and Columbus at night. Maybe we could use the high-powered lights, too."

"Good. Call him and tell him the situation and tell him to get some equipment out here ASAP."

At the entrance they dropped the supplies on the dew-covered grass. Wes took the cell phone and started hunting down Russet. Deke leaned over the edge again, shining the flashlight inside. More debris filtered into the narrowed hole. No way could he or Wes fit into the only access left.

"Gage! I've got some air tanks here. Not sure how to get them down, but we will."

He heard more tapping. Gage still hung in there.

"Cleetus and Daniel are okay for now."

More tapping.

"You won't fit." Bobby's soft voice whispered beside him.

The stark terror in her eyes as she looked into the abyss and slight tremor in her words tore at Deke's gut. Gage finally had a woman worthy of him and he might never know it.

For a moment he considered their options. Wait for the backhoe and only find a dead man in the tunnel? Send the tanks down and pray they didn't knock debris down on him and bury him further? Attempt to go himself and knowingly accomplish the burial? Or…

"Someone has to go down there, at least far enough to get one of these tanks to him. If it's a meth lab, the fumes could kill him." He watched her carefully, making sure she understood what he was asking.

"There are two tanks." She didn't blink, just pulled her lip between her teeth.

"The other tank is for the person risking their life to go in there."

"Right now I'm the only one who'll fit in there, right?"

He nodded.

"Tell me what I have to do."

"I have to tell you I can't guarantee either one of you will come out alive."

"Deke, you're wasting time Gage doesn't have."

Her determination moved him to action. As he helped her on with the equipment, he explained how the air tank and mask worked. He showed her how to turn the voice amplifier on to allow her and Gage to talk with the masks on. He also showed her how he could communicate with them. Next he tied the rope around her to help him control her descent into the tunnel. He didn't tell her that he wanted to be able to haul her up at the first sign of the opening collapsing. Her fear was already a palpable thing.

"Do you know what kind of cavern Gage is in down there?" he asked once she was ready to go down.

"It's not a cavern."

"What is it?"

"It's a room used to hide runaway slaves more than a century ago, dug deep and behind the old Byrd place. Probably fifty feet from here, if I had to make a guess."

"Was that the meth kitchen?"

"No. It was only a place Davis stored the drugs in rock form. Gage suspected the kitchen was elsewhere."

"Okay. That's good. We can't take the chance some of the chemicals aren't getting to him, but the situation sounds better."

After he helped her lie on her stomach on the opening's edge, he laid the other tank in front of her. "Bobby. Once you get down into the tunnel, if it looks like the thing's going to completely collapse tell me and I'll get you out. Understand?"

She nodded.

"Okay. Here we go. Take it slow and careful."

He stood, giving Wes the flashlight to keep the beam shinning in front of her. He wrapped the rope around his body. She slowly wiggled forward, head first, guiding Gage's air tank ahead of her.

God, don't let them lose either of these people.

***

One inch at a time. Just take it one inch at a time. Gage is depending on you.

Dear God, why had she agreed to do this? *Because no one else could.* Because the man she'd fallen in love with was trapped down there.

It was insane. She couldn't do it. She should just pull on the rope, get out before the walls caved in around her.

Gage was trapped down there. He could die before any other help arrived.

No choice.

Bobby pushed the air tank along the solid part of the chasm, not thinking about the dark below or the narrow space surrounding her. Her vision grew dark for a moment, her pulse pounding in her ears.

Stop it! You will not black out.

She would do this. She *had* to do this.

The tank knocked a large stone loose. Dirt and

more stones poured into the hole.

Dammit. She paused. Caught her breath, willed her heart to slow. Think about the man down there. That's all that matters.

"You're doing fine, Bobby." Deke's voice sounded out of the mask's radio. A beacon of reassurance.

If he only knew how badly she wanted to pull on that damn rope. How badly she wanted to crawl back out of this hole. He wouldn't sound so damn reassuring.

"You've gone about twenty feet. Almost halfway."

Crap! Only halfway?

She couldn't do this. Couldn't breathe. Her pulse pounded in her ears like kettledrums marking the orchestra's crescendo and the opera heroine's demise. She had to get out of here.

STOP IT! If you don't go down there, Gage could die.

She paused. Forced air in her lungs. Exhaled slowly. Sweat dripped into one eye. The air mask kept her from wiping it away.

Okay. She was half there. Only a little farther to go.

Gage wasn't too far below.

Carefully watching the tunnel ahead she pushed the tank forward another inch, wiggling up behind it, like an inchworm making its way along a tree branch.

With each movement she focused on Gage's actions.

Big, bad frickin' man! He just had to get the bad guy. Just had to put himself in danger for a town he swore he didn't care about. Yeah, right. Talk about denial.

Now look at the fix the two of us are in!

He's gonna hear about this! Just as soon as they were above ground. He'd damn well better appreciate her playing mole for him.

"He'll appreciate it, Bobby. You're doing great," Deke coached in her ear.

Damn, had she said those words out loud?

She allowed her anger at Gage for running into the damn tunnel after Davis to override the fear bubbling just beneath the surface of her mind. Anger was way more productive than panic.

Suddenly, she heard tapping from below. Her heart swelled and her panic ebbed further with the positive proof he still lived. But why was he tapping instead of talking? Was he injured?

"Gage?" she called, wondering if he could hear her.

No answer. She pushed the tank forward, avoiding the grapefruit-sized rock just in front of her. The light from above barely reached this far down. Another few feet and she'd be in total darkness. She wanted to see his face, hear his voice.

"Gage, dammit can you hear me?"

***

"Gage?"

Gage shook his head.

Bobby? Had he just heard her voice?

No. No way could she be that close to him.

Before the second beam fell and the earth tried to swallow him up he'd seen the size of the shrunken tunnel. She wouldn't be able to get to him. Not in that narrow space above him. She hated small closed rooms, a shaft less than four feet wide would do her in.

Great. Trapped below ground in a small space, seven feet by four feet on three sides, and a couple of beams holding more earth above him wasn't bad enough? Now he was hearing things.

It was his own stupid fault he was trapped. He'd let everyone down. He'd come home to lick his wounds, got caught up in losing Dad and believing danger only existed in the city, not in sleepy little Westen.

Idiot.

How many times over the years as a cop had he found the most innocent-looking situation held the most dangerous outcome? Davis had murdered and manipulated his crimes under the radar for a long time, risking countless lives. Now, the whole town depended on him to protect them from evils such as Davis and he'd failed.

Light flashed above him. Then it was gone. Had he really seen it? Or was it just another hallucination like hearing Bobby call him?

Maybe that beam that hit his head had done more than daze him. Maybe the meth kitchen's explosion spread chemicals down here and they were messing with his brain. He had to be hallucinating.

Ah, but what a great hallucination to have before dying. Bobby's sweet, sexy voice. The voice that reminded him how great she felt writhing beneath him. If he was going to hallucinate, he might as well enjoy it.

"Gage, dammit can you hear me?"

Okay, Bobby just cussed at him. That wasn't a hallucination. She really was just up the narrow shaft from him. What the hell was she doing there? And why had Deke let her climb to the shaft in the first place?

"Bobby!" He croaked out around the dust that clogged his throat.

"Thank God! Are you hurt? Can you reach up into the hole?"

"I'm a little dazed." His dry throat hurt to talk. "Beam hit me. It's blocking part of the passage."

"Okay. I'm coming down farther. I've got an air tank and some bottled water for you. Will they fit?"

"Water, yes. Don't know about the tank."

Pebbles rained down on him. He closed his eyes until they stopped. Something clanked against the beam a foot over his head. Damn, let it hold.

"Bobby, stop."

Bracing his back and feet against the small space's walls for purchase, he wiggled close. His head one foot below the largest beam, he reached up.

Fingers caught with his.

Warm, soft, sweaty fingers.

Bobby.

She'd faced her worst fear to come after him.

Tears filled his eyes. Other than Dad, no one had ever sacrificed so greatly for him.

"Gage," she whispered and he heard the relief in her voice.

He swallowed around the lump in his throat.

"Why?"

"Why am I here? Because you need air until we can get you out of here."

He swallowed again. "No. Why are *you* down

here?"

"Because Deke and Wes wouldn't fit."

"You hate small spaces."

She didn't answer him.

Stupid, stupid, stupid. It took great courage for her to come down here and now he'd reminded her of her fear. What if she panicked now?

"Here take this. You put the cloth thingy over your head." She thrust something into his hand.

Taking the cloth, he fit it over his head. "Ready."

She slipped a bottle of cold water in his hand. "Drink first."

It tasted like manna from heaven. Cold, clean, wet.

As soon as he'd finished it, he dropped the empty bottle below him. The hollow sound of plastic bouncing echoed beneath him. "What's next?"

A hard plastic mask was thrust into his hands.

"This snaps on the front. You inhale deep to seal it."

Following her instructions he fit the air mask in place. Instantly he inhaled clean air. The mask also kept the dirt out of his eyes and mouth.

"Push the button on the side of the mask to amplify your voice so we can hear you."

With one hand, he pushed the button, the other groped above him, only to be met by her fingers. He curled his around them. God, they felt good! She gave his a little squeeze.

"We're going to get you out of here." The confidence in her words brought an ache to his chest.

"You need to get out of that shaft before..." the words clogged his throat. He didn't want to think about her dying here with him. Dying from the thing she feared the most to be with him. He swallowed. "...before it collapses."

"I'm not leaving you alone down here."

The defiance in her voice stroked that vulnerable spot deep inside. She needed to get out of here, but dammit he didn't want to let go of her.

"Why?"

"Why am I not leaving you alone? Because I *need* to know you're alive."

"Why?"

"Why?" Her voice grew soft.

"Tell me." He squeezed her fingers. He wanted to hear the words. Needed to hear the words. Once, before...

"Because I needed to come down here and yell at you for running after Davis. And..."

"And?"

"Because I love you."

It had to be his imagination. His heart swelled in his chest. "I love you, too."

"Hate to break up the romance party," Deke's gravelly voice rumbled in Gage's ear. "But we think we've got an idea how to get you out of there, Gunslinger."

"What's the plan?" He tried not to sound too relieved. Way too much dirt separated him from Bobby and the surface.

"Harold Russet's bringing in a backhoe from the highway construction. We'll dig a side shaft down to you. Shouldn't take...too long to get you out."

"What aren't you telling us?" Bobby asked. She'd

heard the hesitation in Deke's voice, too.

"There's a chance the weight of the backhoe could collapse the whole thing right on top of you."

"Shit."

"Find another way," Bobby ordered, sounding very much like the schoolteacher.

"There's no other way."

"Yes, there is. You find one." Panic laced her words.

"We've looked at all the angles."

"Look again."

"Deke?" Gage needed to hear what Deke didn't want to tell him.

"Yeah?"

"Tell me everything."

"Russet says the spring rains have softened all the ground. With the explosions, we don't have any idea how long you have before it all collapses anyway."

A soft sound filled his ears. Bobby catching her breath on a whimper. His heart tore at her pain.

"Deacon," Gage used his friend's hated name to get his attention. "Get Bobby clear before it starts."

"I'm not leaving you." The pressure on his fingers increased.

"Bobby, you heard him. This whole thing can go at any moment. Thanks to you, I've got the air tank now. If the tunnel collapses, I'll still have some time for them to get to me." He didn't know if that was true, but he prayed so. Getting her out of this trap was more important than whether or not he lived. She was his soul.

"Let me stay," she begged.

His heart broke more.

"I need you to make sure they know just where I am."

"Deke can do that."

"Bobby, please." He swallowed so she wouldn't hear the fear in his words. "Baby, don't make me beg you. I need to know you're up there, safe and sound."

A soft gasp from above. He imagined she had tears coursing down her soft cheeks. She was trying to be brave, for him.

"Okay, I'll go, not because I'm afraid anymore..."

"I know you're not afraid."

"...but because I want you out of there quickly. I haven't finished using that body of yours."

Deke's laughter rumbled in his ear. Heat flushed his cheeks and for one moment he was glad no one could see the stunned look on his face.

Something clanked just above him. Then Bobby slipped her fingers from his. He wanted to grasp them back, cling to her, beg her not to leave him. Suddenly, she slipped a cloth strap in his hand.

"Your air tank is lying just up on this beam. Don't let go of that strap, no matter what. Promise me."

"You got it."

He gripped it tight.

She covered his fisted hand with hers. "I'm leaving the flashlight up here."

Normally, he didn't have a problem with the dark, but the little bit of light above him suddenly eased the tightness in his stomach. Not much, but some. And she knew he needed it. God, what he wouldn't give to hold her in his arms one more time.

"Thank you." It came out in a whisper.

"Ready, Bobby?" Deke asked.

"Take care of her, Deacon." In case I don't make it out of here.

"You got it, Gunslinger." Deke knew what he'd just asked. "She'll be right here when you get out of there."

Hopefully in one piece and still breathing.

"Okay. Get going."

Bobby kept her hand on his. Slowly it moved upward, until just the tips of her fingers touched his flesh.

Then she was gone. His fist clenched around the strap for the air she'd risked her life to bring him. His mind clenched around the words she'd filled his heart with.

I love you.

Chapter Seventeen

The rope pulled her back up the shaft in slow jerks. It seemed to take forever.

"Careful, Deke," she whispered into the mic. Her chest ached so badly every inch she got farther away from Gage.

Each movement could bring tons of soil down, crushing him. *Oh God, how could she leave him down there?* If he didn't make it out of that shaft, she'd just die, too.

She sank her teeth into her lip. Now that he could hear with the radio equipment, no way was she going to let him hear her cry.

Suddenly two pairs of hands grasped her heels.

"Gotcha," Deke said as they hauled her out of the hole.

Once she was on the surface, she squinted at the

bright lights and snatched the mask from her face.

"Get him out of there!"

"We're working as fast as we can." Deke helped her off with the air tank and jacket she'd worn down the shaft. "We need you to draw us a picture of what the underground room and tunnels looked like before the explosions."

She blinked and looked around. Huge stadium-type lights, mounted on truck trailers, sat spread in a semi-circle safely on the barn side of the area. People milled about like ants on an anthill, moving equipment, setting up tables.

Deke led her over to a folding table where several people in hard hats stood looking at charts. She recognized the middle-aged Harold Russet from earlier in the evening among them.

"Ms. Roberts." Taking her elbow, Harold drew her into the group, introducing a twenty-something African-American. "This is André Danner, the construction foreman who's going to operate the backhoe for us. Can you give us some kind of diagram where the tunnels and room were, and maybe how far back the Sheriff might be?"

Didn't they know how little time Gage had? "Why are you just standing here talking? Not doing something?"

"Bobby." Deke laid his hand on her shoulder. "The backhoe weighs nearly five tons. If these men don't maneuver it just right, we'll crush Gage."

A small groan escaped her and both her legs wobbled. She clamped her hands onto Deke's arms to remain vertical.

"Easy. Someone get her a chair."

Suddenly there was a metal chair behind her and she was eased down into it. With shaky fingers she took the pen someone handed her and drew a sketch of the area around where Gage was trapped.

"Good. Excellent." Mr. Russet said, pointing to the large X she'd marked where Gage might be in comparison to the graph. "How far down do you think he is?"

"I'm not sure." Shaking her head. "I'm so bad with distances and it seemed like I crawled a mile to get to him."

"We had a fifty-foot rope tied around her, Harold," Deke said. "Given how much lay on the ground when Bobby got to him, I'd say he's between twenty-five and thirty feet beyond the tunnel entrance."

"Good." Russet nodded. He turned to the backhoe operator and pointed to the map. "If we move the backhoe close to the entrance, but at about a forty-five degree angle from it, we should be able to dig the side shaft on this side of the whole mess."

André sprinted off to his equipment.

"I'm going to go back to the tunnel entrance, Bobby," Deke said as the other men in the group scattered to clear the path for the big rig. "You going to be okay?"

She clutched at his arm. "Just get him out of there, Deke. Please. Hurry."

He pressed a radio into her hands. "Keep him talking. Listening to you should keep him from panicking."

She clutched the radio as he ran to the tunnel

entrance. Bobby stood, shivering from fear more than the early morning air. Suddenly a warm blanket was perched on her shoulders and she was engulfed into firm arms.

"There ya go, honey," Lorna's matter-of-fact voice tickled her ears. "That boy is gonna be okay. You just wait and see."

Bobby leaned into the older woman. "I'm so scared."

"Nonsense," Harriett handed her a cup of hot tea. "Drink this. Deke and the boys here aren't going to let anything happen to the sheriff. They're smart men."

Flanked by Lorna and Harriett, Bobby looked around her and for the first time realized how many people were in the area.

"Gage, you should see this," she said into the radio.

"See what?"

His voice crackling over the radio sounded so good. Each word a testimony that he was still okay.

"Most of the town must be here. Men are helping move debris. The Baptist Ladies Society are serving everyone hot tea and coffee. Lorna and Harriett are with me."

"Why?"

"Because they all care about you."

"But I let them down. Davis killed two—no, three—men, and I didn't have a clue. The drugs. The meth lab. He could've killed more."

"But he didn't. These people know it. And they're here because they love you and need their sheriff saved."

"You tell that boy to stop talking nonsense,"

315

Harriett said loud enough for him to hear.

"Clint's over next to the paramedic's ambulance, along with all your other deputies."

"How are Cleetus and Daniel?" he asked. Bobby held the radio up to Harriett.

"Both on their way to County Hospital," Harriett answered. "Both awake, and doing good. Cleetus' gunshot was a through and through, so Doc says they'll be there overnight at least."

"Good. I'm glad. Tell Cleetus I'm sorry about…"

"Hush. You tell him when you get your fool behind out of this mess."

Bobby gave a whisper of a smile to the nurse's words. She had a feeling she wasn't the only one who planned to chew him out once he was safe and sound above ground.

"What about Emma?"

Bobby's heart clenched. Even in his predicament, the welfare of his cousin and his deputies filled his mind.

"Doc made her stay home. Didn't want her getting hurt out here in the dark."

Harriett didn't say what they were all thinking. Clint didn't want his pregnant wife out here in case her cousin didn't make it out of there.

Bobby slowly inhaled. She would *not* think like that. Positive energy, that's all she'd send his way.

The earth around them rumbled. All movement stopped. Everyone held their collective breath as they watched the backhoe lumber forward.

The earthen prison shook around Gage, more dirt

rained down. Careful not to release his hold on the air tank strap, he wiggled his other arm up to wipe the dirt off his mask. Barely any light shone from the flashlight Bobby left for him.

"Must be the backhoe getting in place."

"Russet says the safest plan is to dig a second shaft on the MacPherson side of where you're trapped. The ground is more stable there, less likely to collapse around you." Deke's voice rumbled in his ear. "How you doing down there?"

"The beams above me are holding. At least for now."

Almost as if they knew he'd been talking about them, both beams shifted above him showering him with more soil.

"Whoa, Deke."

"What's up?"

"Everything just moved."

The rumbling stopped. He held his breath and waited to see if the beams and dirt would crash down on him.

Other than a slight groan from the beams above, nothing else moved.

"Gage?"

"It's okay. Do they have to move closer?"

The radio buzzed then stopped. Had they knocked out his line of communication or were they just deciding on a plan? Or just deciding how much to tell him?

Get a grip, man. Deke wouldn't be anything but upfront. No bullshit, no matter how much. That's the way they'd always been. Yeah, but this time Bobby was listening, too.

Patient.

"Gunslinger?"

"Yeah?"

"Remember the State football championship?"

"Yeah, I was the quarterback and you were the only wide receiver we had on the team."

"Our odds of getting you out are about the same."

Shit. That would be slim to none.

"Ready when you are."

The rumble started again and the side of his prison facing the burned-out barn shook. He clutched the strap to the air tank. The beam from the flashlight shivered and cast eerie shadows above him. His mind on the petite brunette who'd climbed down in the shaft to bring him air and light, he prayed for the first time since his father's death.

As the backhoe lowered its giant arm with the ragged-toothed bucket toward the earth, Bobby inched closer. Her mind knew this was the only way to get Gage out fast. Her heart wanted to believe it. Her fears made her want to scream at them to stop.

The people around her moved closer too. It wasn't just her love buried in that tunnel. These people all had a vested interest in Gage's rescue. Their friend and sheriff was down there. Their worry warmed a tiny piece of her heart. All eyes were glued to the huge piece of machinery.

The bucket pounded the earth.

Bobby squeezed the button on the mic. "Gage?"

"What was that?"

Every time his voice came over the radio she forced herself to inhale. "That's the backhoe trying to break through the ground."

"Hope they don't have to do that too much. I'm taking a bath in dirt right now."

The bucket hit the ground a second time, this time breaking into the grass and soil, scooping it out like a giant ladle.

"They're digging through now."

"Bobby?"

"Yes?"

"I'm sorry about the jail thing that first day."

Now he apologizes?

"It wasn't so bad."

"Just wanted you to know."

In case he died in there? She wouldn't consider the possibility. She wasn't going to let him think like that either.

"You can make it up to me when you get out of there."

The backhoe kept hauling more dirt out of the ground. Each scoop one more foot closer to the level where Gage lay trapped.

Deke jogged over to where Bobby stood.

"We're almost at twenty-five feet."

"How much longer?"

"Maybe another bucketful or two. Harold wants to be actually lower than Gage." He squeezed her hand and jogged back to the digging site.

"Deke says they're almost down to where you are."

"Good. These beams are shaking bad now."

Her heart clenched at the news. "Hang on a little

longer."

"Tell the town I'm sorry things went so bad. That I failed them."

"Stop talking like that! You didn't fail anyone."

"I wish I'd spent more time with them. Lorna, Emma and the boys, Clint, Cleetus, the other deputies. This is where I belong."

She wiped at the tears on her cheeks. "And they want you to stay. You should see how much they all love you. Everyone is working so hard to rescue you. "

Suddenly, the ground shook hard. The land beyond the backhoe erupted, shooting dirt and debris up in the air.

Bobby clenched the mic. "GAGE!"

Chapter Eighteen

The world around Bobby swirled with activity. Frozen like a marble pillar—her eyes riveted on the machine teetering near the side-tunnel—she saw the scene like an old silent-movie reel.

The mayor and a group of men ran toward the huge crater that covered the area where the hidden room once lay. Clint and the deputies swarmed over the area. People shouted for shovels.

The radio clutched to her ear, her only connection to Gage, she strained to hear something.

His voice.

His breathing.

Anything to show her he hadn't been buried alive with the massive implosion.

All she got was static.

The strong, sturdy arms about her shoulders shook.

In a daze, she turned to stare at Lorna. Tears from the older woman's mascara-rimmed eyes streamed down her cheeks like black rivers of despair.

Sniffling sounded from her other side. Bobby looked over to see Harriett wringing her hands, her lips pressed tight in an effort to control her own tears.

Bobby turned to watch the activity at the secondary tunnel.

Why? Why couldn't it have held just a little longer? He'd gone in there to catch a murderer and criminal. He shouldn't pay with his life.

She wanted to scream, to hold her fist to the air and rail at the being who took him from her just when she'd found him.

Suddenly a shout came from the center of the group of men working frantically at the second shaft.

"We've got him!"

A cheer erupted from the crowd.

"Is he breathing?" Someone asked.

"Don't know, hold on!"

Bobby's knees gave out, unable to support her any longer. She sank to the ground, gasping in air like a sponge soaking up water.

"Is he alive?" she whispered, crouched over her trembling knees. She couldn't bear seeing his lifeless form dragged out of the ground.

"I'll find out." Harriett marched into the crowd of men.

"He has to be, Bobby," Lorna said, bending over and hugging her once more. "That boy's got too much ornery in him."

"Oh Lorna, I wish that were true, but he was

trapped. I know it. I saw him down there. Once those timbers gave way…" She just couldn't finish. With Lorna's help, she struggled to her feet.

Wes and Harriett jogged back toward her.

"He's alive," Wes said, his face set in a bleak mask of concern. "But he's unconscious."

"I have to see him." Bobby lurched forward on wobbly legs.

Wes caught her by the elbow to steady her. "He's pretty banged up."

"I don't care."

"Doc's still working on him." Harriett gripped her other arm as Wes lead them over the ruts left in the ground by the backhoe. "Might be best to wait until…"

Bobby narrowed her eyes at the usually unflappable nurse. "Now, Harriett."

She didn't know why she needed to be at Gage's side, but every fiber of her being insisted she get there quickly. As if her very existence depended on touching him.

Sensing her need, the crowd silently parted for them. Gage lay in the center of the group, a white foam collar around his neck. The steady rise and fall of his chest reassured her he still lived. Clint knelt beside him, flashing a light into first one eye, then the other. He glanced up and motioned her closer. The grim set of his features caused her chest to tighten.

"His vitals are good, but he took a hit to the head." He turned Gage's head slightly and pointed to the blood-covered lump on the side.

Shakily she knelt on Gage's other side, laying her hand over his clenched fist. "Will he be okay?"

"The longer he's out, the more worrisome it is."

She had to do something. Blinking back tears, she leaned close to his ear. "Gage." Her hand shook as she stroked his dirt streaked face. "Open your eyes and talk to me."

A moment later his eyes fluttered open. His deep-green gaze, a bit dazed, slowly focused on her. He opened his mouth, but no sound came out.

Thank God. She brushed her lips over his parched ones. "Don't try to talk. You're here. You're alive. That's all that matters."

He lifted his clenched fist and tried to speak again. "I...didn't...let...go."

In his hand was the remnant of the strap to the air tank she'd made him promise not to let go. He'd kept his promise. The man always kept his promises.

Laughter bubbled up inside her. She smiled at him through her tears and covered his hand that clenched the piece of strap. "Yes. You didn't let go."

At that, a cheer resounded through the crowd.

"Gage, you've got a broken arm." Clint braced a plastic splint on Gage's right arm, eliciting a groan from him. "Guess that answers the question if you have feeling in this arm. Can you move your feet?"

Gage wiggled both feet, never taking his gaze off Bobby's. "You came down that hole for me."

The wonder in his eyes caused her heart to trip over a beat. "You risked your life to stop a murderer and protect the town." She brushed his lips with hers once more. "Remind me later to tell you how stupid that was."

Clint stood and signaled for the ambulance crew to

come forward. "I'm taking you to the county hospital to set this arm, get X-rays and for observation overnight. Once the X-rays confirm you didn't have any spinal damage, we'll take the cervical collar off."

After they rolled him onto a board, Gage called his deputies over. "Wes, you're in charge now. Keep everyone out of this area until the DEA people get here. What time is it?"

Bobby glanced at her watch. "Almost six." She looked around and saw the sky growing lighter to the east. The night was nearly gone. It seemed like he'd been trapped down there forever.

"Have Deke check the property on the other side of the Byrd place." Gage continued giving instructions as the paramedics lifted him onto the stretcher. "That's probably where the meth lab is. And no talking to reporters or giving them access until we get the meth lab secured."

"Yes, sir." Wes and the other five deputies started clearing the crowd back from the crater's edge.

Bobby walked beside the stretcher as they wheeled him toward the waiting ambulance. She really didn't have a choice. Gage had released the strap and clutched her hand instead. In all her life she'd never felt anything more comforting.

As they rolled through the crowd, men and women ventured forward to whisper words of comfort and thanks, as well as well-wishes for his quick return. Even the Baptist Ladies group was in attendance, some wiping tears as they patted Gage.

"Tobias," Gage called to the mayor as they passed him.

Tobias came forward, his suit coat long gone, his white shirt sleeves rolled up to his elbows. His arms and the front of his shirt were covered with dirt. Evidence he'd been in the thick of the rescue efforts.

"Davis tripped a booby trap that started all this. I don't think he survived. Make whatever spin you want to the papers for the town's good, *after* Deke and the DEA close down the meth lab."

Tobias patted his shoulder. "Sure thing, Gage. We'll hold down the fort until you get back home. The whole town is proud of you."

The group stopped at the ambulance. Gage looked at the crowd that followed, visibly swallowing. "I'm sorry I let you all down."

"Nonsense." Lorna pushed her way to the front. "You don't have anything to be sorry about, boy. You're our sheriff. You caught the murderer and stopped the drug dealing. Guess you did just what we asked."

Bobby could've hugged the café owner right then, but the paramedics were lifting the stretcher into the ambulance and Gage was tugging her inside with him. "That's enough worrying about the town for now," she said as she sat next to him in the small vehicle. "Let's go get you checked out."

***

By noon Gage's temper and patience were both on a short fuse. After his stint in the hospital for the gunshot wounds, he'd sworn he'd never spend time in one again. Yet here he was. So far today he'd had three different sets of X-rays—one on his arm, which confirmed Clint's field diagnosis of broken bones in his right arm. The other two X-rays were of his neck and spine, which at least got the damn cervical collar removed.

When he'd returned to his hospital room, Bobby had been curled in the bedside chair watching the local news. She'd barely gotten to tell him there weren't any reports about Westen, the explosions, or the drugs, when another orderly appeared to take him for the CAT scan Clint insisted he have.

"Emma will quiz me on the results of every test when I get home," Clint had said and shook his head. "No way am I facing your cousin without all the answers and a bill of clean health for you. She'd make me sleep on the couch for a week if I do."

Knowing Clint's wife would do no such thing to the man she loved, but not wanting to upset her anyway, Gage had let them drag him off again.

Now all he wanted to do was get back to that generic hospital room and the petite brunette who'd filled his mind since the moment he'd seen her hanging over the trash dumpster.

Would she still be there?

She'd promised to stay. Down in that tunnel she'd told him she loved him. He was sure he hadn't dreamt it, but he wanted to hear her say it again. He wanted to make sure she hadn't said it just to give him hope in a hopeless situation. Even to him that sounded pathetic.

As the orderly wheeled him closer to his room, voices, *male voices*, drifted into the hallway.

Who the hell was in his room with Bobby? Between the ache in his injured arm and his throbbing headache, he wasn't in the mood for visitors.

The minute they entered his room some of his irritation disappeared.

"Hey, Sheriff...Gage," Cleetus said from his own wheelchair. His leg was elevated and a thick bandage wrapped around his thigh. "Miz Bobby was telling us all about the tunnels exploding."

"And you getting trapped," Daniel added, seated in the room's only chair. A bandage wound around the top of his head. His color looked a little pale, but at least he was conscious.

Gage scanned the small room until he found Bobby standing by the bed. Despite the dark circles under her eyes, she still looked beautiful and sexy to him. "You two missed all the excitement," he said as Bobby and the orderly helped him back into bed. "Glad you're both okay."

"Doc says we can go home tomorrow," Daniel said.

"I'm sorry we didn't figure out Davis was behind the murders and drugs before you both got injured." A knot of guilt gripped his stomach. These men had looked to him for leadership and his inattention to what was happening in town had nearly gotten them killed.

A soft hand settled on his shoulder. He looked up to see Bobby standing beside him, understanding in her eyes. Taking her hand in his, he brought it to his lips and kissed the knuckles.

"It wasn't your fault," she said.

"Sure wasn't, Sheriff. Mr. Davis fooled all of us. Even old Harley. Those two were as thick as thieves for years." Cleetus shook his head. "He killed his own friend. Did he ever tell you why?"

Gage leaned back in the bed. His men's and Bobby's belief that he wasn't at fault eased the knot in his stomach just a little. Suddenly, the night's events and the day's tests fell on him like that pile of dirt in the tunnel. Wanting to feel the comfort of her close to him, he tugged on Bobby's hand until she perched one hip on the bed beside him. "Seems it was just greed. Simple, everyday greed."

"He killed two people just for money?" Daniel asked.

"Land. I think if someone wanted to look at the county records back to the early eighteen-hundreds, we'll find that Davis was related to the original owners of the land Westen and most of the surrounding farms sit on."

"But didn't the land get sold legally through the years?" Bobby asked, gently leaning her head on his uninjured shoulder.

"He believed it all belonged to him. And he was willing to kill to get it. If your sister's client wants to have his uncle exhumed, I think we'll find Gil Byrd was the first of Davis' victims."

Silence filled the room at the realization that a murderer had lived among them committing crimes with little detection.

A moment later two pretty nurses in deep-blue scrubs strode into the room announcing that Cleetus and Daniel needed to get back to their rooms. Cleetus blushed from his head to his toes, but Daniel's color seemed a bit improved as they bustled them both from the room.

"Could be your deputies might be making a few more calls to the local hospital once they're back on duty." Bobby laughed softly beside him.

"We'll have to keep an eye on their response times from now on."

She glanced at him and he read the curiosity in her eyes. The woman's intelligence was too sexy. Before he could answer her, a knock sounded on the door.

"Hate to interrupt, Gunslinger." Deke stepped into the room. "How's the head?"

"Mild concussion, according to Clint. That's the reason he's making me stay overnight." He lifted his right arm, in a cast from mid-upper arm to wrist. "Compound fracture of both bones in my lower arm."

"Not bad for playing hero."

"I didn't do anything heroic. Stupid's more like it."

"You won't get any argument from me," Bobby muttered beside him.

He chuckled. Pain jolted through his arm and head. "Damn, woman, don't make me laugh, it hurts too much."

"Good, because I didn't think there was anything funny in what I said. You could've died in there."

He felt her body shudder next to his and squeezed her hand. "But I didn't thanks to you, Deke and most of Westen. I know how lucky I was."

"Seems Davis wasn't as lucky." Deke settled into the empty chair beside the bed.

"I take it you found his body?"

"More like parts," Deke said.

"Wild Thing" erupted from Bobby's black bag.

"Oh, crap." She scooted off the bed and fished her

cell out of the bag's depths, scrunching her face like a little girl. "It's Chloe. I'll take this in the hall."

As she walked out of the room, he couldn't take his eyes off her soft, jean-clad hips. He wanted to tell her to stay, but figured she'd rather talk to her sister than hear the details about Richard Davis' demise.

A chuckle sounded from the room's chair. "Man, you've got it bad."

Since he couldn't argue the point with him, Gage flipped Deke off with his good hand. "Tell me what you found out while she's gone."

"The tweaker had the meth lab wired for anyone coming up from that secret room who didn't know the right places to step to trigger it. The DEA and hazmat units will be here for a few weeks cleaning up the mess."

"At least Davis didn't get away with his crime spree. Have the hazmat people said how long those chemicals will contaminate the area?"

Deke coughed hard, the effort shaking his body, a residual affect from the fire he'd nearly died in years ago. "There's where we caught a break."

"How so?"

"Seems your tweaker, Rusty, had used up most of his chemicals. Instead of a chemical reaction, the explosion was from some C4 he'd managed to get his hands on—probably from his days as a demolition expert in the Army. The DEA people think that once they clean out any remnants of the meth from the area, we can bulldoze the remains of the vacant house and the land will be clean for use again."

"Honestly, Chloe, I'm fine." Bobby entered the

room with a disgusted look on her face. She shook her head and rolled her eyes, still listening to her sister. Apparently younger sister was giving her grief. If she knew how close Bobby came to being trapped underground with him, she'd be even more upset.

"There's no need for you to come up here. I'll send you a full report tomorrow. I'm pretty sure the bank will be happy to drop whatever lien they have on the property since it was illegal anyway once the whole story comes out."

Wanting to hold her once more, Gage patted the empty space on his bed. Without thinking she sat beside him and the simple act felt perfectly right. She continued to listen to her sister and he shot Deke a knowing glance. "We'll talk more tomorrow when I get out of here."

Deke gave him a half grin. "Try to get some rest. You both look like death warmed over," he said before walking out of the room.

Bobby yawned as she placed her phone on the bedside table.

"You didn't say goodbye to your sister." He pulled her down to lie beside him, wrapping his uninjured arm around her to hold her close.

She snuggled into his side, her hand resting on his chest. "She's turning into nag sister. I'm too tired to listen to it anymore. You'd think I wasn't capable of taking care of myself after all these years of raising them." Another yawn escaped her. "I should go so you can get some rest."

"Stay." He pulled her a little closer and kissed the top of her head. "I'll sleep better with you right here.

And you're as exhausted as I am."

A few quiet minutes passed.

"You scared me so bad when you went in that tunnel."

"I can't believe you crawled in there to bring me the air tank."

"Told you, I love you. Didn't want you to die because I was scared of closed, dark places. Seemed…" She yawned. "…stupid to me."

"I've made a decision."

"Yes?" She tilted her head back until he saw the question in her dark, sleepy eyes.

"I'm going to run for sheriff again." He held his breath wondering what her reaction would be.

"Figured you would." She smiled, snuggling back against him.

"You did?" Surprised his news hadn't surprised her. "How?"

"Oh, you talked a good game about leaving, but your actions showed how much you love this town and all the people." She yawned again and moved her hand to lie over his heart. "Your mind might've thought it was leaving, but your heart knew better."

"That means if they re-elect me I'll be staying in Westen for at least four more years." He lifted a strand of her hair with his uninjured hand and rubbed the silken strands between his fingers.

"Makes sense. You can't be sheriff long distance."

"Will you stay with me?" he asked, holding his breath as he waited for her answer.

"Mmm…" she snuggled into his side more. "Couldn't think of anywhere I'd rather be," she murmured.

After a minute her breathing grew regular. She'd fallen asleep. Had she really meant what she'd said? Did she know what he was asking?

Her body's warmth seeped into his and the long night's events finally took their toll on him. Content, with her sleeping almost on top of him, his eyes drifted closed.

Minutes later, Clint paused just inside the door, cell phone to his ear.

"Sorry sweetheart, you'll have to talk to your cousin later. He's sleeping. No, I don't think Bobby wants to come spend the night at our place. They're both just fine."

He turned the light out and closed the door. Walking to the nurse's station, he asked for the chart. He crossed out the sleeping pill orders he'd left. Didn't look like Gage was going to need those tonight.

Chapter Nineteen

Jason Clarke pulled the cruiser up in front of the Peaches 'N Cream café at noon the next day. Several news stations from all over the state had trucks parked on Westen's Main Street with groups of reporters and cameramen milling about.

"Just take us over to my house, Jason," Gage said as they came to a stop. Last thing he wanted to do was talk to the press today.

"No can do, Sheriff." Jason jumped out and ran around to open the back door for them. "I'm under strict orders to bring you both here."

Gage struggled out of the cruiser with his good arm, turned and held his hand in to help Bobby out. "Orders? From whom? Last time I looked, I'm still your boss."

The café door opened and Lorna stepped out onto

the sidewalk. "I told that boy to bring you here, Gage. Now get on in here. There's people wanting to talk to you."

Before they could make their way inside, the horde of newsmen swarmed the Westen Inn at the far end of the next block. Moira Dudson stepped out onto the porch, camera lights flashing all around.

"What's she doing here?" Bobby asked.

Gage could only imagine. He clenched his good hand into a fist. "Trying to get the credit for the capture of a major drug supplier, if I know Moira."

Ignoring Lorna, Bobby tucked her hand beneath his casted arm and tugged gently in the Inn's direction. "I think we should go hear what your ex has to say."

The innocent look on her face didn't fool him for a second. Maybe it was the pain pills, but he wanted to find out what Moira was up to, and he *really* wanted to see what Bobby planned.

As they approached, Moira was reading from a piece of paper in her hand. "Working hand-in-hand with the DEA, I've been building a case against the leader of this drug crew."

"More like she was working by mouth to get her information," Bobby muttered beside Gage.

He couldn't help but laugh, which caused several reporters to turn and stare. Bobby took the opportunity to wedge them closer.

Moira continued. "Today's DEA raid resulted in the collapse of a major Methamphetamine production lab here in the heart of central Ohio. Unfortunately, due to the volatile state of the chemicals used in the making of meth, the key operatives were killed in the effort."

Reporters raised their hands for questions.

"So why were you involved in this investigation, Ms. Dudson? Is there a connection between this drug ring and crime in Franklin County?" a young male reporter in front of them asked.

Moira glanced in their direction, visibly blanching when she noticed Gage, but flashed the highly impressed reporter a million-dollar smile nonetheless. "I've been following this ring from Franklin County back to the general area of Westen at which point we contacted the local authorities. So bringing down this meth lab will help reduce the available drug in the capitol."

Bobby reached in and scooped the mic out of the stunned reporter's hand. "Perhaps you can tell us why you knew about this drug connection to the area for months, Ms. Dudson, but chose to keep the information to yourself until last night?"

"I'm sorry," Moira looked back their direction. "What station are you with?"

Before Gage could stop her, Bobby moved forward another step. "I'm with the local authorities. We have reason to believe that you withheld information in an investigation that resulted in the increased danger to the community, continued meth production, and quite possibly the murder of at least two people. Is that how an Assistant District Attorney is supposed to uphold the law, Ms. Dudson?"

Suddenly, the cameras had turned from Moira to Bobby. Gage stood behind her, damn proud she'd taken up the defense of his town.

"I assure you that as soon as the meth source's location was known, Sheriff Justice was notified of the situation." Moira looked around her for some help and found none.

Bobby took another step closer. "Ms. Dudson, can you explain how you came to Westen last night to inform Sheriff Justice," she pointed back to Gage, "of a potential meth lab outside Westen only after he and his men discovered it on their own? And while the local authorities were closing it down, you and the state agencies were nowhere to be found?"

"I was here…" Moira stammered.

"Were you here while the lab exploded?" Bobby stepped onto the porch's bottom step, like a huntress with her prey cornered. "Were you here while the sheriff was trapped underground?"

"Gage?" Moira looked pleadingly at him.

He'd be damned if he'd call Bobby off. It was nice to see someone make his ex squirm.

"If he'd died," Bobby climbed the steps, her voice lowered, but nonetheless threatening and every news camera focused directly on her, "would you find some political angle for your career in that, too?"

The statuesque blonde's face contorted into a mirror of her ugly inner self. She grabbed her bag, shoved her sunglasses on her face, then elbowed her way through the crowd, which contained not only the media, but most of Westen's citizens.

A reporter raised his hand to get Bobby's attention. "So you're saying the sheriff's department closed this lab by themselves?"

"Yes," Bobby said, waving for Gage to come join

her on the porch.

He shook his head and motioned for her to continue, curious to see what kind of spin she'd take and if she'd advertise her burgeoning PI business.

Bobby faced the group of reporters still flocked around the porch. "Sheriff Gage Justice, his deputies and Fire Chief Deacon Reynolds detected the presence of the meth lab this week. They worked quickly to shut down the operation."

"You say there were two murders connected to the drug operation?" another reporter asked.

Bobby looked to Gage for permission. He nodded for her to continue. She proceeded to fill the media and town in on the details.

"That's one helluva spokesman," Tobias said beside Gage.

He glanced to his left. "Yes, she is. By the way, you know she's going to find that public indecency arrest of yours the further into Ruby's files she searches."

"I was barely over eighteen back then, Gage, and drunk as a skunk."

"When she finds it, I'll make sure she buries it once more." Gage grinned. And he would once she got to laugh at Tobias like everyone else in town had.

Tobias blushed clear up to his slightly receding hairline. "Thanks."

"And Tobias?"

"Yeah?"

"She's mine."

The mayor chuckled. "Always knew you were a smart man, Sheriff. By the way, it is still Sheriff, right?"

"You can't get rid of me that easy, Mayor."

"For the record, miss," another reporter asked, drawing Gage's attention back to Bobby's news conference, "what is your affiliation with the local authorities?"

Bobby's gaze met Gage's once more and she flashed a big smile. "I'm just a deputy, sir."

***

"You had a chance to get free publicity for your PI business," Gage said, once the media interviews had ended and they were seated in the Peaches 'N Cream's corner booth.

Most of Westen's citizens, happy to hear Gage planned to run for a second term, had drifted back to their homes or jobs. Gage's cousin Emma and Clint, Deke and all the deputies except Jason, who was still on duty, sat in the café, talking over the night and day's events. Even Cleetus had managed his crutches into the adjoining booth.

The news trucks had packed up and vacated Main Street for other parts of the state. The head of the DEA working the destroyed lab had apologized for not contacting him personally. Apparently, Moira, using her ADA credentials, had convinced them that she was keeping Gage in the loop from the beginning.

Bobby still seethed at the woman's audacity and cruelly selfish ambition. "I'm not sure I'm really cut out to be a PI."

Gage gave her a surprised look. "Sure you are. We couldn't have solved the case without you. Hell we didn't even know we had a case until you came to town."

She laughed. "Oh, please. The only thing I managed to do on my own was dump trash on you."

"Really?" Emma said, grinning at Gage. "I'm thinking that's a story I'd like to hear."

As they all laughed a silver BMW pulled up outside. Wes let out an appreciative whistle. "Oh, baby!"

"Will you look at that?" Deke said.

Bobby's heart sank as the front doors of the very familiar vehicle opened and out stepped a tall gorgeous brunette from each side. "Oh, crap."

"You know them?" Gage asked.

"My sisters."

Everyone turned to stare at her.

"Those two supermodels are *your* sisters?" Clint asked, which gained him his wife's elbow to his ribs. He looked at her. "What?"

Emma gave him a disgusted look while Bobby scooted out of the booth on an intercept course with Chloe and Dylan as they entered the café.

"Sis!" Dylan wrapped her arms around her and hugged tight.

"Are you okay?" Chloe asked after getting her own hug.

"Yes. I told you that yesterday. What are you two doing here? Dylan's supposed to be getting ready for graduation from med school and you have cases to handle."

"We've decided to put an end to this crazy PI scheme of yours, Bobby." Chloe crossed her arms over her chest like she was interrogating a witness. "It's time you came home before you get hurt."

Dylan nodded. "Be reasonable, sis. You're a teacher. You're not cut out for police work."

Her sisters' lack of confidence in her hurt. Bobby wasn't sure how to tell them they were wrong without causing a major family fight in the middle of Lorna's café, but she intended to tell them to mind their own damn business.

"You shouldn't sell your sister short," Gage said, right behind her.

"And you are?" Chloe asked, sizing him up from head to toe.

"Gage Justice, Westen's sheriff."

Chloe raised one eyebrow. "The man who almost got our sister killed?"

Bobby couldn't believe her sister's rudeness. "Chloe Elizabeth Roberts, that was uncalled for."

"I sent you up here to do a simple question-and-answer session with the bank's loan officer, Bobby. Next thing I know, you're involved with dead bodies, drug labs and explosions. You're way over your head here and he's responsible for it. Someone needs to look after you."

"I don't need—" She started to defend herself.

"Your sister not only solved this case and helped stop the drugs being manufactured near our town," Gage stepped up and draped his good arm around her shoulders, pulling her in close so no one would misunderstand their relationship, "she also saved my life."

The shocked looks on her sisters' faces were priceless.

Chloe recovered first. "Well if the case is finished, it's time for you to come home."

"She can't," Gage said firmly.

"I can't?" Bobby looked up at him.

"I need you."

"You do?" Her heart gave a little flutter.

"You're a deputy in Westen. You have a filing system to finish decoding."

"Bobby's a deputy?" Chloe asked.

The renewed shock in her sister's voice irritated Bobby, but the smoldering depth of Gage's gaze held her captive.

"Your sister is a fine deputy. She's courageous, smart, patient and good at solving puzzles. More importantly…" He paused.

"More importantly?" Dylan prodded from behind her.

"She made me fall in love with her." Gage took Bobby's hand in his, bringing it to his lips to press a kiss to her knuckles. "Trapped in that tunnel made me realize how short life is. I don't want to spend another minute without you by my side. Bobby Roberts, will you marry me?"

Behind her, Bobby heard both her sisters suck in their breath, but no protests came from either. Good thing. She'd hate to have to not invite them to her wedding. And by God, she was going to marry this big, slightly autocratic man, and love every second of it.

"Bobby?" Gage asked a bit hesitantly.

Oh, crap! She'd forgotten to answer him. "Yes! Yes, I'll marry you."

He pulled her up against his solid frame and kissed her so passionately it left little doubt to her or anyone else how much he loved her.

Moments later they were separated by well-wishing friends and family. Bobby's sisters both hugged her after she reassured them she loved Gage beyond reason. She introduced them to her new friends and soon-to-be family.

Finally, sheltered in the circle of Gage's arms once more, Bobby smiled at the small gathering as they toasted their engagement with Lorna's sweet tea all around.

"So, Gunslinger, think things will ever get back to normal around here?" Deke asked.

Before Gage could answer, Jason walked into the café. "Sheriff, hate to break up the party, but Ralph's cows are out again."

Bobby and Gage exchanged looks then cracked up.

Life in Westen might never change, but it would *never* be normal.

The End

About the Author

Suzanne Ferrell

Suzanne discovered romance novels in her aunt's hidden stash one summer as a teenager. From that moment on she knew two things: she loved romance stories and someday she'd be writing her own. Her love for romances has only grown over the years. It took her a number of years and a secondary career as a nurse to finally start writing her own stories.

A double finalist in the Romance Writer's of America's 2006 Golden Heart with her manuscripts, KIDNAPPED and HUNTED (Romantic Suspense), Suzanne has also won The Beacon Unpublished and the CTRWA's contests in the erotica categories with her book, The Surrender Of Lacy Morgan.

Suzanne's sexy stories, whether they be her steamy Western eroticas, her on the edge of your seat romantic suspense, or the heart warming small town stories, will keep you thinking about her characters long after their Happy Ever After is achieved.

Visit Suzanne Ferrell's website at:

www.suzanneferrell.com

More Books By Suzanne Ferrell

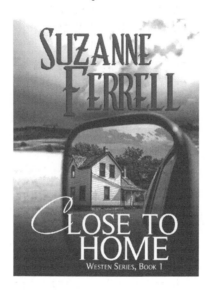

Excerpt:

Chapter One

"**W**hat you need is a man in your life, Emma."

Emma Lewis rolled her eyes at the comment and stacked a pile of celery to chop.

Luckily, she had her back to her boss, Lorna Doone—named after the cookie—the owner of the Peaches 'N Cream café. Not that Lorna would fire her for the action. Lorna thought of herself as the unofficial matchmaker of Westen. Almost daily, she carried on about some part of someone's life in the small Ohio town.

Apparently today was Emma's turn.

"What I need is to get this prep work done before the

lunch crowd gets here." She looked through the pass-through window to where her twin sons sat on stools eating their breakfast at the café's counter. "Benjamin and Brian, I better see all that oatmeal gone or no cookies for later. You hear me?"

"Yes, ma'am," they both muttered, shoving spoonfuls of oatmeal in their mouths.

She glanced at the elderly lady seated next to the boys. Her mother stared off into space, something she'd been doing a little more since Daddy passed away back in the spring. "You okay, Mama?"

Isabelle Lewis blinked then smiled. "Why yes, dear. And Lorna's right. You do need a man in your life."

"Not you, too, Mama." Emma shook her head and began chopping. "Besides, I already have two men in my life." She winked at her sons, which sent them into fits of small boy giggles.

"Mom's right, Em," Rachel, Lorna's daughter, chimed in as she filled the ketchup bottles lined up in a row on the lunch counter. "You need someone, tall, dark, handsome…"

"Like the doc's nephew," Harriett, the doc's nurse, said between sips of Lorna's sweet tea.

"Yeah, him." Rachel leaned one elbow on the counter. "He's so…hot. That's who you need to hook up with, Em."

"Harriett, don't you have patients to see?" Emma peeled two onions and halved them on the cutting board.

"Clint's never been married, has he, Harriett?" Lorna carried out a tray of clean glasses and began lining them up next to the soda fountain.

"No. He came close about a year ago then it all sort of fell apart. Doc and Caroline were concerned about him for a while, but now he's staying in Westen while the Doc takes Caroline cruising around the world."

"The poor guy's heartbroken and in need of a good woman." Rachel looked at Emma through the pass-through. "Someone like our Em, huh?"

"Of course. Besides, Emma works too hard. A man to take care of her would be so wonderful." Mama picked up her toast and scooted down next to Harriett. "How long will Clint be in town this time?"

Emma diced the onion into smaller and smaller pieces.

Dear God, save her. Lorna, Harriett and now her mother. The only person missing was the minister's wife and there'd be no stopping them until they had her dating and marrying the fill-in doctor. Been there, done that, got the T-shirt. Her ex, Dwayne Hazard, cured her of ever trusting a doctor under fifty again. Especially not one as handsome as she remembered Clint Preston.

For a moment she studied her sons, their copper-colored hair shining in the early morning light, heads bent together as they whispered something back and forth. Those were the only two good things she'd gotten from her ex.

She grabbed three roasted chicken breasts and peeled the skin off, then the bones.

"The poor girl hasn't dated anyone since coming home with the boys. Of course they were so small then, they took both of us all day to care for. And they certainly need a father," her mother said.

"That was nearly seven years ago, Isabelle. It's time for her to find someone." Lorna leaned over the counter.

"I'm standing right here," Emma called from the kitchen as she lined the chicken up and chopped with a vengeance.

"What we need is a way to get her to meet the doc's nephew."

"Maybe she could come down with something," Rachel chimed in, her shoulders shaking with hidden mirth.

Emma shot her an I'm-going-to-hurt-you glare.

Rachel's shoulders shook harder.

"No, we wouldn't want him to see her sick," Lorna said, slipping a straw between her lips and chewing on the end. Since she stopped smoking, she'd taken up straw chewing to fill the need for oral fixation.

"Oh, dear no," Mama agreed. "The poor child gets all pale and splotchy when she's running a fever. You remember last winter when she had bronchitis, don't you?"

Harriett nodded. "Sure do. Wasn't a pretty sight at all. What we need is a minor injury."

"I can *hear* you, you know."

What she needed wasn't a man. What she needed was a month's vacation in a sunny place, with a masseuse, good margaritas and a hot tub. Somewhere far away from Westen.

"Oh, yes. Something where he'll have to stitch her up."

"See her as a damsel in distress."

"That's it! Lorna, I'm taking my break." Emma dropped her knife, pulled off her apron, grabbed her tea and stomped out the back door.

"What are we going to do with all these chopped vegetables and chicken?" Lorna called after her.

"Add mayo and cranberries for chicken salad, or make potpie. I don't care!" Emma yelled over her shoulder just before the screen door slammed.

"Poor dear, she really does need someone to help her."

"A man to love her."

"What we need is a good accident."

End of Excerpt

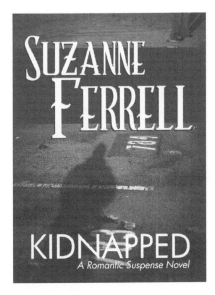

FBI Agent Jake Carlisle is in deep trouble. He's been shot and if he can't get help fast, two lives will be lost—his and that of the young witness whom he's sworn to protect. Desperate, on the run from both the police and the Russian Mafia, he kidnaps a nurse from a hospital parking lot.

ER nurse Samantha Edgars has been living in an emotional vacuum since the death of her daughter. Mentally and physically exhausted following a difficult shift, she's suddenly jolted from her stupor when she's bound and gagged, then tossed into the back of her car. Forced to tend a bleeding FBI agent and his injured witness, she's terrified. But Samantha quickly learns the rogue agent and orphaned boy need more than just her professional skills. Danger is bearing down on them, and she must learn to trust Jake—and her heart— if they're all going to survive.

Praise for Kidnapped:
Loved it! Five Stars
"...very entertaining and well written. Jake, Sami and Nicky were great main characters who supported the plot very well.

If you're looking for a nice and relaxed read I can recommend this one to you." - Book lover (Athens, Greece)

Amazing Story! Five Stars
"This story is one of the better books that I have read in awhile. The interaction between Jake and Sami are electrifying without being outwardly mushy. The plot and interactions molded so well. I will be buying other stories from this author. I found the three main characters and their back-stories both heartbreaking and touching. I highly recommend this story! You won't be disappointed." - Amazon reader (Pennsylvania)

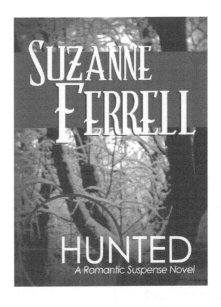

In one fiery explosion Katie Myers' witness protection cover is blown. Unable to trust the Marshals who've been responsible for her safety, she's on the run from the cult leader she put on death row. In desperation she forces a near stranger at gunpoint to help her hide. By-the-book patrolman Matt Edgars is shocked when the woman he's come to rescue points a gun at him and demands he help her leave a crime scene. The stark terror in Katie's beautiful eyes has him breaking rules for the first time in his career. With a hit man on their trail, Matt must break down the walls Katie has built to guard the secrets of her past. If not the cult leader will fulfill his prophecy and take the one woman Matt has ever loved to the grave with him.

Printed in Great Britain
by Amazon.co.uk, Ltd.,
Marston Gate.